BELO

ROBERT
WELBOURN

SRL PUBLISHING

BELONGING

ROBERT WELBOURN

BERO PUBLISHING

SRL Publishing Ltd
London
www.srlpublishing.co.uk

First published worldwide by SRL Publishing in 2023

ISBN: 978-1915073-19-8

1 3 5 7 9 10 8 6 4 2

SRL Publishing and Pen Nib logo are registered trademarks owned by SRL Publishing Ltd.

A CIP catalogue record for this book is available from the British Library

SRL Publishing is a Climate Positive publisher offsetting more carbon emissions than it emits.

Also by Robert Welbourn

Ideal Angels

For Hannah

*This book wouldn't exist without you, because I couldn't
exist without you*

I don't even know if I was looking for the presence of something good or the absence of something bad.
Hermione Hoby, *Virtue*

Do I contradict myself?
Very well then I contradict myself,
(I am large, I contain multitudes.)
Walt Whitman, *Song of Myself*

What did you expect from me?
Senses Fail, *Calling All Cars*

Summer

One

I first meet Max at my office's summer party. He's the first man I'm enamoured with since *The American*, and it feels good.

"Who's your favourite *Avenger*?" I ask him the question without preamble, putting my hand on his forearm from nowhere, without introduction. I aim to startle him into conversation, and it works.

"Er…" he stutters and stumbles, before finding his voice. "I don't really have one?" His answer comes in the form of a question, which tells me that my attempt to knock him off balance has worked.

"Me neither," I admit to him. "Honestly, I fucking hate the *Avengers,* but it's a good conversation starter."

"Yeah I get that," Max replies. "Those movies are fucking e*verywhere*, so I imagine as a spray-and-pray question you probably get quite a lot of answers."

"I do," I say, smiling, "which creates an issue: when

they've finished talking about their favourite, they'll ask me *mine*."

"So, who is *your* favourite *Avenger*?" Max asks with a wink, the crafty bastard. I like him immediately.

This ruins my plan, but by this point it's okay. I ask the *Avengers* question with no preamble or introduction because it usually knocks the other person off balance, and gives you the upper hand in the conversation. I don't normally buy into this pseudo-scientific pick-up-artist bullshit, but I find this is one technique, for me at least, that actually works. Despite this confident conversation with Max, I'm actually a very shy person normally. It's only the alcohol I have in my system at the party that allows me to speak to Max, to touch him, to *engage* him both audibly and physically. It's a thrill.

In case you don't believe me about being shy, let me tell you that I bump into Max in the toilets once, before I've worked up the nerve to talk to him, and it completely throws me. I end up using the urinal next to him without noticing right away. In fact, it takes me a long time to notice, because I'm too busy staring at my dick in my hand, willing it to do one of its two primary functions. I'm a nervous pee-er at the best of times; when I realise Max is next to me, it almost feels like my testicles reverse the drop they made many years ago and return to the warm confines of my insides. Eventually Max leaves, shaking, zipping, washing, drying, exiting. Eventually, I'm able to coax a small stream out of the end of my dick, and I shake, zip, wash, dry, leave. Once I'm back in the party, Max is nowhere to be seen.

I do my best to mingle, try to distract myself from the constant search for him I'm doing out of the corners of my eyes. It's a warm July day, late afternoon verging on early evening, and the company has hired out a local bar which is equal parts indoor and outdoor space. The sun is beating a terrific tempo down from its perch above the cloudless sky, and I find myself spending most of my time indoors; I'm so pale as to nearly be translucent, the human equivalent of an unfried spring roll. Except instead of delicious meat and vegetables, I'm filled with a crippling self-loathing and doubt. Max will soon change this for me.

"Having fun?"

I look to my left, to the sound of the voice, and see Chris standing next to me. I'm leaning on the quiet end of the bar, the bit where the 16-year-olds clump the dirty glasses, out beyond the sign stating this end of the bar offers no service. Chris leans next to me, and we take in the party together.

"Meh," I shrug.

"I get it."

We stand there quietly for a short while; I have absolutely no idea what to say. I like Chris, but beyond work I don't know anything about him. I could ask him the *Avengers* question, but I worry I'll get an actual answer, and when I'm prepared to disappear at any moment should I see Max, I'd hate to leave mid-conversation. Terribly rude.

"I saw the most amazing—"

"—I need a piss bye."

I don't need a piss, but I do need to extricate myself from this situation. I move away from Chris, and halfway across the dance floor I glance over my shoulder to see him looking at me, confusion and a little bit of sadness on his face. I feel bad, but I also don't; I'm sure he'll recover from this trauma.

As I move to the toilets, not needing to piss but having to commit to the lie, I'm accosted by Thomas. He's the one black person in the office, a testament to England perhaps having equality on paper, but still being

7

an incredibly racist country in reality. He's incredibly drunk, and quite grabby.

"Hi Noah," he smiles at me, his mouth forced into a shape somewhere in between genuine pleasure, and drunken leer. I try to ignore him, brush past him and keep walking, but he grabs my arm and won't let me go.

"Hi Thomas," I half say, half sigh, trying to make my exasperation incredibly clear, obvious even to someone as drunk as he clearly is.

"Why won't you fuck me, Noah?"

The question startles me, even though I've heard it a thousand times before. Thomas and I kissed at the Christmas party two years ago, and he just can't let go.

"I—"

"—don't give me all that 'I'm not looking for a relationship, it was one kiss, let it go' bullshit. I know your game."

He's leering at me through one eye, whether through suspicion or drunkenness it's impossible to tell. I don't know what to say to him, but he's still gripping my arm, so I can't leave. He's incredibly strong, and with a person this drunk, who's clearly on the verge of being terribly upset, I don't want to push him.

"Thomas," I say, unable to keep the whine out of my voice. "I'm just going for a piss. Let's talk afterwards?"

He finally releases my arm, and I use the opportunity to move away from him, slip into the toilets, praise God there's an empty cubicle I can lock myself in. I stay there for nearly an hour.

Thomas was yet another casualty of *The American*. Since he left me, I haven't been able to hold down a fully functional relationship. I know it's probably because I'm not over him. How could I be? With what he did to me?

I don't normally come to these work things; I work for money, and that's it. I'm not in it for a career, to better myself, any of that. I work because I have to, because I'll become homeless and starve to death if I don't. Perhaps a bit hyperbolic, but what can you do? The reason I'm here now, instead of at home, happily by myself, is that I'm trying to be more outgoing, and less cynical. I'm of a certain age that was raised mainly by American sitcoms, and so sarcasm is second nature. Though recently, I've come to see it as actually very unhelpful; I used to think no one ever knowing if I was serious or not was amusing, however the older I get, the more I realise it's just a bit odd. I don't want to become *that* guy. So I'm working on myself, trying not to be. I'm not doing very well. But still, baby steps.

I spot Max as soon as he arrives at the party; it's impossible not to. When a person who's as beautiful as Max is enters a room, you can't help but notice. The whole room notices. It isn't like everyone stops and stares, but they all clock him, out of one corner of the eye or another. He's what I imagine Michelangelo's *David* would look like, were he a real man, and also carved in the 21st century. Obviously Max is fully clothed, he isn't displaying himself for all the world to see, but from his outfit, skinny jeans and a very snug white tee shirt, I can tell he has a good body. I'll later learn how much of an understatement this will come to be. I get a glimpse when I grasp his forearm, and it immediately gives me half an erection, the feel of his firm, taught arm in my hand, his muscles working beneath the skin, his body in the act of being alive. Max moves with the confidence of a man who takes care of himself, a man who knows he looks good, but isn't arrogant about it; he looks like he knows he's lucky to have been born so pretty, but he's also aware that it's constant hard work that keeps him this way. Or maybe he just looks like a normal man, in a room full of people he doesn't know, and the couple of drinks I've had are making me think like a fool.

In spite of my sudden and immediate desire, the *Avengers* conversation doesn't happen until much later. He attends the party with Anna, a woman who works in my department, but who isn't on my team. I know her to speak to about work, but nothing otherwise. We're not friends, not even acquaintances. I'd wager she'd have a hard time calling me a colleague if I were described to her. If I was presented to her as a suspect in a murder case, if she was shown a glossy 5x7 of my face, I wouldn't be surprised if she couldn't place me. She'd probably recognise the face, but not be able to give it context within her life. I don't blame her, because I often feel like I'm lacking context. Perhaps she actually knows me really well, to be able to know this about me? Much more likely it's just coincidence.

I wonder if Anna and Max are together; it seems the logical assumption, as they're accompanying each other. But you know what they say about assumptions: most of the time they're usually right, except when they're not. Okay, so maybe *they* don't say that, maybe *I* say that. But maybe I'm part of the mythical 'they'? Someone, somewhere must be? Or must know who is? We all always think about what 'they' say; 'they' must exist, surely? Because of my assumption about their relationship status, as well as the fact I don't know Anna, I'm not comfortable approaching her, ingratiating myself into the various conversations I see her having. I want to, but I don't have an in, I literally know nothing about this woman other than what she does at work; where do you begin with that conversation? Max is involved in all the conversations; for a man who doesn't know anyone, people sure do seem to like him. Every time I see him he's nursing a bottle of beer, sans the label, and I wonder is it the same one each time I see him, or does he simply peel the label off every beer in the same way? I'll ask him about this much later, and he'll smile his knowing smile at me, that glint in his eye that tells me he isn't going to provide an answer because the question doesn't need one, the information he's withholding isn't vital, but he appreciates my interest, nonetheless.

As the party progresses I often lose sight of Max, but frequently I see both of the office hotties, so they'll keep my mind occupied for the time being. There's Daisy, who works on the team next to mine, but frustratingly sits at a desk with her back to me. I hate it, but I reason with myself that it makes the times she turns around and I get to see her face all the sweeter.

"Hi Daisy," I say to her, with a familiarity perhaps out of place considering how little acquainted we are.

"Noah," she smiles at me, "having fun?"

Ah the standard party question. I shrug, not because I'm a disaffected millennial (or not *just* because), but because I genuinely don't know if I am. Discovering such a person as Max exists is great, and not only seeing but now talking to Daisy is also great. But then there's Thomas, who I'm worried will find me and accost me again. There's Chris, who probably thinks our conversation needs a proper ending. There's Anna, the fact she might be Max's girlfriend. Everything is so fraught, I just don't know where I stand. I attempt to communicate all of this with a shrug.

"Are you?" I ask back out of politeness, but even before I finish the question I can see she's lost interest, and I don't blame her. Such boring, standard party fare.

Fuck it, I decide; not now.

"Daisy," I say to the side of her face, as she's turned away from me and is scanning the room, probably looking for a better, more interesting conversation. "You're the most beautiful person I've ever seen."

11

This gets her attention.

"What?" She shouts at me over the music.

"I said," I reply, "you're the most beautiful person I've ever seen." That this isn't true should make me feel cruel, but it doesn't. She's not the most beautiful person I've ever seen, but she's certainly in the top 10. This isn't the time and place for nuances though; I'm trying to give her a compliment, a way of remembering me. It seems to work.

"Thank you," she blushes at me. I can see the genuine joy in her eyes at the compliment, but I can also see her guard come up. She braces herself for what she thinks will come next. It doesn't. I smile and laugh as I speak to try and put her mind at ease.

"Don't worry, I'm not hitting on you." She visibly relaxes, her shoulders dropping, her entire body unclenching. "I know you have a boyfriend, and, honestly, that's the market I'm currently looking in anyway."

It's not, at least it isn't my entire focus. But I don't want to tell Daisy that I want to fuck Max. Too much info. Daisy's smiling now, looking happy. I ask her if she wants a drink but she shakes her head, says she's going for a cigarette. She asks me if I want one but I shake my head, tell her I need another drink. We go our separate ways for the time being, and I walk away from Daisy hopeful that I've made her day a bit better with my compliment. I'm aware I'm most likely vastly overestimating my own importance in her life, but it's nice to pretend.

Everything is better in moderation, so they say. Including moderation. Including beauty. Absence makes the heart grow fonder. I could offer you any number of cliches, if you'd like? A selection of amuse-bouchées to keep you occupied before the main course. Tonight, I can see not only Daisy's entire back, made possible by the top she's wearing, but quite a lot of her front, too. She's gone skinny low-cut jeans with a crop top; there's a lot of flesh on show, and I have a lot of time for it. Once you get past all the generally agreed on attractive parts of a person (breasts, ass, and hair for a woman, chest, arms, and shoulders for a man, face for both, etc.), and move into the subjective, the stomach is where you'll find me. I don't know what it is about them, but I just cannot resist a good stomach. And Daisy's appears to be the best. I'm going to have to resist it, if only because Daisy's so far out of my league, not to mention she has a boyfriend, not to mention I'm horny for Max. But for a time I can't take my eyes off it, and her; whether she's dancing, moving her hips to the beat, her stomach bunching together at alternate sides as her hips rise and fall; whether she's at the bar ordering a drink, standing on the ends of her toes, leaning as far forward as her diminutive frame will allow her, in order to make herself heard over the music; whether she's outside, a cigarette held between two impossibly long and thin fingers, her elbow bending every few moments to move it to and then from her mouth, her mouth forming an 'O' shape as she sucks the smoke in, holding it for a moment before breathing it out. I'm not staring at her, I promise. She's just so fucking beautiful.

The other hottie is a guy named Jason, which for some reason to me, with no basis in fact whatsoever, seems to be a geeky name. It reminds me of Jason Donovan and the TV show *Neighbours*, a small child from the north of England somehow watching an Australian soap of which he follows little, but enjoys a lot, nonetheless. Jason is on my team, sits next to me in fact; and actually, seeing him next to me every day hasn't diminished his attractiveness in my eyes. Perhaps we can all actually get what we want? Perhaps it won't end life as we know it? Two words: doubt it.

Jason has the chiselled jaw of a marble sculpture - one might be again tempted to use *David* as a yardstick, no matter how unfair this may feel - and the body to match. Though unfortunately the attitude to match, too. As the saying goes, he's sexy and he knows it. Jason and Max are a total contradiction in this sense; they're both sexy, and they both seem to be aware of it, but Max is in denial, doesn't believe he's as attractive as other people, or the mirror, tells him he is. Max is humble, he's almost embarrassed to be considered so beautiful, as if it's a burden, a curse, an unconscious privilege, rather than the wonderful reality it actually is. Jason is very much not embarrassed; Jason uses his beauty like a weapon, a tool of oppression. Even though he does the same shitty low wage job as me, as the rest of the team, hell the rest of the department, he thinks his beauty makes him better than the rest of us. The sad thing is, in many ways he's right. There are three main currencies in the world; money, power, and beauty. I have none; Jason has beauty. He may have wealth and power that I'm not aware of, but I couldn't say, where I know for a fact he has beauty. So whilst we may be equally cash poor, failures of the neo-liberal system from which we cannot escape, Jason at least can trade on his beauty, he can be the master of those transactions that require a little something more than money can buy. If I sound incredibly bitter, it's because I'm incredibly bitter.

Normally arrogance is a huge turn off for me, but as there's never going to be anything between Jason and I, I don't mind it. (He'd be so pleased, so *humbled*, if he knew that in my head I was making allowances for him. I mean really, who do I think I am? Woah, don't open that can of worms.) I fantasise about Jason regularly, laying on my bed with my dick in my hand, impatiently waiting for the blood to reach it, for the soft flesh to become hard, for me to have my very own, if only temporary, marble sculpture. The best thing about fantasies is that they are just that; as such, in my head Jason is wonderful. He looks the same, however he's shy, retiring, I have to coax him out of his shell. He's never been with another guy, he tells me nervously, as I take his hand in mind. It's okay, I tell him, I'll guide him, I'll be gentle. Then before I know it fantasy Jason is coming in my mouth whilst in reality, I'm coming on my own stomach. Not the most graceful way to spend your evenings, but it happens to us all every now and then. At least, I hope it does. It can't just be me, surely?

When I finally find Max again, what feels like several lifetimes later but is in reality probably only an hour at the most, I find him heading towards the club's main bar just before midnight. I stumble up to him, wanting to intercept him before he reaches the bar; I have a full bottle of beer in my hand, so can't use wanting a drink as an excuse to be near him, to engage him in conversation. In my drunken stupor I drop the beer; my mind decides this is the best course of action, and then carries it out almost before I've realised. I don't mind it though; sometimes, in my darker times, I've fantasised about a life on Valium, or Xanax, or some such tranquilliser. I'd like to live out my life passively; I don't want to kill myself, but I'm happy just to wait for my death. Life is relentless, and it'd be nice to take a break every now and then. Weekends are never long enough, and actual time off work always disappears before you've barely adjusted. But 5, 6 years on Valium? Maybe then I'd finally be able to relax and catch up with myself. Maybe in those 5 or 6 drug-induced, drug-addled years, I'd be able to place myself in relation to the world around me. Although I doubt it; what I haven't achieved sober in 24 years, I doubt I'll achieve inebriated in one fourth of that. And anyway, sometimes I feel like I'm skating through life so much I wonder if Valium would actually make a difference? Do I need to take apathy in pill form, when I'm living apathy in human form? Who even fucking knows.

Before I first approached Max, he had looked tall from a distance. Standing next to him I'd realised he's even bigger than I'd imagined. I'm six feet tall, and he towers over me. He must be 6"4 or 5, easily. I think about using this as my second opening line, but stop myself as a sober(ish) part of my brain shouts loud enough for me to hear that he's probably had that used as an opening line so many times it makes him want to scream. I drunkenly tap Max on the shoulder, hoping I'm being suave and sophisticated, but knowing the odds are that I'm not. More physical contact though, look at me doing a decent impression of a normal human being. I have no idea what I'm going to say to him; I simply tap his shoulder until he looks at me with a quizzical expression, and I open my mouth to see what words, if any, fall out. (This is fairly typical for me, not just when I'm drunkenly hitting on friends of colleagues, but of all life; I have no plan, no idea what's going on, I just lurch forward head-first, and hope things work themselves out. They often do. I'm a very fucked up person, but I'm not going to sit here and deny my Western white privilege. If I were straight as opposed to bi, I don't think I could have been handed many more advantages, both at birth, and then continually through life. I may not be rich, but at least I'm not a black man in America going for a job, Or a Brazilian tourist in England simply running for a tube).

"So how do you and Anna know each other?" My

words are louder than I intend, even taking into account the fact I have to shout over the club's music, which is blaring at an almost unbearable level, and I wince as I see Max flinch. Not off to the most auspicious of starts. But I persevere nonetheless, because fuck it, why not. "Sorry, I just sort of dived in there. Again." I thrust my hand towards him with perhaps too much zeal, but he shakes in nonetheless, his grip firm without being painful, almost tender, the flesh in his palm soft as it rubs against mine; my hands have never done a real day's work in their life, but compared to Max's they feel like stone, like relics from another age. I want to end the handshake out of embarrassment at how my hand must feel to him, but I also don't want to let go of him, I don't want to end our physicality. In this brief moment, Max is the only thing anchoring me to the planet. I'm terrified that if I let go of his hand, there'll be nothing to stop me from drifting off. Back to my home planet? You tell me. Perhaps it's my drunken state, my intoxicated brain making connections that aren't there, but did I feel something between us? Not quite an electricity, but a spark, something at the beginning of that long and winding, and hopefully not too lonely, road?

When Max eventually replies it's with a slight lisp, and a definite glottal stop, but even as I register these imperfections in his speech I realise I find them endearing, rather than discouraging. They serve to form his character, they're the foundations upon which I build my image of Max. There's the Max standing in front of me, like a dam, a well of information being carefully held back, and then there's the Max in my head, the one I slowly piece together as I gain more information about him. It's like an hour glass; I'm at the bottom, empty, and each grain of sand is a fact about Max, a facet of his personality. Eventuality, hopefully, I'll have it all; he'll have given himself over to me totally, and I'll be full of him, and he'll have emptied himself into me. His lisp and glottal stopping are the first two parts of what I hope will eventually become a whole; I hope Max will become fully formed in my head, because that'll mean I know enough about him.

"We're old friends," he says, the wording flowing perfectly as expected until the climax of his response, at which point the word 'friends' becomes 'friendth'. A tiny imperfection in what has so far been a perfect man, an Adonis, a titan of masculinity. "How do you know Anna?"

"We work together. Not on the same team," I elaborate, my words rushing out in a torrent of nerves as I realise with a start that I am, in fact, not too drunk to fear rejection. But it is, in fact, too late to back out of this conversation. Not that I'd have been able to if I'd tried; we've exchanged somewhere in the area of 20 words, and Max already has a hold on me. I remember a line from a book that has haunted me ever since I read it: *he's going to break my heart, and I'm going to let him.* "We're not on the same team, but same department. We're not close," I finish with, in my nervous state adding extra, unnecessary information, just saying whatever words form in my mouth and roll off my tongue and past my lips.

"That's cool," Max says, clearly already losing interest in me, the weird drunk loner approaching him at this weird office party full of strangers. For the second time. I don't blame him. What am I even saying?

"So how'd she drag you along here?"

"The promise of free booze," he says, laughing to himself. I laugh too, though I'm not sure why.

"Wait," I say, confused, stopping laughing, looking around to see if there are any signs I've missed, any indicators that what I've been handing money over for should in fact have been free, the financial side of the transaction removed, changing the receiving of each drink from a transaction down to a gift. "Is it a free bar? I've been paying for my drinks all night."

Max is looking at me, a glint in his soft brown eyes. It's a look I can't read.

"No no, no free bar. Anna is paying for my drinks." Drinkth. As he says this he holds up his nearly empty glass, as if it offers some sort of proof of Anna's fiduciary generosity.

I laugh, hoping the sound will cover my nervous excitement, my embarrassment at having misinterpreted his words. Max seems nonplussed; he's looking around the club, perhaps looking for Anna, perhaps wanting to be rescued from this conversation, from the strange man saying strange words to him. No, not strange; much, much worse than strange: mundane.

The drinks situation worms away at me as well; I hadn't considered it previously, but now I do think about it, there *should* be a free bar. This company makes hundreds of millions and pays us little people a big old slice of fuck all. The least they could do is give us some free booze. But then again, if the top bosses get smaller bonuses, however will they afford to support all their mistresses and coke habits? Oh woe is them. I'll keep paying for beer if it allows them to keep ruining the world. After all, the CEO definitely works so hard he deserves millions, where the rest of us do so little, we deserve what little we get.

"Fair enough," I say, knowing I have to reply but struggling to find the right words. I'm about to say something, say anything, when Anna appears. She hooks her arm through Max's and smiles a polite but blank smile at me, the smile you give to strangers in the street, to people you recognise but can't place. To people you don't know, and don't care to.

Anna says something to Max, something I can't hear over the music, and he smiles, laughs, bends down to her level and says something back. She laughs too, and before I know it they both shout a goodbye at me that feels incredibly abrupt, before turning and exiting the scene. I'm left standing there, suddenly and irreparably alone, my new and instant love taken from me, my heart left bereft. I order and drink another beer, and the feeling soon passes. It's amazing what a bit of alcohol, plus years of low-grade mental health problems, can do to a person's ability to not care. It'd be wonderful, if I could in any way control it.

Who the fuck am I kidding? I've said perhaps ten sentences to Max, probably even fewer, and yet once he's gone there's a hole in my life, a hole in me. I get attached to people far too easily, and I curse myself when I realise it's happened again. I realise I'll have to speak to Anna in the office on Monday, try and find out more about Max. Namely his sexual preference, and his dating status. If he's gay, or at least bi, and single, then I'll be happy. Any other response, I'll deal with when I get it. I don't want to think about that right now. My therapist says I need to focus less on the past and the future and spend more time living in the present. It's something I have to do consciously, it isn't my natural state, and so standing alone in the club, in the early hours of the morning, I resolve to do what she says.

I buy another beer, still not free, to replace the one I've just imbibed, and make my way to the dance floor. Soon someone starts dancing with me; in the flashing of the disco lights I can't make out many details of them except that they're human and upright, i.e. not too drunk to make it non-consensual, so they'll do. It turns out that the mysterious person is male, and I take him home and we writhe around with each other for several hours, a pile of flesh, sweaty limbs thrusting this way and that, movement crescendoing in his ejaculating inside me, and me ejaculating on the sheets in front of us. I collapse, spent, and before I know it I'm waking up, it's Saturday morning, and he's gone. Once again, I am alone.

Two

I wish I could say, in terms of employment, that I do something interesting, that my office is NASA, or even the NSA, one letter away from glory. I could tell you that I work in intelligence gathering for MI5, or I work in fraud and anti-corruption for the police major crimes unit. I mean to be fair, I could tell you these things; the problem is I'd be lying. What I do is admin for a mid-sized stock trading platform. One that specifically is only allowed to do what customers ask, we're not allowed to give advice. Oh no, that's a big, huge no-no. That's the first thing they told us, on our very first morning, myself and several other people huddled too early into a too small, too cold meeting room. This was a couple of years ago now, but I can still remember it vividly; the nervousness of starting a new job, having to ask where the toilets are, what the deal with lunch and the canteen is, trying to remember names and faces, all the while looking for anyone particularly attractive. Even if they just end up being office-attractive, as opposed to regular-attractive, I find you need at least one pretty face to look at, to give you some respite from the never-ending monotony of data entry. According to the pointless e-learning they made us do, I'm supposed to take my eyes off my computer screen for ten minutes every hour, to rest them. I choose to spend those ten minutes staring at beautiful people. Sue me.

(Please don't sue me, I have neither a lawyer, nor means of getting one. And anyway, even if you win, you have nothing to gain; I have nothing to lose.)

The job is a late-stage capitalist classic; the only purpose my company serves is to create wealth. Under the guise of creating wealth for the customers, it creates wealth for itself. Each little thing I do in a customer's account levies a charge on the account; the charges are only fractional, when compared to the size of accounts they're levied from, but when the volume of charges is multiplied by the number of customers the company boasts, it ends up being quite the sum of money each month. I'm fairly certain, *fairly*, that it's more than I get paid. Because my labour is being exploited; of this fact I'm 100% certain.

The job makes me feel ill, if I'm being completely honest. It's one thing to be poor; I know I'm poor, there's no escaping it. Life is becoming a constant struggle just to survive for my generation, we're all constantly treading water, upward mobility is a thing of the past. It's one thing for this to be the case, but God, the awareness of it is inescapable. I love the internet, it's absolutely revolutionised the world; but it hasn't half made us all hyper-aware of everything all the time. I know it's good to be aware, but when it's 24 hours a day, 7 days a week, sometimes you just need a break.

Sometimes I do believe that ignorance must be bliss. It certainly doesn't help when I spend my days earning my meagre salary by looking at the vast sums of money these people hold, *hoard*, like some sort of fictional dragon, just sitting on it, willing people to try and take it so they have an excuse to burn their bones. Money I could use so much, that they just sit on, and watch grow. If I were to wager, I'd say 99% of the company's customers hate socialism, and absolutely have no awareness of the irony of getting richer and richer from interest, dividends, growth, etc. They hate people who sit around wanting money for nothing, they shout, from the tops of their ivory towers, in which they sit around earning money for nothing.

I'd never do it, I'm not the kind of person to, I'm not interesting or exciting enough, and plus the world simply doesn't work that way; but still, I'd fucking love to steal from them. From all those rich fuckers who hold their money with the company I work for (almost said *my* company then, that would have been a Freudian slip on a Marx/Engels level). It'd be so easy; I could simply open an account in my own name, transfer a shitload of wealth, and then disappear. That would be going nuclear, taking my life past the point of no return. That is, if anyone found out. These old cunts are so rich they probably wouldn't even notice some money going missing. And even if they did, they'd put it down to a bad investment, or something. It's funny, these people have so much money that losing some doesn't affect them. If one of the company's clients lost, say, 80% of their net worth, they'd still be in the 1%. If I were to lose 80% of mine, I'd be completely and utterly ruined. I'm a whisker away from ruin at all times anyway; one unexpected bill, let alone a massive decrease in personal wealth, could completely and utterly fuck me over. Although actually, mathematically, if we're being technical, if I lost 80% of my worth I'd be fine, because 80% of nothing is nothing, so I wouldn't actually lose anything. But you understand the point I'm trying to make.

If I wanted to be subtle, to try and commit theft in a way that only ruined my life later, not immediately, I could move small amounts, fractions of shares, and build my portfolio over time. Like I say, I'm never going to do either, but the temptation is always there. When did my life become so much day dreaming? Probably when I left uni, with a master's degree, a whole lot of hope, and a whole lot of naivete, not to mention a whole lot of debt, and upon struggling to find a job, any job at all, I realised how truly shit the real world is.

Flash forward from induction day to today, and I've worked at the company for two years. I know all the names and faces I need to know, I know where to piss, and I know where to eat. I know when I get paid. That's basically all I need from the job.

Three

It's two days after the summer party and my alarm emits
the usual shrill beeping that, as always, infests my dreams
before dragging me out of them and back to reality. I flail
one arm vaguely in its direction, before remembering that
I'm an adult now, and it's my phone from which the
alarm sounds, it's no longer an alarm clock I can silence
simply by batting. I roll over, the sheets being pulled with
me and wrapped around my body like a cheap mummy,
or a human burrito, and I pick up my phone, using two
hands to hold it steady, and eventually I'm able to swipe
my left index finger across the bottom of the screen,
silencing the infernal noise maker, pleasing my metal god,
for now at least. I look at the time, even though I know
what it'll say; in this age of digital alarms our wake-up
times can be very specific. When I was a teenager,
through school and onto college, I had an old school
alarm clock. It was small, the shell made from a sky-blue

plastic, and for some reason it was rectangular. It worked fine as a clock, you always knew approximately what time it was from just a glance, but when it came to setting the alarm, when I wanted a time much more specific, you had to move the alarm hand to approximately where you wanted it to go, and hope that the time it awoke you was a reasonable facsimile of the time you wanted it to wake you. My getting up time for all those years was 7:40: on a rectangular clock, it wasn't easy to get this time exactly. The clock's hands didn't turn in perfect circles, like they do on the majority of circular, *normal* clocks. I'm not bitter about it, despite how this probably sounds; in fact I've already devoted far too much time and energy talking about a simple piece of plastic housing, with lots of complex metallic parts inside, that served a single function, which was to rouse me from sleep. It's funny, the way I take this clock for granted; clocks are incredible inventions, able to keep ticking perfectly in time for god knows how long. They're so common that we all take them for granted, but I'd wager if I'd have taken that clock apart, I could have sat in front of it for a thousand years and not got it back together in the correct way. I would have stopped it, in taking it apart, and it never would have started it again. There's probably a lesson in there somewhere. There's also lots more hyperbole, because why not? Life is so boring, a little exaggeration adds a little spice.

But as it is with my phone alarm, I glance at the time, knowing full well it'll be 7am, and being confirmed right. It's Monday morning again; how is it always Monday morning? Though there are seven days in a week, and every day has a morning, afternoon, and evening, it seems to be Monday morning a lot more often than it is, say, Friday afternoon. Though both come exactly once per week, were I a betting man I'd say Monday morning comes round tenfold in comparison to even a Wednesday morning, or a Tuesday evening. Let alone a Friday morning, afternoon, or evening. Something about time being relative, is that what Einstein meant? Or is it just that I hate my job so much that Monday morning makes the biggest impression on me, of all the times of all the days, and so it's most memorable? If you were to ask me, I'd actually have said that I'd remember Monday mornings the least, because they're traumatic enough that my brain could hide the memory of them, but alas, that isn't the case. Fuck you brain.

Well, no matter how I try to explain it away, no matter how much I try to deny it, fight it, run from it, it is Monday morning. That's an empirical fact, an unchallengeable piece of information that's true, no matter what else is going on. Monday mornings aren't trees in uninhabited forests. Even if no one's around to experience it, Monday morning happens. It is inevitable.

This Monday is like most others for me; a slight hangover from the four beers I drank last night; a dry mouth from said beers, as well as a night of sleeping no doubt with my mouth hanging open, dignified as ever, a parody of a corpse in a horror film, face locked in a look of shock. There is nothing shocking me into this way of sleeping though, thankfully, I just have terrible sinuses. I have done for as long as I remember; I often think about doing something about it, booking an appointment with the GP, or whoever it is that deals with noses, and going from there. But I haven't done it yet, and figure I probably never will. I'm that type of lazy that goes out of his way to be lazy. If I put half as much effort into doing things as I do into not doing them, I could probably end up king of the world. However, that's far too much effort. I'd rather put the effort into not doing anything. My sinuses fall into this category perfectly; because I divide everything in my life into categories. Well, I divide all knowledge anyway. There are three categories: don't know and don't care; don't know, care but don't care enough to find out; don't know, want to know. My sinuses fall into category two; I don't know what's wrong with them, I'm curious what's wrong with them, but I'm not curious enough to actually find out. To be honest, the majority of all knowledge, where I'm concerned, falls into this category. You could probably sum up my life with that category; I don't know, and I do actually care, just not very much, not enough to *do* anything. Doing things is a con.

(Side note: no matter how hard I work, I'll never become king of the world. There are two reasons for this: 1) because there's no such thing, and 2) because I'm working class, so the ceiling I have to aim for is very low; I'd be lucky to be the world king's jester, or his pisspot. The world will keep me in my lane, no matter how hard I try to swerve.)

I go through the usual Monday morning — well every weekday morning — routine. I turn on the shower, standing outside it testing the temperature of the water with one hand, waiting for it to warm enough for me to get in. I'm not one of those people who turns the water on and gets in immediately; I genuinely think those people may be sociopaths. (I obviously don't think this; the word sociopath is thrown around all too easily these days, it's definitely en vogue. Most people who are called sociopaths are just dickheads really - but sociopath is a much more socially acceptable phrase to use, particularly in the media.) I let the water get lukewarm, and no more; it's barely after seven in the morning, and my phone tells me it's already 24 degrees, and only going to get hotter. The humidity is also up, which I hate. I love warm temperatures, but I hate humidity; it's like we, as humans, can't have anything nice without some sort of compromise. I love the heat, I wait all winter for it, praying for it to come like an ancient farmer praying to gods he can't see that he'll have a bountiful harvest. I pray for the sun, and for warmer temperatures, and rejoice when they arrive. But then, inevitably, they bring the humidity with them, and the joy I feel is tempered. In this way, I guess the farmer and I are no different; we're both slaves to that giant ball of gas in space that provides life to every single thing of which we're aware. Times change, but people don't. Not really.

I hate that sticky heat. You know the heat where you sit in shorts and a tee-shirt, if that, and feel woefully overdressed? When every movement feels like a titan moving a mountain; an act as simple as reaching for a cold drink, feeling the drops of condensation on the glass cooling your fingers for a blessed fraction of a second, becomes a Sisyphean task. Just breathing becomes a labour of love, the air almost hot enough that it might be preferable to have it outside your body, would that not result in your death. Don't get me wrong, I'd take 30 degrees and 90% humidity over winter any day of the year; I'd quite happily live somewhere like LA, where even on the coldest days the temperature is still in double figures, and the rainfall is minimal. They don't get proper seasons in LA, it's just summer about 98% of the time. That would be fine and dandy by me. I know people who say they'd have to hate a warm Christmas, that it would feel wrong, and whilst I understand and appreciate this: not me. I'd love to spend Christmas on the beach. I think it'd be so weird, so outside the realm of my past experiences, I might go insane. Were I to sit, on December 25th, and watch the waves flow in and out, swallowing sand only to regurgitate it a second later, like some sort of mother bird. To look into the distance and see the beach appear to shimmer, see the sand dance in the heat waves, it would be glorious. One day I'll make it happen. Maybe. Do I really want to, if it'll make me go insane? How do I know I'm not already insane? How do any of us? Why am I getting so existentially side-tracked?

The last time I went to LA I was by myself, and on the flight out from Heathrow I sat in a row of three seats with an old Swedish lesbian couple. We got talking, as you do after a couple of drinks, and I found out they were on their way to LA for the winter (the flight being in October). They said they were both retired and had had enough of the cold; they spent winters in LA, before heading back to their native Sweden for the summer. They lived in a 12-month summer, running from the cold faster than it could catch up. I envied them this. I don't have many wants in my life, I live a very simple existence; if I can achieve a situation like this, where I'm never cold, I'll be happy. Or at least, I'll be slightly less unhappy.

For a time anyway, before the old dissatisfaction kicks back in. We humans are funny creatures that way; we'll beg and beg and beg for something, but if you give it to us, there's a good chance we won't know what to do with ourselves. We laugh at dogs chasing cars, but how different are we, humans chasing dreams? We certainly wouldn't know what to do if we caught them.

A cool shower, pissing and brushing my teeth in it to conserve water, quickly dress, then I grab my phone, wallet, keys, and I'm out the door. Time to face another week.

The walk to the office takes about 20 minutes; I could probably do it in ten, but my pace unconsciously slows down the closer I get. It's kind of like halving a number; the closer to zero you get, the more it slows down. Unfortunately, however, where the halved number never reaches zero, I do reach work. Fuck you numbers, want to swap?

I'm like a petulant child in many respects; if you were to ask me my thoughts about going into the office each morning, my response would most likely be a very immature "I don't wanna!" Today is no different. In fact, today is even more boring than most days, because I arrive at the office ready for some Summer Party Hot Gossip, ready to find out who did what with whom, where; upon arrival, and after some discreet enquiries, I find myself incredibly disappointed. One of the few positives about working in an office is that, be it at a Christmas party, summer party, random work drinks out, whatever the occasion, if there's alcohol involved at least one person, *at least*, is going to drink too much, and do something stupid. Like Christmas 2019 for example, when Phil took too much coke and tried to fight the CEO. Or Summer 2018, when Lisa and Becky decided they wanted to be together, each leaving a boyfriend initially incredibly aroused, before soon succumbing to the dawning realisation that this wasn't some sort of fantasy come to life, it wasn't wish fulfilment; if anything, it was the exact opposite. Both boyfriends thought all of their dreams had come true. It just so happened that, unbeknownst to them, their dreams were nightmares.

I'm hoping for, expecting, awaiting, things as juicy this Monday morning, but there's nothing. It seems everyone who attended was very mature, very reserved, very well behaved. How incredibly tedious and underwhelming. A pretty good microcosm for life, then, when you think about it.

Unlike life, however, things become a lot less boring once I'm at my desk. I turn on my computer, load up my emails, excited to see what crap has arrived in there since 5pm on Friday. Once Outlook has warmed up they begin to trickle through; here's one from the facilities team, warning about a fire alarm test. Here's one from the CEO, talking about some corporate bullshit no one actually cares about. Here's one from Anna; no big deal, I think, it'll just be some boring work question. I double click on the preview to bring it full size onto my screen, and I'm pleasantly surprised to find it's nothing work related at all. Anna has written, *Noah, despite the way you acted, Max found you very interesting, and he was wondering if he could get your number?*

I'm stunned. I read the email a second, then a third time, to make sure I'm reading it correctly. *Max found you very interesting.* My heart beats in triple time. *He was wondering if he could get your number.* Erm, fuck yes he can. I don't even reply with words, simply type in my mobile number and press send. I then click to my outbox, staring at the email until it disappears. I go to my sent box and lo and behold, there it is. The email has gone to Anna, and there's nothing I can do about it now. I take my phone out of my pocket, place it on the desk in front of me, and will it to vibrate. I'll find myself doing this a lot over the coming days and weeks. Doubly so, once I meet Lucy.

Four

Summer in the city; the city being Leeds, not New York or LA or Paris or Milan, oh no, nothing so sexy and exciting as that. Not that Leeds isn't without its charm. At least as far as cities in England go anyway. I think it's Birmingham that's called England's second city, but that's a historic nickname that I don't think rings true anymore. And not just because my therapist told me that historical conclusions are not always helpful, and it's healthy to regularly review thoughts and feelings to see if they still apply. For example, I've always considered myself a coward, and when I told my therapist this she asked me why, and I couldn't answer. So perhaps I'm not a coward after all? I can't say just yet, I'm still on the fence; my therapist was referring to the way I talk about myself, but I think the logic applies in a multitude of other scenarios too, particularly this one.

Birmingham is a magnificent city, don't get me wrong, I'm not here to shit all over it; but it seems to, at some point, have reach its self-imposed limit. What I mean by that is that I've been a few times, three or four, and the city just has an air to it; to me, that air is that Birmingham made great strides forward in terms of progress until about 1984, then decided it was happy, and ceased. The citizens, without any sort of formal agreement, without even speaking a word, simply decided they'd had enough of progress, they'd reached a place they wanted to be, and stopped there. I'm sure in 1984 Birmingham was a beacon of progress - someone older than me will have to weigh in, as that was a long time before I was born. But what was true in 1984 isn't necessarily true now; Birmingham is almost an homage to the past, to a certain way of living. It's less of a city, almost a pastoral love letter to a certain type of industrial progress. Being a city built on canals, that used to be the gateway between London and north of England and Scotland, no doubt once carried a great amount of prestige. But then is not now. Now Birmingham is a city being left behind. And seemingly aware of it, yet unwilling to do anything to prevent it.

Leeds on the other hand, Leeds is a different kettle of fish altogether (whatever that metaphor actually means - I stopped trying to explain language a few years ago, in my second year of uni. The English language is a nightmare, and kudos to anyone who learns it as a second language. I can barely speak and understand it and it's my native tongue). Leeds is progress personified. Or should that be citified? Outside of London it's definitely the most technologically advanced city. In terms of disruptive industries like digital marketing, it's second only to London. And now with Channel Four opening a new building, it'll only continue to grow. And continue to move forward. Birmingham is growing, but staying still. Staying in the past.

(I apologise for using a phrase such as 'disruptive industry'; that's one of those phrases invented by some business idiot, like 'synergy', which at first you laugh upon hearing, then start to use sarcastically, and before you know it it's in your everyday vernacular. You have no idea how, but your tongue has turned the joke back on you, and there's nothing you can do except accept your fate. Except accept. Except accept. Say that ten times quickly after a few pints.)

I've lived in Leeds for just over six years: I came here to go to uni, and never left. I think that's the story of a huge percentage of the city's residents. The average population can't be much over 30, and that's factoring in all the elderly raising the average. The population declines massively in summer, as waves of students leave, off to explore in their time off, to see the world for a short while, taking a break from the insides of lecture halls and seminar rooms, to explore pubs on a different shore. The slightly older crowd left uni but still ostensibly young, the 'young professionals', they filter off too, to festivals, to summer camps, they go to America to volunteer, to Asia to volunteer, they go somewhere to assuage their capitalist consciences, somewhere they can chip away at the mountain of guilt which their privilege has afforded them. I'm not here to criticise or to judge; I did exactly the same thing. My first summer out of uni, the first time in 18 years I hadn't been in full time education, I was shocked with what I was faced with; namely, the world entire.

The thing about childhood is that there's always someone there, if not holding your hand, then at least guiding you in the right direction. Childhood, and into your teenage years, is a river. We all ride it, admittedly some in bigger, comfier boats than others; I went down it in a mid-sized rowing boat, just my mother, my sister, and I. Dad died a long time ago. We never really recovered.

As a child, then a pre-teen, then a teenager, you float down that river, the lazy river of life. What problems you have, though they may feel the size of the world itself, are fairly minor. Clothes to wear, friends to make, hobbies to pick up, sports to play, dates to try and get; they define your life, but only within its existing parameters. You can change everything about yourself, but you'll still be on that river; the river is relentless and doesn't let go until it's time. But then when it is time, it's almost like going over a waterfall. You've spent 20-odd years growing up, learning things, trying to carve out a space for yourself, and then all of a sudden it's so long, good luck, enjoy whatever you end up doing.

That's how I've ended up in this meaningless, dead end admin job. I wasn't prepared to have to live my own life. Because if you ask me, that's the one thing that childhood doesn't teach you. I know that $a^2+b^2=c^2$; I know that the first world war was ostensibly started by the assassination of the Archduke Franz Ferdinand. I know that the band Franz Ferdinand took their name from that man; I know that Charles Dickens wrote some of the most amazing literature in history, before abandoning his wife and nine or ten children to take up with his 19-year-old mistress. I know all of these things, these insignificant, highly irrelevant things; and yet I don't know how to live my own life.

So it is, I just sort of stumble through it, lurching wildly from one day to the next, like a drunk driver crossing lines between lanes, no cares, no clues; my theory on life, at least at the moment (I subscribe to moral relativity, and extended this to my entire life; everything is relative, everything should be capable of being changed based on new evidence. Hence why this is only my theory *currently*. This may change any time, with any information. It may remain forever. The future is unknown - I'm undecided if this is a good or a bad thing), is that if I can make it back to the safety of my bed without having killed anyone or causing any major accidents or fires or any other destructive force which being guilty of will ruin my life, then all is okay. So far, so good. No deaths to attribute to me, and any major accidents or fires I caused are unbeknownst to me, and no one official like the Police or whatever has come knocking on my door, so I can only plead ignorance in this case. Whoever said ignorance is *not* bliss is full of shit. Ignorance is a wonderful thing. In small doses anyway. Ignorance in large doses leads to Brexit, and we all know how well *that's* going.

Summer in the city; it isn't stifling hot like New York or LA, it isn't unbearable. It's difficult, but difficult in a good way; I'm a summer person, I like the sunshine and I like daylight. I've never really checked it out, but I assume I suffer from SAD. Season Affective Disorder. Like I say, I've never confirmed with a doctor — file it under 'care, but don't care enough to find out' — or other kind of trained professional, but that fact I feel incredibly sad from around October to April probably doesn't bode well. I'm sure most people don't feel overwhelmingly sad for six months of the year.

And don't discount the other six months, from May to September; I feel incredibly sad then, but it isn't weather related. I'm just generally sad in those months, in spite of the sunshine and warm temperatures.

Summer in Leeds means topless locals. But not in the good way your mind, if it's anything like mine, probably immediately leapt to the conclusion of. When temperatures in this country hit a certain number, a certain type of person decides it's acceptable to walk around without anything covering their top half. You know what I mean, this isn't news to anyone who's spent any time in this country. Like life's little ironies, it's never the people you *want* to see topless that you get to see topless. You could line up 100 English citizens, put them in order of size and attractiveness, and I guarantee the bottom echelon are the ones who'll use the sun as an excuse to get topless. It's never the top echelon, the beautiful men and women (and everything in between) who show themselves. But perhaps this is for the best; we all need to want. If I saw Jason topless every day for six months, there's a chance I genuinely might just die. I know that sounds melodramatic, but it's the truth. A truth we'll never have to put to the test, thankfully, so I can say it's a truth and no one can prove otherwise. It's never people like Max and Lucy who get topless when the sun comes out; sure, I've seen them both topless, indeed completely naked, myriad times, but it isn't the same. Don't get me wrong, it's much, much better, but it isn't the same.

Summer in the city means remembering that English buildings were constructed to keep the hot air inside, not to allow it to dissipate. Which means excellent insulation, no air conditioning. In winter, it's incredible. In summer, it's torture. On this Monday morning, when I sit at my desk pretending to work, waiting for Max to message me, if he's even going to, the temperature hits 30 degrees when the clock is barely past 10am. It's going to be another scorching day. And yet another reason being in an office frustrates and depresses me in equal measure.

I've been exaggerating the temperatures and the seasons that transpire in England. It's true we get all four seasons, like most of the world. However, despite the fact they're split in four equal sections of three months, the weather doesn't work like that. Summer is officially

June, July, and August. However, the sunshine first appears in April, staying for a couple of weeks before disappearing. May gets one week, maybe two of nice weather; June begins to slowly ramp things up, turning the dial up a notch every few days, until July arrives, and brings proper summer. It's usually nice for most of the month, same goes for August; the sun is out in full force, unbidden by clouds or rain. The country comes into full bloom, both flora and fauna. The people bloom too; it definitely isn't just me that's affected by the changing seasons. Summer brings a sense of optimism, of hope. When the sun's shining, doom seems a little bit less likely than normal. The months pass too quickly though, and soon August gives way to September; summer winds its way down, and we usually get a week or so of sun in September, and perhaps, if we're lucky, an Indian summer in October. We don't have one sustained summer period, instead we have three months of good weather stretched across seven or eight months. If nothing else, it keeps us all on our toes. And gives us not just something to talk about, but also something to complain about. And if we English people have nothing to complain about, well I dread to think. I don't think such a situation has ever arisen. Although now that I think about it, I'm sure we'd just start complaining about having nothing to complain about, and we'd all breathe a huge sigh of relief.

(Note to self: research the origins of the phrase "Indian summer": it feels like exactly the kind of phrase passed down from older generations that probably arose from some form of bigotry or ignorance. Google whether it's okay to say or not and adjust behaviour accordingly. PS boomers: it's literally this easy to change your behaviour. So just do it already.)

Sitting in an office in 30-degree heat in a shirt and tie

with no air conditioning doing work I'm pretty sure makes literally no difference to the world. I'm fairly certain if I did no work for a year, no one would notice. I do no work for large parts of most days and it's not once been mentioned to me. Some days I definitely do no work at all; I'm not trying to get fired, I'd starve if I did. But I also think that being made unemployed and being unable to pay my rent, as opposed to now, when I'm just barely able to pay my rent, might force me into some kind of reckoning. I work in this job because after my Master's degree I had no one to tell me what to do next, and this job came up whilst I was trying to figure it out. It's been a few years, and I've made no progress. I've become comfortable in my routine. Comfortable in my discomfort. Maybe I need that fear to kick start my life. Or more likely, I'll work shitty jobs forever, spending my life scraping by to make rent. Why? Because I'm a millennial, that's why. Isn't this what we do?

Five

Max doesn't message me for two weeks. After ten days I'm close to giving up hope, not just with Max, but giving up on the entire world; then I meet Lucy.

You know how in this country, the second the sun comes out everyone dashes off to the nearest beer garden, or alfresco cafe, the nearest *anything* that has outdoor seating and sells alcohol? Well, in Leeds this is epitomised by Belgrave Music Hall; it has a rooftop terrace, high above the city, which provides wonderful panoramic views. Admittedly, they're only views of the urban nightmare, but that's the best most of us can hope to see in the 21st century, so we learn to appreciate it. On a good, sunny day you need to arrive at Belgrave no later than three in order to secure a table, which will provide seating for up to six people. If you arrive before four you might get a seat, but no accompanying table. If you arrive before five, you might just squeeze into the remaining standing room. Any time after, and you should be so fucking lucky, buddy. Not happening. On the rooftop of Belgrave Music Hall is where I meet Lucy.

We operate in three shifts at work; the first arrives at 7am, leaving at 3pm. The second arrives at 9am, and leaves at 5pm, the office classic. The third arrives at 3pm, leaving at 11pm. I work exclusively on the 9-5; my team does something, I'm not sure what, but it does something which means we all need to be there during office hours. I feel bad for the other teams, who operate on a rota, and so struggle with long term consistency, but really I don't mind. I help others where I can, don't get me wrong, and I always try to leave things better than I found them; if I was being honest, I'd say my empathy stretches almost too far sometimes, and if not stopped I may actually set myself on fire to keep someone else warm. However, this doesn't apply where work is concerned. Work is the worst part of my life; I despise every single second of it, and I despise the person I have to become whilst I'm there. I'm not me; I'm not even close to being me. Any office that says they want to be a family, and have people act like themselves, is full of shit. Particularly my office; if I was being myself, why would I go to work? I only go now for the money; if money were no issue, I'd never work again. I might volunteer if I got bored, which I'm sure I would eventually, but travel would keep me occupied for a long time. I hope so anyway; travel is all I want to do with my life, so if it turns out to be shit, then I'm screwed. Then I'll really not know what I'm living for.

But anyway, sometimes, when the amount of fucks I'm giving reaches dangerously close to zero, I'll take advantage of the confusion and slip out with the morning crew at 3pm. We only have managers working the morning and night shifts, none work the day; by having managers on the morning and night shifts, there's guaranteed to always be at least one on duty. Sure, it means there can never be a full picture of the office, and manager's shifts don't overlap, so issues can't be passed from day to night. It also means the day shift, my team's shift, is often left to our own devices. We have a manager, but she works morning or night, not day like the rest of us, so she'll either leave halfway through our shift, or turn up halfway through it. On the day I meet Lucy, she's on holiday. The sun is out, I'm parched and in need of a drink, something definitely alcoholic, and I just really, really can't be arsed. That's the crux of the matter, if I'm being honest. I could ruminate all day on Marx, capital, seizing the means of production and all that jazz, but ultimately, on this day, it comes down to this: I. Cannot. Be. Fucking. Bothered.

I made my decision to leave early at approximately 9:01am; the only problem with this is that in my head I know I have a short day, so the second I make the decision to leave, I start waiting. Which is all well and good, except I have six hours to wait. Time really drags when you're clock watching for six hours. 360 minutes. 21,600 seconds. It's actually a long time, especially when you're wishing it away. But what can you do? I'm convinced that sitting in the office waiting to go to the pub is the closest an adult can get to replicating that feeling of Christmas Eve as a child. I can still remember it now; the excitement, the anticipation, the fear. Even as a child, though I didn't know it at the time, and only came to understand it later, I feared disappointment. The disappointment of not getting what I wanted? Sure. The disappointment of getting *exactly* what I wanted? Absolutely, that too. More so, if I'm being honest.

I remember Christmas Eves sitting up in the living room, being allowed to stay up much later than normal, one of the small concessions my parents would make. We'd watch a film, or just watch some TV show, my sister Emma and I too excited to concentrate, my parents already too over it to care. Eventually they'd shuttle us up to bed, and then the real waiting began. And that's how it is in the office, staring at the small clock in the corner of my computer screen, each sixty second revolution of the second hand seeming to take forever, and then when it finally makes its way past 12 and starts again, I swear sometimes the minute hand doesn't move, and the minute is repeated. Relative time again; I used to think it was about just women, love, sex, tits, but now I realise it's basically about everything. Women is just the example people use, because it's basically universal.

On this particular day I sneak out of the office with the three o'clock crowd. Will I be missed at work? Potentially. There's always a chance someone, maybe Jason, might notice I've gone. Do I care? On a sunny day like this, it's hard to. A few of the work crowd are going to Belgrave so I tag along, uninvited, perhaps unwanted, definitely uncaring. One good thing about going out with work, aside from the fact that you get to see people in a new light, is that you can get lost in a crowd. In this instance, no one knows who invited me, but it doesn't matter. Everyone knows I normally work until five, but I tell anyone who asks I've used holiday time to leave early, and no one questions it. A work do involves a crowd just large enough to provide the right level of anonymity. I love it. The anonymity that is. I fucking hate the work do part of the scenario.

I spot Lucy the second we sit down on the roof. Having left work at three, we're there early enough to have our pick of the seats; I guide us to one I know will stay in the sunshine until late; we won't be one of those tables who suddenly start shivering once the sun goes down enough to stop heating them; we won't have to leave before closing time, cold and out of the spirit of summer. To be fair, even if we were one of those tables I wouldn't leave anyway, but it's nice to have a reason that isn't just stubbornness of character. Or something like that. It's nice to live logically for a change, not just acting out of fear based on emotions that may or may not be real.

I see Lucy right away; blonde hair, blue eyes, beautiful smile, small boobs. I notice, and appreciate, these things in this order. I'm not drunk enough to talk to her, having barely had a sip of a drink yet, but she's also so beautiful I can't wait until I am drunk before I do talk to her. What if someone gets there first? What if, by the time I'm drunk enough to start chatting to her, someone else has already started talking, and she's fallen in love with him, or her, or them? Unlikely I know, but not beyond the realms of possibility. I sit there, agonising over what to do, before it hits me. This is an extreme situation, so I'm going to have to go for extreme measures.

Belgrave has a bar on the rooftop, a tiny little thing crammed into a kind of bastardised garden shed. It's ridiculous, really, but it means you don't have to go down three or four flights of stairs to get a drink, so it's entirely brilliant. Sitting at the table, ostensibly with the work crowd, but really only one of two people who exist in that moment, I wait for Lucy to go to the shed-cum-bar. At this point I of course don't know that she's called Lucy, I only know that she's beautiful and I want to suck on her nipples, but it's easier to apply her name retroactively than it is to call her something demeaning, refer to her by her appearance, as if that's all she is. It seems to take an age, but she eventually gets up and goes and gets herself a drink. I watch her, and once she's sitting back down, I go up to the bar. I catch the

attention of the woman who served Lucy, and ask her to
send the same drink over to her, compliments of me. I
ask her to wait until I'm seated; I head back to my group
sheepishly, knowing things are set in motion. I imagine
nothing will come of it; she'll get the drink, ask the
woman about it. The woman will point me out, and
perhaps Lucy will smile, or say thanks, and that'll be it.
The last thing I expect is her to approach me and start
talking.

A few moments after I sit down, Lucy approaches me
and starts talking.

Five

My father died when I was seven years old. Emma was nine. It's been so long now I can no longer remember what he looked like. My mother has pictures of him in the house still, but there seem to be fewer and fewer each time I visit her. I've often wondered how it works, when you're widowed. At what point do you stop wearing your wedding ring? Do you ever? When you start dating again, if you do, what happens if you fall in love? Do you have to remove the pictures of the deceased, and replace them with pictures of the living? Can you have pictures of both?

If heaven exists, who do you spend eternity with? Being widowed must be an administrative nightmare, I can't even imagine. Luckily (luckily?) when my mother went through it, I was too young to understand the full ramifications. I knew what it meant for us in practical terms; there'd be three of us, not four, living in the house. We had to tighten our belts, literally; my mother's wage alone barely kept us going, and smaller portions of food meant smaller children developing. I know Emma looks back on it almost fondly; she's a model now, the small body that malnutrition never really allowed to develop is apparently just what the modelling industry is looking for. I'm proud of her. Though I wish she'd do fewer topless adverts; I'm not a prude or anything, it's just that seeing my sister's breasts, particularly when I least expect it, knocks me for six. I really don't know how to feel. This isn't a situation that most people find themselves in, so there isn't a rulebook or anything. I haven't even dared ask my therapist what you're supposed to do when your sister gives you an erection. How on earth do you broach that subject?

My father died of a massive heart attack. He went off to work like any other morning, was presumably just travelling through the time of the day like any other day, and then boom. Well, not even boom; from *du-dum, du-dum, du-dum*, to nothing. Just like that, a life ended. Everything he did, everything he was, all gone. Snuffed out like a candle. Except he didn't even leave a smell. You know that lovely smell that permeates a room once you've extinguished a candle? My father didn't even leave us so much as that. What he did was leave us alone and leave us to fend for ourselves. Like I said, we never got over it. My mother didn't cope then, and I honestly don't think she copes now. It used to make me sad, and angry, and then sad again; now it makes me nothing. One of the things my therapist is trying to teach me is to actually live by the words of the serenity prayer. You know the one I mean: God grant me the courage to change the things I can, the power to accept the things I can't, and the wisdom to know the difference. I don't think that's it verbatim, but I assume you know the one I mean. My therapist is trying to teach me to let go of things I can't control. It's tough, and over the last year or so I'm not sure we've gotten very far, but I know we have improved. I know this because it no longer upsets or angers me that my mother isn't over the death of her husband, a death that happened 17 years ago. I should not be mad at her, because I'm not over it either, and thus would have to be mad at myself. But who's ever taken that good a look at themselves? We're all hypocrites, we just don't all acknowledge it. That would mean leaving the path of least resistance, and does anyone really ever want to do that? I certainly fucking don't. The less resistance, the happier I am. Maybe that's where I'd finally be happy, in a vacuum? If not happy, then perhaps dead; either way, my unhappiness would be a thing of the past.

Did I talk about life's little ironies before? Here's another one; my father died of a heart attack. My mother has since had a heart transplant. My family is run by hearts, one way or another. My sister and I have had whispered conversations, around the dining table after my mother has gone off to bed, about which way we think it'll go for each of us. Will we be like our father, absolutely fine until we're absolutely not? Or like our mother, getting a little unwell, enough so that we have tests, and a much, much bigger problem is spotted and solved before it takes a real hold of us? My sister wants to go like our father. I don't want either, but if I had to choose I'd take the same path as my mother. At least I'd be alive. Above all things, I'm not ready to die.

I miss my father every day, but in some ways I'm glad he's dead. That sounds horrible but bear with me; he was a wonderful man, that I remember. He was kind, caring, he worked hard to provide for us. He wasn't a genius, he was never going to change the world, never going to cure cancer or anything, but he carved out a little corner of the planet for himself, and he made it better. So why am I glad he's dead? Well, it's an excuse isn't it? Particularly growing up, it's amazing the things you can get away with by having a dead dad. It's amazing the things people will forgive, because you've been through trauma. I'd recommend trauma to everyone, were it not so traumatic.

I'd never normally say this, but fuck it, whilst we're learning all about Noah; having a dead dad really, really helps getting girls. Never overestimate the sympathy vote, because it really does work.

"Thanks for the drink," Lucy says, by way of an opening.

"You're welcome. I hope it wasn't too presumptuous or anything?"

"Not at all, I totally appreciate it. Plus, it's pretty old school. Did you know I've never had someone buy me a drink in this way before?

"I don't believe that," I say to Lucy, half flattering her, half telling the truth. I find it difficult to think no one has ever bought a woman this beautiful a drink in this way before, but then again what I'd done was so old fashioned, why would anyone do it? Did people even still meet in bars, or was it all online? There must be some IRL talking, right? Somewhere? Do the normies do it? I can see people talking from where I'm sitting talking to Lucy, so presumably they must do? If I can't trust my eyes or my ears, what can I trust? Perhaps that's a question for George Orwell.

"It's true," she smiles back at me, half proud, half bashful (I think - I'm not a great reader of people. When you barely understand yourself, you hardly even try to understand others. It's too complicated, without a doubt). I can sense a playfulness to her, a flirtiness I'm dying to try and coax more out of. This girl is interesting, I tell myself. This girl has potential. For the first time since I met him, I forget Max exists. Well, I nearly do.

"But you must have had a lot of drinks bought for you in, like, more traditional ways?"

She doesn't answer this with words but with a look; her head is angled down as she sips her drink through her straw, but her eyes look up at me, teasing me, as if telling me that I know the answer, and to stop asking such stupid questions. It isn't a rebuke though, far from it. If anything it's more like a challenge.

"Noah," I reach my hand out as I say this, offering it to her. I'm quietly relieved when she accepts.

"Lucy."

Her grip is firm without being over the top. She shakes my hand briskly and efficiently, two quick pumps up and down, before removing her hand and placing it back on her drink. Whether this is the one I bought her, or the one she had before I don't know, so I ask her if she'd like another. She acquiesces, and we make our way to the shed bar.

The woman who served us both earlier has since left and been replaced by a man. The bar is crowded, bodies jostling for position, but Lucy simply strolls up and pushes her way through the crowd almost as if they're not there. She gets served immediately; not very professional from the barman, to overlook all these people who have clearly been here longer than she has, but I don't blame him; Lucy is perhaps the most beautiful women I've ever seen in the flesh. And this isn't one of those beauty is in the eye of the beholder moments: Lucy's beauty is objective, is an empirical fact. The way the guy behind the bar acts towards her and around her is proof enough, if looking at her face wasn't.

Beauty of course means different things to different people; some people find true beauty in nature, in the bright colours of a spring flower, or the rustle of the leaves on a sturdy oak tree as a soft summer breeze passes through, causing a ripple effect that shakes the tree and makes it look even more alive than it already is. Some people find beauty in the man-made, in giant buildings, fast cars; others find it in art, poetry. Beauty is everywhere, and it means something different to every single one of us; there's a dictionary definition of beauty, and then there are nearly eight billion individual definitions too. And then there's Lucy; I don't care what you consider beautiful, I don't care if you're straight, gay, bi, poly, whatever. Lucy is beautiful, and there's no denying it.

It isn't just the way she looks too, although in this sense she's next to flawless. She has blonde hair, parted in a straight line down the centre of her head, falling to just below her shoulders. It sits on them, as if biding its time; and then when Lucy moves her head her hair takes the spot light, moving as if it's one solid block, rolling from side to side like a wave, passing back and forth, to and from the shore. Always leaving, always returning. Never quite there, never quite gone. Always filled with potential, but always just tantalisingly out of reach.

Her hair frames her face, and to glance at her she could be a work of fine art, a tribute to realism, the definition of it. She has blue eyes, set either side of a quite small, quite hooked nose. But it isn't the kind of hooked that calls to mind a cartoon witch; it's a soft hook, a tiny one inclining upwards so little as to barely be noticeable. It doesn't curve up with negative connotations, only positive; it's just another beautiful feature of this beautiful woman. You might consider it a flaw, but only in the sense that Da Vinci, when painting the ceiling of the Sistine Chapel may have made a single incorrect brush stroke. It could be said to be a flaw, but it's not noticeable, and it serves as part of something greater than itself. It's the kind of imperfection that's necessary to make you completely understand how perfect everything else is. It's *realistic*. And anyway, it's not like noses are one of those parts of the body that are ever particularly attractive in their own right. But if they're taken away, their absence destroys the face upon which they should sit.

Her skin is flawless, at least from the distance at which I regard her. White as porcelain, she's perhaps only bettered in this sense by me; I've never met anyone paler than me, and with the exception of albinos, I don't think there is anyone. She has the kind of skin you want to touch; not in a creepy, leering way, but in an appreciative way, the way you would run your fingers over a particularly smooth rock you find on the beach, or the way you might trail your hand through tall grass as you run amongst it, feeling a freedom you haven't felt since you were a child.

Lucy has blue eyes, which when combined with her hair become a bit cliche, give her that Aryan chic, but this is a metaphor so grounded in nonsense, stemming from one of the greatest monstrous regimes in human history, that I wonder why I make the comparison. Why, when faced with great beauty, do I often resort to cliches. Why can I never find my own words to describe the person or thing in front of me? Why do I resort to empty platitudes? If I had to guess, I'd say it's because I'm a true romantic at heart, a real believer in true love and all that crap; and so when faced with great beauty, I forget myself. I lose all sense of myself, my brain curdles like so much old milk, and I become a stammering mess. My brain becomes unable to find any new words, so resorts to pulling words from TV shows and films, from songs and poems. It's easier to speak through someone else's words, I think, not just because it means you don't have to do anything original, to engage your brain, but also because if it goes wrong you can just blame the person who originally said the words. Can't be mad at my words if they're not mine. Right?

Whatever the reason for my banality, it isn't important right now. What is important is that Lucy is handing me a drink, something I take a sip of without even wondering what it is, and then we're making our way back through the crowd. I start to make my way back to the group from which she plucked me, but her hand placed gently on my upper arm stops me. Honestly, I could have been about to score the winning goal in the World Cup final, and if Lucy put her hand on my arm I'd stop, and do whatever she told me to do. I fall in love so fast that just this one bit of physical contact, our first apart from the brief handshake, is enough to plant a flag inside me. I thought I was completely and utterly, irrepressibly in love with Max. Well, it turns out there was still space in my heart, and that space has now been filled by Lucy. I'm in love with two people, two people with whom I've never even had a full conversation each. Sometimes I really do hate myself.

Lucy's touching my arm was to indicate that where I was stood as she touched me was fine. I look around and we're far enough away from my group that we're afforded some little privacy, even as we're surrounded by people. These people around us are strangers, people I've never met, and judging by her lack of acknowledgement of them Lucy hasn't met either. So now it's just the two of us, standing in the crowd, surrounded by people but completely alone. It's my second favourite way to be when I'm with a beautiful woman.

Even though her hand is back on her glass, I can still feel its ghost on my warm. My whole body is warm from the summer sun, and yet this small patch of my arm feels

55

like it's on fire. But not in a scary, dangerous way; in an exciting, endless-possibilities way. The way she touched me, gently, but with a confidence and a surety, leaves me stumped, stunned, confused, a little aroused, and completely lost in Lucy. Her eyes are so blue, and everything she says and does is reflected in them. You know they say about psychopaths that when they smile it doesn't reach their eyes? Everything Lucy does reaches her eyes. I don't know what the opposite of a psychopath is, but whatever it is, it's Lucy. A goddess? An angel amongst mere mortals? A normal human woman in the presence of a desperate mess of a creature that resembles man?

Now that we both have drinks, and we've found a place to put ourselves, I realise I'm going to have to talk to her. But how? What can I even say to this woman? Any words that come out of my mouth will fall so short of the standard that her mere existence demands, I don't know that I have it in me. I can see her looking at me, those blue eyes of hers inviting me, and so I open my mouth, and hope against hope that I don't sound too much like a twat.

"So what do you do…" I begin, hating myself before the question is even out of my mouth, sounding completely and utterly like a twat, delighted when Lucy interrupts me.

"Nope," she says, loudly and firmly. Her reaction confuses me.

"Nope to anything in particular," I ask her, "or just nope in general?"

"Nope to your question."

The conversation is moving so fast it takes me a moment to remember what I was even going to say.

I look at her and she smiles back at me, revealing two rows of straight white teeth, as well as quite a lot of gum, something again that might be considered a flaw in and of itself, but when it's part of the collage of humanity that is Lucy, it's basically perfect.

(Incidentally, I think teeth are the only part of the world where straight and white isn't a pair of terms to strike fear into the hearts of mortal men (and women).)

"My question?" I ask her, half laughing.

"Your question," she says, laughing with me, but offering no further information.

"What about my question—" I begin before she cuts me off.

"Fuck your question." I'm taken aback, but not unpleasantly, by her directness. (I'll learn in time that Lucy is an incredibly direct person, and I'll learn to rely on it, because I myself am a very indecisive one.)

"I have a job, I earn money, I use it to pay my bills and what little I have left over I use for fun."

I'm stunned into silence by her reply. Whilst I will eventually become used to how forthright she is, initially I'm knocked for six. Despite having a family, a mother, a dad for a certain amount of time, I was basically raised by television and movies. In my mannerisms, my speech, all of that, I think I'm much more American than I am English. But it isn't just being American that's resulted from being raised by media; I'm not used to strong, confident, self-assured women. The media has only prepared me for pliant, supplicant women; I've obviously met enough women that I know this is a ridiculous notion, and I'm working to dispel myself of it, but it's difficult. We humans do so much subconsciously; by the time Lucy and I had even spoken for the first time, I'd imagine I'd made somewhere in the region of 10,000 assumptions about her. And as I say, subconsciously; I didn't look at Lucy and decide in my head that she's submissive, my subconscious drew upon thousands of years of Western sexism and made the assumption for me. It's a pleasant surprise finding out just how wrong I am.

"I have a job, but that isn't what I *do*, it isn't who I *am*."

I don't say anything, simply regard her silently, fascinated, hoping she'll go on.

"Do you have a job?" She doesn't allow me time to answer. "I'm sure you do, and I'm sure you go to work, and each month pay your rent and bills, and then try to live your life on what little is left over." She's incredibly correct. "But I'm sure that isn't, like, reflective of you as a person, is it?"

Now she waits for a response. I'm not sure what to offer as one; she's nailed it completely, and really there isn't much more to say on the subject. I think she can sense that she has me on the back foot, because she gives me that look again, sucking on her straw, eyeing me with amusement. I'm amused too, though I'm not sure why. I think I'm just mirroring her movements, her actions; I want to not just be with her, and be around her, but I want to be her, I want to be who she is. This woman, the ephemeral beauty, like a portrait brought to life, a woman of such unbridled beauty, such unquestioning confidence, a woman who is everything a person should be, and yet unapologetic either way. I don't want to be a woman; I want to be *Lucy*.

Whether I'm taking too long in answering, or whether this was part of her plan all along, with a flourish she finishes her drink, places the empty glass down on a nearby table, and after glancing at her phone says, "I've got to go, it was nice meeting you," and then she's gone.

I stand rooted to the spot, stunned. Did that just happen? Was I really talking to a woman named Lucy, or did I imagine the whole thing? The only evidence I have is the half full glass in my hand, and the sight of the empty glass I can see just a few feet away. Lucy exists in my memories, but even now I'm already beginning to doubt she was ever real, and I'm beginning to suspect that she was a figment of my imagination. Has my mental health finally deteriorated to the point where I'm hallucinating? If so, this can't be good. But really though, she was real, right? You saw her?

I'm on the verge of having a complete and utter nervous breakdown when I'm saved by the bell. My phone vibrates in my pocket, and without thinking I pull it out, and gently depress the button on the side which causes the screen to light up. It's a notification from Instagram; I have one new follower. I open the app and click on the notifications tab, and there is indeed one new follower. Welcome, On_Wings_of_Lead, I wonder who you are. The name is more like something from MySpace than Instagram, and for a second I wonder if I've been transported to an alternate reality where Tom never sold MySpace, Facebook never took off, and Democracy still exists as something more than a mocking taunt. If only, if only.

The profile is private, which I always find equal parts frustrating and ridiculous; frustrating because it's impossible to digitally stalk someone when they've maxed their privacy setting, ridiculous because it's like, what are you hiding? If it's private enough to keep from people, why put it online at all? I'm sure smarter people than me find privacy settings a tiny hurdle; once something is online, then it exists forever, and pretty much in the public eye. Especially where social media is concerned. For better or worse — definitely worse — social media exists, and we all just have to deal with it. I'm aware of criticising social media whilst being an active participant in it; but this is half the problem, you basically have to be on it. It's like Capitalism; yes I want to destroy it, but yes I do also live under it and participate in it. That's half the reason for wanting to destroy it in the first place. At the very least we need one viable alternative; isn't competition the cornerstone of Capitalism anyway? And if it's so good, why does it fear competition? Why is it so scared of the free market? Because the free market is self-regulating, right? Right!?

The profile may be private, but if I squint I can make some features of the profile picture out. Namely blonde hair; when I say some features, I mean one feature, just this one. But it's enough to get my heart racing; is it Lucy? I press follow back, and then I do with (potential) Lucy as I did with Max; I wait.

Six

Another of life's little ironies: did you know that the box my anti-depressants comes in makes really good roach material for when one is rolling a joint? I've said that to a few people jokingly, just to gauge their reaction. Each telling is mostly met with amusement tinged with genuine concern, which I think is how people approach me in general. I'm the friend who makes a lot of jokes about suicide, depression, that kind of thing, that are borderline at best. You know what I mean, every friend group has that guy. Or woman; this kind of self-deprecating humour isn't exclusively a male trait. I do think it is exclusively an English trait, or a British one anyway. I think it's the kind of wry British humour that you just don't find anywhere else in the world. Say what you will about Britain, and I can think of a thing or two that I'd start with, we're a funny people. Ha-ha funny that is. We're the other kind of funny too, but that's not to what

I'm currently referring.

If you asked me, I'd say I smoke a bit of weed, not a great deal, and certainly not too much. It's all incredibly subjective though isn't it? I have friends who would consider one drag of one joint too much for an entire lifetime; I have other friends who, if they're not stoned by 9am, consider it time wasted. I'd put myself somewhere roughly in the middle; I smoke weed some days, not all. I can sleep just fine without it, but I'd be lying if I said I didn't sleep better with it. I don't exclusively masturbate when I'm high, but I try to most of the time. It just feels better. No one can deny that; weed makes most things feel better. Which I guess is why so many people, myself included, smoke it. Or eat it, or whatever it. Imbibe it I guess is the catch-all term I'm looking for. And I guess that's why it's illegal in this country too; can't have the proletariat being too happy; because if we're happy in one way, we might start to imagine we can be happy in other ways. And we might start to question why we're not. And then comes revolution.

Of course, everyone smokes weed for different improvements; it makes masturbating better, ergo it must make sex better. That logic follows surely? I can't say I know, I've never had sex whilst high. Well, I've never had sex whilst *only* high. Every time I've been high and had sex, I've been drunk too. And it's not the same. It's fun, yes, but a different kind of fun. Plus, sometimes it's also super *not* fun; whilst weed makes orgasms better, I find it makes them harder to achieve. With alcohol, I get aroused really easily, but again find it difficult to finish. I also find it difficult to maintain an erection. Basically I'm just trying, right now, to avoid using the phrase 'whiskey dick'. But evidently I failed at that task. So anyway you can imagine how I am in bed when I'm both drunk *and* high; it's carnage. And unfortunately, it isn't the kind of carnage from which genius occurs. It's the kind of carnage that makes the news, and leaves people hospitalised. Not literally, obviously, but you get where I'm going with the metaphor.

I smoke weed because the improvement I'm chasing is that it allows me to live in the present. (I also love having the munchies because I love eating, plus the weed makes everything taste so much better. I used to be a fat kid, is it obvious?) One of the things my therapist thinks, which I guess I already knew, but didn't realise it until she told me, is that I don't live in the present enough. I spend too much time either fixated on the past, or waiting for the future. As I say, this was not incredibly surprising information for me to hear. I definitely live in the past too much. Or dwell on it, as popular phraseology would have it. I've been told, by my therapist, but also by articles I've read online (sources checked, don't worry, I'm not a maniac) that this is a symptom of anxiety. The anxious person, I've read, spends a lot of time revisiting things; be it dwelling in the past, like I do, rehashing old memories, be they good or bad; they watch the same TV shows and movies repeatedly, read the same books, listen to a small amount of music, but listen to it a large amount. Basically, the anxious person does things they've already done, because they know how it's going to turn out. This was another thing that I had no idea about, but then when I read it, it made so much I know about myself click. It was incredibly satisfying, first reading this, to know the things I did, whilst probably not absolutely normal, not at least by the strictest definition of the word, were not completely *abnormal*. Sure, they were outside the norm, but not so far out as, say, eating babies, or smearing your own faeces everywhere. I haven't gone that far beyond the pale yet, anyway.

I spend so much time pouring over my memories, reliving them in my head. Even the bad ones. The thing is, to me it isn't just about what's good or what's bad, it's about what's unknown. Most of the time I'd rather relive an old, painful memory, than live in the present, and make a new memory. It's ridiculous isn't it? If I purposefully relive a bad memory, there's a 100% chance I'll have a bad time. Whereas, if I live in the present, and work on making new memories, statistically there's at least a 1% chance I'll have a good time, right? I mean really, in this instance, where we're thinking in a vacuum, surely the odds are straight up 50/50 between good and bad time? And yet, something in my brain would rather I take the 100% chance of a bad time, because it's a known thing. Rather than a 50% chance something good might happen, which leads to a 50% chance of something bad, I opt for 100% chance of bad. There's as good a chance something wonderful will happen as there is something terrible, and yet I opt for definitely terrible. Tell me again that mental illnesses can be cured by time outdoors and exercise?

I spend a lot of time waiting for the future, too. I'm only 24, a couple of years out of my four-year uni course, a couple of years into full-time work, proper adult life. I'm waiting, because I have a question I need answering, and the answer can only come from the passage of time. The question is this; is this all there is? I mean, really, *is this it?* After everything you hear in childhood, after everything everyone has told me about growing up, about potential and hard work, and dreams and hopes and aspirations, are you telling me that's all basically bullshit? And that actually, when you told me I could grow up to be anything I wanted to be, what you meant was that most likely I'd spend 40 hours a week for 50 years in Microsoft Excel? Is that the truth you conveniently failed to mention? Because it would have been good to know, so once I graduated university I could have blown my fucking brains out. Surely that'd be better than this?

I'm waiting, always waiting for something. Something good has to happen, right? Something good has to be brewing? I'm always looking to the future, waiting for that thing. For some reason, *this* unknown is a good thing. Not like the other unknowns, which were bad. This is what little optimism survived adolescence making itself known. You wouldn't think, to look at me, or to hear me talk, that deep down I'm an optimist. Probably because it is so deep down; another emotion reined in, like a wild horse put in a stable, left to calm. I am my own bucking bronco.

I need to leave the future to itself, leave the past to *itself,* and be in the present more. And yet, I don't know how. You heard me right; I basically don't know how to be alive as a human. It's crazy. Literally, as well as metaphorically, it's crazy. But it is what it is. And so I smoke weed to keep myself in the present, whilst attending weekly therapy sessions to learn how to be in the present without drugs. I literally pay a woman to teach me how to be alive. Isn't that the thing your parents are supposed to teach you? Well perhaps when a parent dies, and the children outnumber the remaining parent, some things get lost. Perhaps.

Another one of life's little ironies; I got a cat to help with my mental health problems and ended up naming her after a woman who killed herself. Sometimes, I just can't fucking help myself.

Seven

It takes Max two weeks to reach out, but when he finally does we text for a little while before he asks if I want to meet up. I very fucking much want to meet up; obviously I don't say this to him, and merely agree, trying to play it cool. I behave over text the way I wish I could in real life; I'm calm, confident, composed. All the things I very much am not in person. Max and I arrange to meet one day, for me to accompany him with some shopping he has to do. It's a weird one, outside the box, but I roll with it. If Max had asked me to go on a shit tasting, I would have said yes. Wouldn't even have hesitated.

Because of life's little ironies, I see Lucy on what is Max and mine's official first date.

I don't think it's entirely a *date* date, per se; I accompany him as he shops for presents for his nephews. We go to a shopping centre in the city, and the amount of people immediately makes my anxiety stand up on its hackles. I'm alert, my eyes zipping from one side to the other; I'm not looking for anything in particular, just surveying the scene. Big crowds don't make me nervous because of the threat of terrorism, they just make me anxious in general. Too many people, too little space. Too many conflicting things happening all at once. I hate it. But for Max, I'll do it. For Max, there's so much I'll do. I'll give myself to him entirely.

He has two nephews, he tells me, and their birthdays fall within a week of each other. It's incredibly stressful in the build up to that week, he elaborates, particularly for his sister, who has to try and balance the delicate needs of two young children, trying to please both without upsetting either; the build-up is stressful, he says, looking for two presents, making sure not to accidentally favour one or the other; basically doing all the things you have to do around children, making all the allowances you have to make, to ensure these tiny humans that are remarkably similar to drunk adults remain happy. It's stressful in the build-up, but blissful the rest of the year. He tells me all his family's birthdays fall within a single three-month window each year; Max hates these three months, but loves the other nine, for their absence. The other nine, he tells me, he can relax, not have to worry about missing a birthday, not have to panic realising he has to go to a party, he doesn't have a present, all the shops are closed. I guess it's the uncle dream variation of turning up naked to a lecture, or unstudied for an exam.

When I ask Max about this day later, *after*, he'll act surprised when I call it a date. "We never dated," he'll tell me, with a rueful look on his face, and whilst I can see in his eyes he knows as well as I do that this is *not* true, that we *did* date, I don't say anything, I simply let the words wash over me, storing them away to pour over later, to over-analyse, and to weep. I call it a date not because I really think it is a date, but because of this intense need I have to categorise things. That's such a human trait, the need to fit everything into little boxes. It's a fucking nightmare, honestly. And mostly completely pointless. Of course, I do spend far too long pouring over Max's words, but that comes later. For now, let me try and stick to the present.

Order, that's the name of the game. The world is a big, cold, cruel, unfeeling planet full of confusion and surprise. I don't like it, the lack of control I have. And so I try to impose order onto things, whenever and wherever I can. It doesn't work, most of the time I'm just as confused as ever, but I'm reassured by the attempt, and that's better than nothing. It is better to have categorised and still be lost, than never categorise at all. I don't think those are Shakespeare's exact words, but I think their spirit rings true.

So I'm trailing Max around store after store; his nephews are three and five, he tells me, so should be easy to buy for in theory, but apparently it never works out that way. Even when he asks his sister, and she gives him an up-to-date list of the kids' likes and dislikes, he still misses as often as he hits. Like last Christmas, for example; due to the size of the extended family, Max says, now his sister is married and they have kids, there are all kinds of relatives to appease, relatives who appear from god knows where for the first time in years, wanting to hold the baby, telling the baby how pretty he is, setting him unrealistic expectations for later life. Due to the influx of family, both discovered and gained, Max tells me, last Christmas was the first time he saw his nephews over the festive period for a few years. The first Christmas since both boys will understand and appreciate what's going on; he saw the older boy on his first Christmas, but the kid obviously had no idea what was going on. It was an adult's party for kids; a chance for everyone to relive their childhood, he tells me ruefully, half a smile on his face. A chance for everyone to play with toys and forget about adult life for a time. It nearly worked, he says, but doesn't elaborate, and I don't push the matter. The time for probing questions will come, I hope. Now is the time to listen and understand.

Last Christmas Max had turned up at his sister's on Christmas eve, mid-afternoon, just like they'd planned. His sister had one spare room and Max had reserved it months previously, as soon as he'd found out the kids would be there. All the other relatives not only live within walking distance, but they also own cars; Max fits neither criteria. He lives an hour away by car, an hour and a half if he has to take the two trains and a taxi from the second station to his sister's front door, as is the case on this cold Christmas eve. His lack of flexibility with travel gives him the edge it takes to be allowed the one spare room; he tells me he feels bad that this means others can't drink because they have to drive on Christmas day; "but I also don't really care too much," he adds. "If Uncle Ken has to drive so he can't get drunk and start spouting crap about refugees, so be it. The world will not have lost anything."

He'd caught up with the kids, his sister and her partner, they'd all had a merry time. Max went to bed feeling good, he told me, feeling optimistic about the day ahead. "Christmas is always a bit rough for me," he tells me, as we enter yet another toy shop, browse more aisles of what I can only assume are the same toys that have been in every other shop. The joys of the 'free' market. I wonder what's taking him so long, but don't say anything; the longer it takes, the more time we spend together on this non-date date. The more time I get to be in his presence.

He doesn't elaborate on why Christmas can be rough for him, and again I don't ask. As I trail him around the toy store, I realise I'm happy not asking these things, because in my head I've already decided we'll be spending a lot of time together, and so there'll be time for me to learn all about him. This doesn't turn out to be true, but there was no way for me to know that then. I think back to who I was in these days; young(er), optimistic, in lust. With two people. Something I hadn't experienced before and haven't since. On TV and in films it usually sucks when someone loves two people; there's usually a reckoning, a watershed moment where the person is forced to choose the one he really loves. Real life doesn't work like that; I'm 24 and haven't had a single reckoning in my life. I can't imagine a scenario where I would, to be honest. That kind of thing just doesn't happen in the real world, only in Tinseltown. Hollywood, for those of you too young to know what Tinseltown means. At least I'm pretty sure it means Hollywood?

This optimism for a good Christmas with his sibling and nephews was ruined as soon as presents were opened, Max tells me. Despite the fact he'd queried with his sister, done a lot of research for the right toys, even sent her links to double check before he bought anything; it was all for naught. Each kid had, in that way that kids do, decided that in fact they no longer liked their own hobbies, but liked those of their brother. But they also decided, they each wanted their brother's toy, but didn't want to give up their own. You can imagine how well that went.

Max's sister insisted he hadn't ruined Christmas, but he knew he had. "I didn't ruin it *intentionally*, obviously, but to say I didn't ruin it is just, like, being nice, or being polite, whatever." He says it with a wave of the hand, as if to bat away the confusion over terminology. "It wasn't my fault, but my actions led to Christmas being shit." He glottal stopped on the word 'shit', which I hadn't even known was possible. What should have been pronounced with a hard T-sound was pronounced "shi-", as if he'd been interrupted, or was stretching the word out for effect. Actually, he just didn't pronounce a lot of words properly. But I didn't mind; if anything, it was a part of his character that just made me more attracted to him. Every flaw he had made him seem more human, and therefore more attainable. When you're young, and I think we're all guilty of this, we put those we like, or love, or lust for, on a pedestal. The problem being that, if you're lucky enough to have this person, for a kiss, or for the rest of your life, they can't possibly live up to the expectations you've set for them. You end up bitter with them, and yet you can't tell them; you poison the relationship through your own stubbornness, and end yet another good thing, something that had potential, but which you ruined. You fucking idiot.

But Max is different; Max is flawed, Max is definitely not on a pedestal, and far from perfect. But you like this about him. Max is kind, caring, diligent; you know all this just from how much effort he's putting into his nephews' birthday presents. But Max is also clumsy, somewhat awkward; his nose is slightly crooked, he speech is imperfect. I'm not saying these things to slight him, just to give some balance. Max has some wonderful, wonderful qualities. He also has some awful ones. But that's love, or at least lust that might turn into love; you take the good with the bad.

I'm tired and want to stop shopping, but I'll never say this. I want this moment, no matter how much it aches me physically, to last forever. The physical pain will be worth it for the mental joy. But of course it doesn't last forever, and soon he finds two items that he deems appropriate, that are current with what his nephews supposedly enjoy. "They might hate it by the time I give it to them," he says to me with a wry smile. "But fuck 'em. It's the thought that counts, right? And I've thought about this way too much." He rubs his temples as he says this, as we stand in the queue to pay, as if the thoughts have poisoned him. I want to reach out and touch him, feel his skin on mine, but I stop myself. Don't rush, Noah, just take your time. Don't scare this one away.

When we reach the front of the queue Max has some polite flirtation with the cashier, a man who looks older than us, but still younger than 30. Not too old, in other words. I'm surprised to find I'm relieved when the transaction is complete, when the cashier hands Max his bag, and the two of us leave him to serve the next customer. I want to say something to Max, comment on the sexy cashier who clearly had fallen irreparably in love with him, but what could I say? Max belonged to me no more than he belonged to the cashier. So I didn't say anything, instead suggested we go for a drink before heading home, hopefully to either his place or mine, but much more likely going home separately to our own dwellings, to be parted again. Hopefully only temporarily, however.

The day is warm, cloudy so as not to be completely sunny, but with patches breaking through every now and then. We find a pub, a placed called The Cross Keys, one of the million pubs in this country with that name, and I send Max to find a table whilst I go to the bar, get us a beer each, and place his in front of him when I find him sitting at a table in the back, looking exhausted at having been shopping, and delighted to be sitting down with a beer now it's over.

I pick my glass up and move it towards his in what is obviously a toast, but I panic when I realise I have nothing to say. What the hell am I doing? Why am I even toasting anyway? The panic starts to try to take hold of me, and the hand holding the glass begins to shake. I want to put it down, move it back into a more normal position, but the panic has frozen me. Luckily Max hasn't noticed; he's on his phone, doom-scrolling through one app or another no doubt, liking something, sharing something else, commenting on yet another post. I will my hand to move, to do anything; even if it suddenly opened, my fingers lost their grip on the glass and it fell, glass and beer cascading in all directions, most likely soaking us both; that would be better than this, would be better than being stuck here, hand floating, making me look completely and utterly ridiculous, like some sort of fucked up Madam Tussauds waxwork.

I'm just beginning to move from panic into being genuinely upset and a bit scared when I'm startled into movement. I don't have time to rejoice in my success, because before I know it I have a face full of blonde hair, and when it pulls back the face under it is Lucy's, and she's invited herself to sit down. Max is still looking at his phone, gives no indication he's noticed the newcomer.

"Look who it is," Lucy says to me, beaming. But the smile on her face doesn't quite reach her eyes. There's something else there, and I brace myself, waiting for it to come out. "So why haven't you replied to me?"

I'm confused for a moment, before the panic returns. Lucy had messaged me last night, but I was so busy thinking about today with Max that I completely forgot to replies. It was one of those *I'll read it now and reply later, oops I never replied* kind of things. We all do it, all the time, but it doesn't make it any less awkward when confronted with the fact. I can't look at her so I look at Max instead; he's put his phone down, and finally seems to have registered the presence of a third person at our table. I move to introduce her, not only because it's the polite thing to do, but because it's an easy way to change the subject away from my embarrassment, but Lucy beats me to the punch.

"Lucy," she says, holding out a hand, the same one I shook all that time ago, when we first met. I watch as she grasps Max's outstretched hand and gives those two small, firm pumps again before quickly letting go. Her hand looks tiny in his, dwarfed by his giant man hands; it looks small and delicate, like the hand of a child. But I bet she has some power in there, can get some power behind her hand, if she really wants to. A part of me gets excited that I might find out one day.

"Max," Max begins, but Lucy cuts him off.

"Oh my god, have you been there today?" She's pointing at the shopping bags, the ones with the presents from the last toy store we went to. She reaches behind herself and produces a bag from the very same store. Max and I both laugh at the sight of it.

"It's my niece's birthday next week, so I'm doing the proper aunt thing."

Max and I look at each other and burst into laughter. Lucy looks confused, until I'm able to stifle the laughter enough to explain our mirth to her.

"It's Max's nephews' birthdays next week, so he's been doing the proper uncle thing." I can't help but laugh again, and soon all three of us are. People in the pub look at us, but thankfully no one approaches us to try and find the reason behind our nearly maniacal laughter. How would you explain that we're laughing this hard at the coincidence that two people went to the same shop? You have to be there.

The laughter eventually subsides, and Max and Lucy launch into an in-depth conversation about the joys of aunt/uncle-hood, the joys of there being kids in the family, but of them having no responsibility towards them. Lucy in particular making references to her body, how having nephews and nieces is amazing because it's kids, but without literally ripping yourself open. She says something about her breasts but I don't hear it because she cups them as she does, and I'm entranced. I'm entranced by her confidence, not just to do this in public, but with two people she barely knows, one who she's just met in fact. For the first time since we met up earlier in the day I'm not thinking about Max. I'm lustful, but in a different direction.

I'm not a part of this conversation, my sister having precisely no children, so I simply sit back with my beer and watch them. They're both very animated, both gesture a lot whilst they speak, move with an almost over the top air. They get along like a house on fire, which fills me with a mixture of joy and terror.

I think I love both of these people. I think I love Max, and I think I love Lucy. If they fall in love with each other I'm going to kill myself.

Eight

Even though the city is much less crowded in the summer, the students home with their parents, or holidaying with their parents money, it always feels much busier. I think it's because the sunshine brings everyone outdoors, and into the public eye. People, like me, frankly, who've spent all winter and spring hiding indoors from the driving rain and biting winds, finally emerge, like butterflies completing their transfiguration. We spread our wings, baying towards the sun not unlike an ancient civilisation, practically worshipping it not directly, but through our actions.

You can see the heat shimmering on the ground, making the bottom few inches of the visible world seem like fuzz, as if we're all floating to get to where we need to be. Floating on the bright light and beautiful warm air, carried along as willing participants in this sudden shift into good weather.

The greenery that has been rearing its head all spring finally comes to fruition in summer; the city becomes a wash of greens, yellows, reds, primary colours providing a dash of life to what has been a grey existence for a little while now. "Leeds in bloom", I think they call it, and I never understood what the point of this kind of thing was when I was younger, it seemed like so much wasted time and effort, not to mention money, though now I understand it completely. Living in an apartment in the city centre, in the height of the urban jungle, you don't get to see much greenery, much natural life. There are three things about city living I don't like; it never gets fully quiet, it never gets fully dark, and it's far too grey.

When you live in such a large city, the light and noise pollution are a constant. Sure, they drop away as day turns to night, and the early hours are so close to silent you can almost taste it, like it's some tangible thing, but the silence is never complete. There's always a person, a car, a train, some sign of life. It's reassuring in a way, to know that you're not alone, that the world is still spinning, even if few are around to witness it, to experience it. I experience it often; I've never been much of a sleeper; my mum tells me I got it from my dad. Apparently he was up early every day, regardless of what he was doing the previous night, what time he went to bed. He didn't drink, I know this, and that must have helped with the early mornings. Alcohol and getting up and going are not two things that generally combine well.

The darkness is held at bay by a million streetlights, a million closed offices that still have all their lights on for some reason. The city is lit up like it's a holiday, there's a celebration going on. Regardless of whether it's just another Tuesday. I read a book once about sailors in the English navy in the 1800s who could see Saturn at night; there isn't much about the 1800s I'd like to port into today's world but being able to see distant planets is definitely one thing.

I used to take walks in the early hours sometimes, when I really couldn't sleep. I never quite had insomnia, but I don't think I was ever far away. Some nights I would lay in bed, TV or music on, only half watching or listening, not really awake, not really asleep. I lived these nights in the void, in the in-between space, between what is and what isn't. Because that's how I felt on those nights, there and not there.

Walking around the city used to fill me with a naked thrill. When I was growing up, you'd see suburbia after dark; the streets, houses, the local park. The thing is, it all looked the same. When you live your entire life in one place, for many, many years, you begin to come to know it inside out. You don't need light from the sun to recognise the houses and streets, to know where you are and where you're going. In the city, though, it's different. Generally, as a rule you only go into the city during the day. And so you know it as a day place, every image of it in your memory is of it during the day, lit up by natural light, existing in its natural state. Once the sun has gone down, it's a totally different animal.

The place becomes unrecognisable; but that isn't all there is to it. It's something different, something almost carnal; it's like seeing a beautiful woman without her clothes on. Seeing the buildings at night, lit up by their own internal lighting, lit up by street lights, it's a queer thrill. I feel like a thief, skulking around streets I shouldn't be on. It feels illegal, frankly, to be walking around in the small hours, seeing things that most people never see. Whilst it feels illegal, it doesn't feel immoral. It feels wrong, but it also feels so incredibly right. I'm very much a day time person; I love the sun, thrive in warm temperatures, would quite happily live somewhere where it's summer all year round and winter never arrives; and yet, there's something about walking around the city, at night, in the dark, that creates a feeling in me I've never been able to replicate in any other way.

Nine

The weeks pass and days become routine. July slips into August, which passes in a warm, fuzzy haze. The shimmer that usually only floats just above the ground seems to envelop the entire city; it's like every day is foggy, and lurking inside the fog is something unknown, waiting to be discovered. But it's an optimistic unknown, as if something good is waiting; even though the heat turns sticky, the humidity rises and life in a city without air conditioning becomes a chore, even as people get grumpy, short of temper, quick to anger; even through all of this, it's the hope that shines through. In a country that's as grey and dull as often as England is, a few weeks of good sunshine can turn the mood of the entire country. Perhaps the economy will recover from Brexit. Perhaps we'll stop being a laughingstock in Europe. Perhaps the Nazis that have been rising will fall back again, and we'll all be ok. Of course, eventually the sun disappears, taking all of this good feeling with it, and soon we're back once again to being a small, petty island, isolating ourselves from the rest of the world and then claiming we didn't want to be a part of it anyway, like a man rejected, a man who tried to turn a friendship into something it wasn't, a man who's incapable of amicably walking away, and assumes there must be something wrong with the woman who rejected him, and is vocal about it. I've known a few of these men in my time, and my question has always been this, often thought but never uttered aloud: why does a woman *refusing* to sleep with you make her a slut and a whore? If anything, isn't it the opposite? If you lashed out at her for being frigid, it'd be equally as offensive and embarrassing, but at least there'd be a logic to it. But calling them sluts and whores, you only make yourself sound stupid. Well, more stupid; attacking someone for the simple act of not wanting to be with you makes you stupid, regardless of the words you use to articulate this stupidity. Just walk away my friend, she isn't interested. Not everyone can be stuck with the Herculean task of dating two people simultaneously. I feel very modern doing this, considering the world around me seems to be moving backwards in time. To pick up a newspaper in this country, you'd think it was the 1950s. And yet, to be dating two people, one a woman, the other a man, it feels like I'm doing my bit for futurism. I'm trying to drag some part of the country into the 21st century, whether it wants to be there or not.

I fall into a routine of seeing Max twice a week, Lucy twice a week, and then having the other three days to myself to do with as I wish. I usually ended up seeing one if not both of them; it seems like nearly all the time I'm with Max we run into Lucy, and when I'm with Lucy we run into Max. Without ever really having met properly, officially, Lucy and Max are becoming acquaintances. I know I should be happy about this but I can't be; there are always doubts in the back of my mind, a lingering feeling that they're going to fall madly in love with each other and abandon me. I wouldn't kill myself, that was hyperbole, and yet if this scenario did come to pass, it would probably be the end of me. It'd break me, no doubt, and potentially beyond repair. What was hyperbole before is now a vast sea of melodrama, and I'm drowning in it. It's fun to play with language like this though, isn't it?

Max and I do lots of sporting activities; he tends to monopolise my weekends, which is something that if you'd asked me in advance I would have rejected with disgust, but now it's happening I don't mind it. We go running in the morning, 5 or 10k depending on what mood he's in, how our bodies feel, whether we're hungover or not. Most Saturday afternoons we play tag rugby; I can't say I love the game, but I don't mind it. I've even scored a try, so I know I'm definitely contributing. After rugby we usually go home, shower, sometimes separately, often together, and then go to bed, oftentimes to sleep, usually not.

The time I have alone with Max, from when we get home from rugby, until the time we get out of bed and start to face the evening, is my favourite time of the week. I get to see Max being truly Max, in all his forms. After the games he's tired, he's sweaty and his body aches. I don't touch him when he's like this, but I love to look at him, hear him, smell him. The smell of sweat normally turns my stomach, but with Max it's different; he doesn't smell sweaty like he's unwashed, even though he is; no, he smells sweaty like a hero, like a champion. Sitting there next to him, one of us driving, the other sorting the music, putting on a podcast, doing whatever, I feel like he's just left the scene of a great battle, rather than a simple game of non-contact sport. He smells how I imagine Perseus smelled having finally vanquished Medusa and saved Andromeda; it doesn't matter if the game ended with a win, a loss, or a draw; when I'm with Max after the game, this is all that matters.

I hate to ascribe myself to stereotypes of masculinity, I hate to reinforce gender roles, but there's no denying that these things exist because they were at one time true, or at least a half truth. An attractive man doing quote unquote manly things is a truth self-evident. Max doing anything is my constitution.

I love to see Max in the shower too; he's in great shape, takes excellent care of himself. He runs five days a week, always running at least 35k a week. He lifts weights in the gym three times a week, and on top of rugby he also plays squash and football. I have no idea where he gets not only the time, but the energy and the inclination; when he told me about his exercise routines, I was exhausted just listening to him. But it's worth it, for the body he's built. If I don't join him in the shower, often I'll just watch. I love to watch him wash the layers of sweat off, first with just water, then lathering himself up with soap. The way his hands, his big, masculine hands, caress his body so gently, as if it were made of porcelain and liable to shatter at any point. He rubs his left hand up and down his right arm, under his armpit and across his chest, where he switches over and uses his right hand to wash his left arm. He has no tattoos or piercings, no scars or moles or marks of any kind. Forgive the continued toxic masculinity, but I can't help myself; Max looks exactly how a man should look.

I'd be lying if I said he doesn't make me self-conscious; I exercise with him, running and playing rugby, but I do little over and above that. I'm not fat, not too thin; I don't know how you'd describe me. I just have a body? I don't have a six pack and abs, but I don't have a gut. My chest and stomach are flat, all the way down from my shoulders to my groin. I don't have a particular body shape, but I also don't *not* have a particular body shape. I just kind of... am. Or should I say, my body just *is*. As for myself, I can't say for certain that I am, indeed *am*. Just because you can see, hear, feel me, doesn't necessarily mean I exist.

When Max and I are both showered and dried, feeling more like ourselves, I love climbing into bed. The smell of sweat has been replaced by body wash, usually strawberry or cherry; I now associate these smells with him. If I'm in a supermarket, or passing a roadside farm stall, and see or smell strawberries, my mind instantly goes to Max. I can't help it. Lying in bed with him, sometimes jumping straight at each other, sometimes lying side by side just relaxing, sometimes kissing softly, caressing each other gently; whilst these things are happening and more, it's his smell upon which I focus. I think his smell is as much a part of his masculinity as his sculpted body; sure he smells sweaty sometimes, but only when he's meant to. He always smells right, and no matter how he smells, he always smells good. I could drink him in, get lost inside him, have him lost inside me. It doesn't matter as long as we're together.

This time we spend in bed together I never want to end. It always does; we always get up, get dressed, even if it's only to go to the living room of his flat to watch TV. We always go to his place; I have a roommate, he doesn't. It seems the only logical thing to do. Some nights we go out drinking, or to the cinema, or to one of his friend's, or one of mine. Some nights we watch a film, do a jigsaw, go to bed early and lay side by side in silence, each reading our own book. It doesn't matter. What matters is I spend time with Max, time that I enjoy. Because, really, isn't that the ultimate goal? Sure, to be rich would be nice, to not have to work a mind numbing, soul destroying late-stage Capitalist job would be nice; to be able to cure a disease would be nice, or save babies from a fire. Whatever. There are a lot of nice things, but I don't aim for these. I aim much lower; I aim to be happy. Some days, more so on the days I'm with Max, I begin to think this may actually be possible.

Lucy often makes me think that once I've started ejaculating, I'll never be able to stop. That's crude as hell, I know, and probably not the kind of thing I should be saying about another human being, but I feel like it's the best way to sum up how she makes me feel. My relationship with Lucy is a lot more carnal than the one I share with Max; with Max we spend a lot of time doing things, going to museums, gigs, art shows, all that kind of thing. We have sex regularly, don't get me wrong; but there's more to our relationship than that. Sometimes with Lucy it feels like it's all about the sex; which sometimes is great, sometimes leaves me worried.

Lucy is, for want of a less cliched word, insatiable. She's practically a fucking machine sometimes, and I can barely keep up. We go out and do things, the same as Max and I do, but whenever we do it always just feels like a preamble to sex. We go to bars and drink, we go to clubs and drink, we go to art shows and gigs and friends houses and house parties and we drink. And always, always the alcohol feels like liquid foreplay, liquid seduction. I sometimes think Lucy only drinks because it makes her less uptight, more easy going. I think it allows her to become the person she wants to be. She's very outgoing, very sociable, but she lacks a lot of confidence.

Why exactly, I'm not so sure. She's hinted at dark things in her past, things that affected her deeply, but the way she mentions them it's not the kind of thing you can ask about; it's one of those where you have to wait for the other person to offer the information, you can't go seeking it. She'll tell me when she's ready, if she ever is. And if she ever wants to. I'm not going to pressure her. Of course I want to know, but as I say, my relationship with Lucy is different to that of mine with Max; if Max had hinted about a lot of dark things in his past, I'd be trying to worm them out of him. With Lucy, I'm mostly just worming her body out of her clothes.

One thing I'm keen to keep at the forefront of my relationships with Max and Lucy is that I want there to be a complete lack of pressure. I've developed hard feelings for them both, that's absolutely true, but I'll never let them show. I keep it cool, keep it light and breezy; I'll keep pretending that everything's always fine, even if inside I'm falling apart at the thought of losing one or both of them. It's just easier that way. Clay from *Less Than Zero* put it best when he said "I don't want to care. If I care about things, it'll just be worse, it'll just be another thing to worry about. It's less painful if I don't care."

Less painful: sure.

Lucy has this one blue dress, and I don't think I've still yet recovered from the first time I saw her wearing it. There wasn't anything particularly mind blowing about it; her breasts weren't on show, there wasn't a flap in the back like in a baby grow, presenting her rear end to the world; it's just a regular dress, worn by an incredible woman. To be honest, Lucy could probably go the Marilyn Monroe route of wearing a garbage bag, and still be the best dressed person in any room. I went round to her flat; she wanted a quiet night in, she was going to cook, we'd watch a film, just generally have a chill one. When she opened the door wearing that dress, every other thought went out of my head.

I forgot basic language; she smiled and said hello to me, I simply stared at her. After a few seconds of this she laughed uncomfortably, before asking if everything was ok. It was more than ok, but I couldn't find the words to articulate what I was feeling, so I forced myself to nod, and followed her into the flat, closing the door behind me. She stopped in the doorway between the hall and the kitchen; I have no idea if she'd planned to do something, say something, or what. I didn't find out, because before she could do anything I had grabbed her in my arms and was kissing her deeply, passionately. I couldn't help myself at the sight of her in that dress; I wanted her, needed her, had to have her. I needed to become her, to become just a small part of her. I didn't want to climb on top of her, I wanted to climb inside her, combine our singular people into one person, one being with one consciousness, one train of thought, one goal.

She extricated herself from my grasp with a smile and said she didn't know what had come over me. I told her that I'd missed her, and the second I'd seen her I couldn't help myself. She smiled at me again then, but this time it was a smile filled with mischief. She pushed past me and moved away from the kitchen, into her bedroom. I didn't hesitate to follow her.

She sat on the edge of the bed but when I entered I reached out for her and pulled her to her feet. I briefly held her body against mine, basking in the feeling of her, before I turned, closed the door behind me, and then pushed her up against it. I couldn't help myself still, I just had to have her. We kissed passionately before I pulled away and started kissing her neck, her shoulders, the top of her chest. The dress lay on her shoulders, sleeveless, and I ran my hands up and down the length of her arms, savouring the feeling of her skin. It was soft, a sparse dotting of hair on her forearms. She was warm, and the feeling comforted me, and made me think of the home I've never really had. I've never really felt I belonged anywhere; well, I hadn't until I saw Lucy in that dress. When she'd opened the door, and I'd first laid eyes on it, I knew she was my home.

The dress was loose fitting, falling down her chest, curving above the tops of her breasts, allowing enough sight of them to remind you they were there, and they existed, but covered enough that all subtlety was not thrown out of the window. I eased down first one shoulder, then the other; the dress fell away having its support removed, and then she was standing in front of me, breasts on show. I began to touch them, knead them hungrily, before I moved down and took first one, then the other nipple in my mouth. Lucy's soft moans and gasps encouraged me, and as I continued to play with her breasts, my left hand went wandering.

The dress curved in at her waist, and then out again at her hips; only the top half had fallen down when I bared her shoulders, and so I had to reach all the way down to just above her knees, where the dress ended, so I could slide my hand back up, but this time inside her dress. As my hand moved upwards, tracing the soft skin of her thigh, feeling the warmth I was moving towards; my hand was soon high enough for me to become aware that she wasn't wearing underwear; I'd known as soon as I opened the door she wasn't wearing a bra; that I could see her left nipple piercing, that it was pushing against the fabric of the dress, had only served to turn me on even more. And now, finding out that she wasn't just braless, but completely devoid of underwear, I nearly went over the edge. My hand found her vagina; she was shaved, and

I caressed her pubis for a moment, savouring the softness of her baldness, holding out for as long as I could so I could prolong the moment. I didn't manage to hold out for long. She was still moaning and softly gasping, and she bit down on my shoulder as I slid first one, then a second finger inside her. She was already wet, and my hand moved in and out of her easily.

My penis was so erect it hurt; against the tightness of my jeans it began to feel trapped, pressured. It need release, in both senses of the word; it needed to be freed, and it needed to fuck. And that's what it, and I, did. I didn't finger Lucy for long; quite quickly I took my hand back from under her dress, spun her around, and pushed her gently by the shoulders so she was bent over in front of me. I didn't bother taking off her dress, simply lifted it up and began to fuck her, really pounding her. We didn't make love then, we didn't do anything close; we fucked, like two animals fighting at the watering hole. The sounds we each made were not pretty, and we probably didn't look like much either, but I don't think she cared, and I didn't either. The sex lasted probably less than a minute, but we both finished, and soon collapsed onto the bed, into each other's arms.

As we lay there, me still fully dressed with just my penis sticking out of my fly, her still wearing the dress, although her top half was exposed, I felt a rush of feelings I couldn't fully understand then, and can't fully describe now. I felt like we'd shared something that was much, much more than sex. We'd had sex plenty of times before, and would do plenty of times afterwards, but we've never done anything like that again. I don't think we could if we tried. I think it was such a perfect storm of circumstance that it can never be repeated; sometimes the universe aligns just for you. Well that night it wasn't just for me, it was for both of us.

Eventually we got up off the bed and left the bedroom smelling firmly of sex. We actually made it to the kitchen this time, and as Lucy cooked, I opened the wine, and between us we polished off a full bottle before the meal was even ready.

That was a pleasant evening, I think; I honestly don't remember much of it, past the sex. That's a feeling I've been chasing ever since, and no amount of fucking, or drinking, taking drugs, no nothing has come close to replicating it.

I'm aware that what I have with both Max and Lucy can't last forever; I don't think dating two people, and keeping them secret from each other, is sustainable in the long term, unless you devote your entire lifestyle to it, live on a commune or something, become totally outside society's rules, live entirely by your own. Although saying that, I do know a few other people who have made it work, so perhaps it can last, and we'll all be together forever. If we're not, that dress easily made up my mind should I ever have to choose:

Lucy, Lucy, Lucy.

I am the opposite of Sylvia Plath, the woman for whom I named my cat. She said, "I am. I am. I am." If you were to ask me about Noah, I would say, "I am not. I am not. I am not."

Some people spend so much time trying to read between the lines that they forget to read the actual lines themselves. This isn't aimed at any person in particular, or referencing any event in particular, it's just a thought that flits its way into my head as I walk home from work, one that I consider for a few minutes, before being replaced by another thought.

This is how my walk home is on this particular day;

one disconnected thought following another, not so much a train of thought as a motorway of thoughts, each car a single idea flitting across the surface, bearing little to no connection to any of the other thoughts around it. Summer is winding down for another year, and though the temperature continues to rise, the days are becoming shorter. I've always hated this, it seems like such bullshit; that technically the first day of summer is the longest day doesn't sit right, because it means that each summer day is shorter than the one before it. This feels like the opposite of how it should be; as the days get warmer, they get longer too, until they crescendo into one boiling, bright, hellish day. And then things can all be downhill after that, the days becoming colder and shorter. This obviously can never be the case, but it's something I think about with a frequency that's almost worrying. I wish I could explain why; my therapist seems to think I have an aversion to responsibility; she's right, but I was alarmed when she told me, alarmed at the speed with which she'd figured it out. My anger towards the shortening of summer days is something like this; I spend all winter waiting for summer, baying for it like a pack of hyenas waiting for their injured target to bleed to death so they can feast on its flesh without fear of reprisal. I salivate, I sit and wonder what the warm weather will bring. Inevitably, my anxiety will begin to rise, and I'll spend all summer chasing that excited feeling, the optimism and promise that the thought of summer brought to me. It often doesn't appear, leaving me disappointed and flat. How do I react to this? By taking responsibility for my own life, my own actions, owning my disappointment? If you've been paying any attention at all you'll know that's absolutely not the case. What I do is find an external source to blame for my disappointment; in this case, it's the shortening of the days. It isn't my own failure to live my life properly that makes me sad, oh no, it's the idea that even as they warm up, the days are getting shorter. It's not my fault I'm unhappy; nothing is ever *my* fault.

I walk the familiar route between office and flat, one I've walked in both directions for five of the seven days, 48 of the 52 weeks, for the past couple of years. I don't have to think about where I'm going, the muscle memory in my feet taking me to my home, my cat, my bed. My thoughts are particularly prevalent today because I'm not listening to music; it's not that I don't want to, or my phone has died or I've forgotten my headphones or something. It's that there isn't any music I want to listen to; everything I have saved on Spotify, the artists, albums, the playlists I've haphazardly created; none of it is working for me today. I could listen to some new music, but I'm about as likely to go sky diving, or become Prime Minister. I'm not 100% certain, but around 90% this fear of new music is my anxiety showing itself again. It goes back to safety and certainty vs the unknown. New music may end up being scary or rubbish. I might listen to the new Lorde single, or some old Blondie B-sides I've never heard before, and they might turn out to be crap. Then what do I do? A good song changes your life, doesn't it? You remember the first time you heard some songs, you remember where you were, what you were doing, but perhaps most importantly, you remember how the song made you *feel*. And how it still probably makes you feel. What if there's a new Blondie song, but it doesn't make me feel the way I felt when I first heard 'X Offender'? Same question with Lorde and 'Supercut'. Then what? Am I supposed to just continue with my life as if everything is absolutely fine?

It's eight o'clock as I pass down Briggate, the main shopping street in Leeds. It's pedestrianised and lined with shops either side; if you're not looking to spend money, you're in the wrong place. I walk past Harvey Nichols, the doorman wearing top and tails, occasionally deigning to open the door for someone, be they a seasoned shopper, or just an excited tourist.

Not every unit is alive and buzzing with life; more and more shops move out of the street and aren't replaced. The high street really is dying in this country, and to me it's no more evident anywhere than it is on Briggate. Although I'd say that there's a 99% chance of bias in this statement; I can hardly say that Leicester Square is the epitome of the death of the high street when I haven't been there in who knows how long. Obviously the physical representation of the death of the high street is, for me, the street I walk down twice a day, most days.

It's still warm, even as the sun goes down; I don't normally leave this late but I've been doing some precious overtime, trying desperately to make my next pay cheque slightly larger. I'd forgotten how expensive it is dating people. It's doubly expensive dating two people. When you're with someone, you have to do things, go out, socialise. And everything costs money. Even if Max and I or Lucy and I go to a museum, all of which have free entry, we usually end up having lunch or dinner, or at least going for a drink. Nothing in life is free, I've come to realise. I think that's one of the main reasons why we're all so fucking unhappy all the time. Capitalism has evolved into late-stage Capitalism, and now we're no longer human, we're simply currency for exchange. We are human capital, as Marx put it, we're simply worker bees. Sure, we have the illusion of freedom; we choose where we live, where we work, when we go out, when we stay in. This is probably the dictionary definition of freedom (Freedom, noun: the power to act, speak, or think as one wants), but once you put it under a bit of scrutiny, it falls apart. It's all well and good saying that we're free to do what we want, to say what we want; but what about that time a few months ago, in our daily morning buzz meeting at work, when we received a memo reminding us about our social media presence outside of work, because someone at one of our rival firms had jokingly tweeted about running someone over because they were late for work and had been fired in order to protect the company's reputation.

It's all well and good saying we have freedom, but I imagine if I went into the office tomorrow and called my boss a cunt, I'd be free to leave the building, free to find another job. At which point I'd be free to not be able to pay my rent, and free to get kicked out of my flat, free to become homeless. And isn't homelessness the ultimate freedom; you're not tied down by possessions, by a home; you're not even limited in where you sleep each night. The world is yours to explore. Want to be harassed by drunks under a bridge? Go for it! Want to be moved along by police for literally no reason? You choose the spot, they'll find you.

Freedom is also the name of an excellent book by Jonathan Franzen, which I highly recommend.

Despite the hour and the day, Leeds is still teeming with people as I walk home. It's Thursday, which is generally accepted as the unofficial student night in the city. And so as I walk home I'm thronged either side by groups of youths, some all-male, some all-female, a lot mixed. The females huddle in packs, flesh on show, wanting to be able to have fun without fearing for their lives. The males try not to huddle too much, they don't want to appear intimidating. The majority of them just want to have a drink, have a dance, meet someone pretty and fall in love, that is after falling into bed. Of course, even if just by the law of averages, some of these men are on the prowl, date rape drugs in their pockets, horror on their minds. It's of course impossible to tell who these people are; it's nights like this you're particularly glad you're male, and so the chances of anything bad happening are minimal. Not zero, but as close to zero as to be basically infinitesimal.

The groups of youth are so full of life, so full of optimism and hope. Was I ever like this? I'm only 24 for Christ's sake, only a few years older than these people I see as children. When did I get so old? Has the 9-5 worn me down so much that, at 24, I'm a bitter old man? Perhaps. More likely it's simple jealousy; oh to be young, to be free, to be able to go drinking on a school night knowing you can sleep the following day away and suffer no consequences. Oh to be free, not trapped as a wage slave.

Sylvia the cat is waiting for me in the hallway of the flat I share with my friend when I finally arrive home. My flatmate is nowhere to be seen, so the flat is dark, the only light from the waning sun, the residual glare of a streetlight a few buildings up the street. Sylvia meows at me, perhaps a hello, perhaps a request for food. Perhaps she's wondering where I've been; the overtime was a last-minute thing, so I didn't get chance to warn her before I set off this morning. She seems to be mad at me for this, meowing at me until I move to stroke her, then running out of reach when I try. I take off my shoes, savouring the feeling of freedom in my feet, and follow her down the hallway, both of our footsteps muted on the laminate flooring, hers by the soft pads upon which she walks, mine by my socks. She leads me into the main area of the flat, the space that comprises the living room/kitchen/dining room — although dining room is generous, it's more that there's enough room between the kitchen cabinets and the couch my flatmate and I share to squeeze in a small table. I've eaten at it once, when Lucy came over and we had a staying in date night. I don't know that Tom, my roommate, ever has.

I feed Sylvia, removing the mush she calls food from the pouch and tipping it into a bowl. She meows and rubs around my legs as I do this, clearly impatient for her dinner. I put it down, and despite how awful it looks, she eats it with relish. I suppose for an animal that, did we live somewhere else, would be out all-night hunting small animals, a bit of processed food isn't so bad.

Whilst she eats I move towards my bedroom, loosening my tie as I walk, debating whether to take a shower. I'm knackered and want nothing more than to slump on the couch and watch TV until bedtime, but I'm sticky too, a hot mess, and so in the end I take all my clothes off, leave them in a pile in the corner, along with a hundred other pieces of clothing that are too dirty to hang up or put away, and too clean to wash. I turn on the water and as I stand with just my hand in it, waiting for the temperature to hit an acceptable level, I hear my phone ring. It's in my bedroom, and I can't be bothered to answer it. It rings a couple more times then stops; a minute after I step into the water it begins to ring again, and I ignore it again.

I wash myself slowly, savouring the feeling of the water removing the stains of the day from my skin. I emerge feeling reborn, and with just a towel wrapped around my waist. I pick up my phone as I sit down on my bed, and check the missed calls. One from Max, one from Lucy. I can't help but smile. They've both texted me too, asking my plans for the evening, whether they can see me or not.

I initially don't know if I have the energy to see them, but I know I will. Even if for no other reason than to feel wanted, to be seen. It's an incredible feeling to have these two people seeking my time and attention, and I'm as flattered as I am scared. I've never been in this situation before; what happens when it inevitably comes crashing down? Who cares what happens? Murphy's law; whatever can happen, will happen. As it is, I lay down in the bed, Sylvia joining me, happier now she has a full belly. She lays on the bed next to me purring away, seemingly content with life, and I feel the same way. Maybe things aren't always perfect, but things could also be a hell of a lot worse.

Autumn

Ten

Autumn brings with it new colours, and though they're no less bright, in actuality, from the summer colours, there's a melancholy to them. As if they know, somehow, that they're ushering in the beginning of the end of yet another year. Green and yellow is replaced by red and gold, and as the season progresses, the leaves make their way from branches to the ground, piling up, swept up by the wind, blown by moving traffic, kicked by little children. The colours are a stark contrast to the grey that's settled across the city; any idea, any faint inkling of sunshine has gone, and the best that can be hoped for is that it'll be dry, it won't be too cold, the wind won't howl too loud.

I don't hate my job as much at this time of year; I still hate it, it's just easier to stomach when the weather outside is less inviting. I used to work with a woman who altered her working pattern based on the time of year, and the weather forecast. It's something almost Pagan in a way, very ritualistic; to get up earlier with the sun, in order to finish work earlier, and spend more time in it. To come into work later in the winter, finding fewer reasons to get out of bed, finding the idea of stepping from that comfort zone and into the real world a terrifying one.

I still hate my job because, regardless of the season, it's the same old crap. I get up earlier than I feel like I should have to, than I feel like any human should have to, I shower and dress, I walk to work, I sit at my desk. Every day is the same; open Outlook and check my emails, reply to the few that require it, delete most of them. Open Excel, put some numbers in some cells, make some graphs, maybe a pie chart if the data is particularly interesting. Eat some lunch, maybe go for a lunchtime walk, depending on the weather; and then it's back to my desk, back to my computer, and the afternoon is spent much the same as the morning.

Regardless of the season it's the same old drudgery for the same old crappy salary; the only real difference may be that I do more overtime in autumn and winter; there really is very little that's particularly inviting about living in the north of England at this time of year. That's not entirely true; there's very little that's inviting about living in *urban* northern England at this time of year. On the rare occasions I break out of the city, being whisked away by Max or Lucy on a day trip, then the weather seems apt to the surroundings.

I'm not going to go into great depth about the Yorkshire countryside; if you're that interested, go and read *Wuthering Heights*. It's from that book, and everything else by the Brontes, that makes me think that the moors are made for inclement weather. When they're sunny it feels like a trap, a diversion, some sort of trick. When it's particularly dark or cold, or lashing it down with rain, it feels false, put on, a show, though I don't know for whom. However, when it's dry but cold, grey but not too dark, when the wind lashes in a way that feels almost sinister; then I feel like I'm in the right place at the right time. There's something about being up there, on what feels like the top of the world, nothing to see except fields, occasionally broken up by dry stone walls. When I'm with Max or Lucy it feels like we're the only two people in the world; and not in a cute, romantic type way, but in a scary, dystopian way. It's easy to feel alone up there, to feel lost, to feel, please excuse the pun, *un-moored*.

I spend a lot of time this autumn with Max; his family owns a bed and breakfast in north Leeds, and he still helps out from time to time, when things are particularly busy. Like now, for example; it's the Bronte society's birthday, or the anniversary of one of the Bronte's birthdays, or something, and so people have come from all over the world to visit their old home, to see the Parsonage where the great works of literature were written. Haworth gets so booked up that people end up in hotels all over West Yorkshire; they've travelled halfway around the world to be here, after all, so what's another 20 or 30 miles? Negligible at best.

Max tells me he likes it when the B&B is full, because he knows that's when his parents will be making the most money; he tells me he also hates it when the B&B is full, because his parents refuse to hire more staff, and they always end up pleading with him to come back. At a period such as this one, where the busy time lasts a couple of weeks, he goes back and stays in his old childhood bedroom.

"This isn't something my parents ask me to do, it just makes sense. When you run a live-in B&B, you might

101

only end up working five hours in a day, but those five hours can be spread anywhere from 12:01am to 11:59pm. It just doesn't make sense," he continues, "to go back and forth, particularly if I'm only needed for half an hour, and then by the time I get home I'm needed again."

He tells me he sublets his flat on Air BnB for this time, and though I know this is highly illegal, I don't say anything. Why would I? I love this man; I love him to the extent I would forgive much worse crimes than simply trying to maximise his income. I'm not sure why it's illegal anyway; I mean, I understand why, and yet it goes against the whole money-at-all-costs mantra that this country runs on these days. It's illegal because it contributes to the sky-high cost of renting, the unaffordable cost of buying; and yet, these rising costs haven't been slowed at all by this law. I think, like Max, most people do it anyway. They just don't tell anyone. Of course Max has told me, but that's different; his penis has been inside my mouth, I think that creates some sort of bond between us, a mutual pact of silence.

I find the idea of having grown up in a B&B fascinating, and pepper Max with questions. It's clearly just part of life for him, nothing extraordinary, and though I can sense his annoyance at my constant stream of questions, he doesn't tell me to stop asking, or refuse to answer. He patiently responds to each query, and I like him all the more for it. His tolerance of me is nothing short of heroic; if there's two things I am, it's inquisitive to the point of fault, and self-aware. I know how annoying I can be, asking question after question, not just to Max but Lucy too, to friends, colleagues, everyone and anyone, but I can't stop myself. I have this incessant need for information that can only be silenced by gaining information. I know what you're thinking; isn't it normal to try and learn about those you care about, to get to know them better? And yes, of course it is; but what I do goes above and beyond that. I'm less a reporter asking questions for a story, more a detective asking questions in order to lock them up for life. I can't help myself.

With Max and the B&B, I quickly graduate from simple questions like "who cleans the rooms after the guests have checked out?" or "what should I avoid on the breakfast menu?" to "what was it like growing up in a house full of transient people?", "does it feel strange to think that the home you grew up in is part of a thousand anecdotes strangers tell people?" and "does it feel odd knowing your permanent home was also a temporary home to countless strangers, does it make it feel less like your home or even more so?" I don't think Max understands these questions, or the reasons I have for asking them, but he indulges me, he answers as best he can, knowing me, knowing that once you break past this barrier I put up, one of information, identity, the need for knowledge, that deep down I'm actually a fairly normal person. Or at least, as normal as anyone. Which I don't think is too normal.

Max's childhood bedroom is small, tiny really; my guess is that the bigger rooms are rented out. I imagine his parent's room is similarly tiny, for the same reason. Max tells me he guesses, but doesn't know, hasn't really thought about it. It's the kind of thing I can't help but think about. It may just be because of the B&B, but there could be a million other reasons Max's room is so small. It could be the obvious; it's a room built for a child, and in it stand two grown men, a combination of people the room was never designed to house. It could be that Max's parents didn't like him, and thus tried to punish him, but without him really knowing. It may be that, despite being the smallest room, is the warmest in winter, so his parents actually did something really nice for him, and are very kind, caring people. I venture forth all these theories and Max just smiles at me, indulging me; he shrugs his shoulders, suggests we go to the bar and have a drink.

The idea of a drink sounds good, but not in the B&B. I still have so many questions, and I think Max's tongue might be loosened not just by alcohol but by being off-site, being on neutral ground. I wonder if he's scared of saying anything particularly damning in a place where he may be overheard, and what he's saying may be misinterpreted. We all like to think words have one meaning, and that what is heard is what was said, what was intended, but this simply isn't true, is it? Direct, face to face speech is perhaps the best way to communicate, the best way to avoid misunderstandings or mistakes, but that doesn't mean they don't happen. Someone can tell you their tone, and you still might get it wrong. It's not anything malicious, at least not all the time; it's just something incredibly human.

Eleven

Autumn also brings with it a lot of phone calls from my mum. She's quite happy to leave me be for most of the summer, mostly because she's busy herself, has better things to do than speak to me. Which is fine with me; I love my mum, but I loathe speaking on the phone. I have absolutely no idea why, I always have done. It's one of those things I don't care enough about to try and find a reason for.

The main reason she calls is to see if I have any information on my sister. Emma lives in New York, it being essential to do so for her modelling job. But even before she moved across the pond and settled in the Big Apple, she lived in the Big Smoke. (Now without the idioms: even before she moved across the Atlantic Ocean and settled in New York City, she lived in London - this is what I mean about speech being misinterpreted. We spend so much time speaking in metaphors, that it's easy to miss someone's true meaning. The problem is, there's no solution - if we all spoke literally all the time, the world would cease to function. We need that fluff in our language to make life a little more interesting. I picture it to be like lying - sure, lying is bad, but sometimes it's necessary. Lying and metaphors, two necessary evils.)

Emma was spotted by a modelling scout at age 15, at an under-18s nightclub in Leeds. What a model scout was doing at an under-18s night is something I've often dwelled over, and I can only come to one conclusion; I just hope it wasn't as sinister as I know men usually tend to be. I hope it was scouting, and nothing more. Even though this is sinister to an extent, it's a lot less sinister than other things that might have, may have, *could have* taken place.

Emma became somewhat of a phenom; although only having been 'discovered' that same year, she made the cover of *Elle* aged only 15. There was something of an uproar at the time, you may remember; she appeared on that cover topless. She was covered up, her barely-there breasts hidden by her hands, as well as her name splashed in size whatever font, but still. My mum didn't mind; well, she gave her permission for Emma to do it. Whether she minded or not is a different story. I've asked her many times, but other than nearly admitting to something before catching herself one Christmas when she was drunk, she's never talked about that cover, Emma being so naked, so young. I was 13 at the time, and didn't understand it. All I knew was that Emma was suddenly everywhere; no matter where I went, I couldn't escape her. It wasn't just that magazine cover; she appeared on the cover of *Vogue, Teen Vogue, Cosmopolitan, Marie Claire, Good Housekeeping, Socialist Weekly, Sociopath Quarterly*; she was in print ads, on TV and before films. She was on the radio, she came through our door on flyers. It was enough to see her in the house, at the age when I still considered girls as disgusting, before I grew a bit, hit puberty, changed my mind. It was too much for me; I was almost glad when my mum took her and moved to London for a year.

I know for a fact my mum didn't want to do that, but since our dad died she hasn't really been able to say no to us. Emma's career, whilst blossoming in Leeds, would never continue there, could only ever be burgeoning at best in such an unimportant city, at least in terms of the global scale. She had to move somewhere bigger, more important, to really kick start it; London was the compromise gesture. Emma wanted to go to New York straight away; that was one of the few times my mum put her foot down. The arguments were incredible; my mum sent me to my room, but it was only a gesture, only for show. They argued so loudly I might as well have been right there, eating popcorn like it was the summer blockbuster.

Emma accused my mum of stifling her career; my mom screamed back that she was 16 and didn't even have a career yet. Emma accused my mum of jealousy; my mum assured her she was trying to protect her. Emma said my mum was ruining her life; at that my mum just laughed. I think it must have dawned on her she was arguing with a 16-year-old, and her daughter to boot; my mum was willing to treat Emma like an adult, but only to a certain point. Past that point, my mum would remind Emma that not only was she her daughter, but that she was only 16 years old. If she wanted to, my mum could withdraw all her permissions, and my sister wouldn't be able to do anything until she was 18. I don't think it was a serious threat; in fact I know it wasn't because the arguments went round and round for weeks, every night the same points put forward by the same parties with the same vested interest in the outcome. What seemed to me like years later, the arguments stopped. My mum announced she was moving to London with Emma, and my aunt and uncle, just migrating back from Australia, would live in the house for a year and look after me. It had all worked out perfectly! So said my mum. I had some disagreements, but didn't raise them. My sister was happy, my mum was happy; so what if I was unhappy? I was probably just being selfish, I told myself. It was actually *me* that was jealous, not my mum. I waved them off the day they left the house, car laden with their respective items; my mum's stuff mostly books, Emma's mostly clothes and make-up. Once they'd gone, I cheerfully told my aunt and uncle I was going for a nap, and went up to my room and spent the rest of the day crying.

When my mum came back to Leeds, Emma stayed in London, and remained there until she moved to New York. I know she went all over the world; I follow her on Instagram, and we speak occasionally, although not too often, at least not as often as most siblings do. I still see her face everywhere, and as I said before, I see more of her from time to time than any brother should see of his sister. But it is what it is; I think I've always had a little crush on her; my subconscious apparently felt like the true Freudian way, that of being in love with your mother, was a bit much, and so chose my sister as a surrogate. As it is, I've done as much sexually with my sister as the majority of people have done with their mothers. We all have twisted thoughts and secret, passionate desires we can never, ever share with anyone. This is mine.

My mum calls to ask for updates about Emma because, as rarely as Emma and I speak, it's still more common than the contact between Emma and my mum.

It isn't spiteful, there's no old resentment from Emma about not being able to move to New York aged 16, at least as far as I know. There's no malice in it at all, it's simply a combination of Emma being incredibly busy, there being a big time difference between the east coast of America and the north of England, and Emma mainly communicating via text or social media, and my mum participating in neither. My mum isn't even that old, she only turned 50 three years ago. Yet she refuses to get a smartphone. I don't know why, and I tell her regularly how weird I find it. She takes a strange kind of pride in it, as if there's time and energy to devote to being a Luddite in this day and age. I don't know how she does it; I think even if I were able to sleep properly, get a full eight hours interrupted, I still wouldn't because I'd need to regularly check my phone. I'm addicted to it, I'm not going to sit here and pretend I'm not. But what can you do? Smartphones are necessary, and it's not like I'm addicted to fucking little girls, or shooting heroin, or anything like that. At least being addicted to my smartphone only harms me, and that's no one's business but my own.

The calls between my mum and I are stilted, broken up; they're a jigsaw with half the pieces missing, we're both just trying to make something out of what remains. Our family was never close, but with dad dying, and Emma being so absent, what little proximity we had faded a long time ago. My mum tries to keep it together, but only half-heartedly. I sometimes think she'd be happier if we just admitted that we had nothing in common other than being mother and son, and cut off contact altogether. I sometimes think I would be too.

"Hello?" I phrase it as a question, even though my phone screen told me it was my mum calling before I slid the bar across with my index finger and answered.

"Hi Noah, it's your mum."

"Hi mum, how're you?

"I'm ok thanks, same as ever really. How're you?

"Same, same."

This is as far as we can get before the awkwardness kicks in. I know she wants to ask about Emma, that's why she's called, but I know she doesn't want to give the impression that that's the only reason she's called. She doesn't want to offend me by only being interested in my sister. I wish she would, because then she'd see I'm not offended, that I really don't care either way, and we could move past this awkward dance we do each time we speak.

"How's—"

"She's fine." I interrupt my mother, giving her the answer she wants without forcing her to ask the question that so pains her. "I haven't spoken to her for a while, but last time we spoke she was good, and based on her Insta she's doing really well."

"Based on her what?"

I proceed to explain Instagram to my mum for approximately the five thousandth time. It's social media mum, you share pictures and stories mum, she has several million followers mum, it's how celebrities connect with fans and also show off mum. Round and round we go, having the same conversation. Do you ever feel like your life is only actually a week long, and you're just living it over and over again?

Twelve

I don't see much of Lucy in the autumn; she has some high-flying job in PR, and that means she follows the sun around a lot of the year. So in summer she's in England, and it's wonderful, but in the other seasons she might find herself in France, Spain, the Netherlands, or places much more distant; Tokyo, LA, Hawaii, Hanoi. My job doesn't afford those sorts of perks. I can't even work from home.

Lucy is a little older than me - 26 to my 24 - and a lot more mature. That she's the same age as my sister, and even looks a little like her, is not lost on me. They've actually met once, although I haven't told either of them. I like to keep my relationships siloed, particularly where sex is involved. With Lucy, not with Emma. Obviously. Her age is one of the reasons that she's much more advanced in her career too; the other one is that she has a passion for her job, one that I'm sorely lacking in mine.

I'd probably say she actually has a *career*, whatever that really means; I'm still a floating voter, I haven't committed myself to anything yet. Mostly because I haven't found anything I want to do. No, that's not true; I haven't found anything I want to do that I can *afford* to do, or that I have the right access, background, connections, and privilege to do. I'd obviously love to work for the *New Yorker* or *The Atlantic* or something like that; no chance I'll ever get my foot in the door though. For one thing, I live in the wrong country. Secondly, my only point of access is their fiction submission inbox, with which I occasionally grace a short story. I haven't had anything published, and judging by the number of rejections I've had, I doubt I will. But I'll keep trying; that's what's keeping me in this shitty office job right now, the hope something better will come along. The alternative is I accept that financial admin is what I do, and commit to that. It'll be a dark, dark day in my life when that happens. It may also be the last one. That's absolutely not hyperbole.

Lucy travels so much she doesn't even keep a permanent flat in Leeds; in the spring and summer she uses an Air BnB, and then in autumn and winter she packs all her things up and moves them back into her parents' house, somewhere down south. Somewhere wealthy down south. I can't imagine basically moving house every half a year, it'd drive me crazy. I'm the kind that struggles to settle as it is; if I knew I'd be moving in six months, there'd be no point settling because I'd then be moving in another six months, and I think I'd lose my mind. Not that my current situation feels any more permanent. I'm a few months into a 12-month contract on my flat; I've lived here for just over 18 months, and don't plan to move any time soon, unless something happens. And yet still, I don't feel settled. Though that has less to do with the flat, or my work or home or social situation, and more to do with me, and my mental health complexities. I think Graham Greene said it perfectly in *The Quiet American*: "From childhood I have never believed in permanence, and yet I had longed for it. Always I was afraid of losing happiness." Although, afraid of losing happiness? I think I'm more afraid of finding it.

Greene was writing about a man sent to South East Asia to report on the war; I live in the same city I grew up in, that my mum lives in, that my dad lived in all his life, that my sister grew up in and deigns to come back to every now and then. I'm slightly different from Greene's protagonist, and yet the basic emotions are the same. I think that's true of all humanity; our stories may be different, our specifics, the day to day, but the basic emotions are the same. We're all the same, really, inside, and we all think and feel the same things.

Lucy manages some celebs for the firm she works for, which is based in Leeds where it was founded about twenty years ago, but has offices in London, New York, and hubs elsewhere. It truly is a global firm, and Lucy does a lot of global work. She's told me so much about it, but for some reason the words just don't stick in my brain. I know she has some very famous clients, household names she works with. I remember being impressed when she told me; perhaps a pop star, a couple of movie stars? Certainly people I'd like to meet, and would try not to fawn over, though would, and would hate myself for it afterwards. I try to be different, but I'm just as human as everyone else.

I don't really know much about Lucy, about her history anyway, her origins. She loves to talk about her job, where it takes her, the campaigns she works on. When she's out of the country I check her Instagram feed relentlessly, my heart beating faster with each new post. She's regularly in bikinis, and I regularly masturbate over the pictures. Just before she went away for the first time since we'd met she asked me if I'd ever done this; I said no, of course, the lie slipping off my tongue so easily it was a little scary. She'd looked at me, clearly unbelieving, giving me a wry smile, a little poke with one finger, telling me she wouldn't be mad if I had, in fact she might even find it quite sexy. I'd repeated my denial, and she'd repeated her disbelief, and her lack of fear of the truth; we'd gone back and forth like this for several minutes, me denying, her cajoling, until I gave up and told her yes, of course I'd masturbated to her pictures, most men who'd been on her profile at any point probably had, she must have known that surely? I knew I'd gone too far as soon as these words came out of my mouth; in my frustration at her repeated questioning I'd somehow made her out to be the bad guy, I'd victim blamed her.

I immediately went into apologetic mode, telling her I was sorry over and over, but it was too late, the damage had been done. What had I been thinking? Frustration is not an excuse; Lucy is a human female living in England; she's free to post virtually anything she wants on her Instagram. Her body belongs to her, and her only, who the fuck do I think I am telling her that men pleasure themselves to images and thoughts of her, and she's naive if she doesn't know this? I'll tell you who I am; I'm no one. I'm just another white man telling a woman who they can and can't do, what is and isn't their fault. Lucy is just another woman trying to live her life, I'm just another man trying to make it all about me.

Luckily she didn't stay mad at me for long; I think, as much as she was angry at what I'd said, and particularly the way in which I'd said it, frustration spilling over into vitriol, my almost telling her off; as much as she was angry with this, my immediate contrition went a long way to absolving me of my guilt. That I was literally on the floor, on my knees, helped too. I don't think Lucy would be upset if I told you that she likes having her ego stroked. Let's face it, who doesn't? Cliches are often cliches because they're true; I literally fell at her feet. She loved it.

I didn't mention it before, but Lucy's birthday is two days after Emma's. Obviously there's no way I could have possibly known that when we met; and yet, it's more fuel to the bastardised Freudian fire I keep burning; I wonder if anyone else has made these connections, or if it's just me. Is it almost going to become a self-fulfilling prophecy? I'm so worried that people will find out I've sub-consciously chosen to sleep with a woman remarkably similar to my sister, that I'm going to accidentally out myself as someone who has chosen to sleep with a woman remarkably similar to my sister? I dread to think what my mum would say. I dread even more to think what she'd think; what she'd want to say but would hold back for decency's sake, for the sake of our future relationship, for the sake of my relationship with Emma.

Lucy knows all about Emma, I've told her in great detail. She knows about the modelling, living in New York; Lucy does some work with models, and some in New York, so I'm just waiting for their paths to cross again, this time with one knowing the other, knowing who they are. Their relationship then will be defined not just by their proximity to each other, but their shared proximity to me too. I may get away with it if they do happen to meet, because I haven't actually told Emma about Lucy. It's not that I'm particularly withholding knowledge, it's just that Emma and I aren't *that* close.

Because we speak so infrequently, and for such short amounts of time when we do, Lucy simply hasn't come up as a topic. There's also the fact that Emma and I haven't actually spoken since I met Lucy. That may have a bearing on things.

I'm at the B&B with Max when I feel my phone vibrating against my leg. Slipping it out of my pocket, I smile when I see Lucy's name on the screen. Excusing myself to Max with a gesture, I step outside and answer it.

"Hey, you," she says after I say hello, and those two words are enough to melt my heart. I'd do anything for this woman.

"How's...?" I purposefully leave a gap, letting her fill in the location. It's a little game we play, one I'm not entirely sure either of us like, but both play because we think the other does.

"Schiphol? It's good thank you, Amsterdam is good." I had absolutely no idea that's where she was. Had she told me and I forgotten? Probably. "What are you doing this weekend? My office wants me in London for the next couple of weeks, working on the new Vogue cover. It isn't your sister, don't worry." She laughs, but I don't. Could she hear my immediate panic over the phone? Did I somehow make it audible? Or are we just such similar people she knows what I'm thinking almost before I do? "It's good timing actually, because my parents are away, and the dog needs looking after." It's always 'the dog', never Nellie, or her, or anything else; just 'the dog'. I call her Nellie because I feel like I should, it feels like the polite thing to do. I haven't met any of her family, immediate or extended, and yet I feel like it's for them I should call Nellie by her name. It feels like a mark of respect for my position as an outsider; once I've met her family, and potentially ingratiated myself into it, then I

116

can call Nellie 'the dog', refer to her colloquially, as if I'm just another person. Until then, it's always Nellie.

"How is Nellie?" I ask.

"Huh? What?" I can hear the muted sound of a tannoy announcement. There's a few seconds of silence on the line, before Lucy's back with me. "I have to go, I'm boarding. I get back to London tonight; do you want to get a train down tomorrow morning? I'll meet you at King's Cross?"

"Sure," I say, though immediately begin to panic again. A train to London, when buying the ticket this late, will cost me what, £150? £200? That'll about wipe me out, and I don't get paid for another fortnight. Still, I go online on my phone and do it anyway, choosing an e-ticket in an attempt to do my part to fight off Capitalism's destruction of the planet and all its resources. If we're house- and dog-sitting hopefully we'll stay in all weekend, and I won't have to spend any money. We'll eat her parents' food, drink their alcohol, I'll make love to their daughter. And I'll survive another month, pay 4 more weeks of rent, stave off homelessness for the next little block of time.

Lucy has long since hung up on me, and dropping my phone back into my pocket I push the old wooden door to the pub open and make my way back inside, lift the section of the bar that allows travel back and forth, smiling at Max's mum who glances over to see who the interloper is, smiling when she sees it's only me, and I make my way up the back stairs to find Max. He's in his room, fresh out of the shower, looking once again like something unreal, impossibly attractive, a tribute to the perfection of man. I want to take the towel off and make love to him, but I know he's wary about doing anything in the B&B, particularly when his parents are there too. They know he's gay, or bi, or whatever, not-straight, and

117

know that we're seeing each other, and yet around them
he doesn't act openly not-straight, and they don't act like
he's not-straight. Nothing homophobic happens, at least
not outright; it's more of a generational thing, an inbuilt,
unspoken homophobia. It makes me sad, but when I
brought it up with Max he dismissed it. He told me that,
as much as he hates it, he loves his parents, and knows
they they're not malicious, just ignorant. He doesn't mind
keeping a lid on it for the time he sees them, because it's
worth it to maintain the relationship. I'm not sure I agree,
but keep my concerns to myself; they're his parents, it's
his family's B&B. It's nothing to do with me.

Instead of making love to him I kiss him, quickly, he
doesn't even like to do that, not even in the safety of his
own bedroom, which he's long since made sure his
parents knock and wait for a response before entering. I
tell him that was my mum on the phone, and she's
invited me for the weekend. I don't know why I lie; he
knows Lucy exists, and she Max. I haven't told them the
extent just yet of my relationships with them, but they're
not idiots, they've surely figured it out? But Max doesn't
question the lie, and so a difficult conversation is
avoided. I spend the rest of the day helping out around
the B&B, eventually giving Max another surreptitious kiss
before I hop on a bus back to my flat, as he ties an apron
around his waist and proceeds for an evening of playing
waiter.

Thirteen

There's a sadness in Max's grey eyes that only becomes evident once you find yourself within a certain proximity of him. From a distance, or even from what might be considered enough space to not be impolite during a conversation, you'd never notice it. From normal social distance his eyes are convivial, they're awake and alive and they almost, *almost* invite you in. But whilst an invitation is always teased, you're taunted by the thought of one, for most people Max's eyes never truly deliver that invitation. It makes me so much more delighted to know that I've made it behind the curtain, that I've been not only invited in, but accepted once I arrive. For someone so outgoing, so outwardly social, Max has a lot of reservations that a person must navigate in order to find themself in his inner circle. I can't believe my luck that I've somehow managed to be one of the lucky few.

The sadness in Max's eyes doesn't tell the whole

story; there's a hardness there too. The two are differing sides of the same coin, and both arose for the same reason; as well as having a sister, Max has three older brothers. There are five of the Fleming siblings, and Max is the youngest. He tells me, though from the assumptions I've already made I had guessed, that his childhood and passing through puberty and into adulthood was one continuous battle. It was a battle to be seen, he tells me. Max says that when he was growing up, he wanted his parents to have more children. He wanted at least one baby brother, so that he could switch allegiances, and go from being the victim, to being another bully. He feels horrible about the way he used to wish and wish for this mythical punching bag brought to life, but it seems that Max was named for nominative determinism; upon his arrival, his family was full.

Max is only 19 now; he tells me the reason he hasn't gone to uni yet is that he's saving up. He'd like to go, indeed plans to, but his parents barely get by at the best of times so can't help him with his fees. He's eligible for a student loan, but I'm not the first to tell him to avoid them if possible; it turns out that when they say it's an interest free loan, what they're doing there is lying. There very much is interest on it. And with the government now having decided to lower the threshold at which you start making repayments, it makes less sense to take one than it ever has. Not that the alternative route is any better; Max tells me the course he wants to do, set design, at the uni he wants to do it at, Oxford, which he's clever enough to have earned a place at, are asking for so much money it should be a crime. It never will be; stealing from the poor is fine, it's only when you steal from the rich that anyone actually pays any attention. So as long as Max continues to be priced out of following his dreams, he has a job working behind a bar, and helps his parents out when they need it. He tells me he might as well try and save for a deposit on a house whilst he's at it. He doesn't think he'll ever be able to afford to go to uni, and the sadness inside him is amplified beyond measurable levels as he admits this.

I learn everything I know about Max piecemeal; it's not that he's a closed book, he's just quite a guarded person, and doesn't proffer much information. You have to needle it out of him, asking the right questions at the right time, hoping you have him in an environment in which he feels safe enough to open up and share.

I'll eventually learn that Max actually has four brothers, however the fourth has been completely and utterly ostracised from the family. I'll learn at an even later date that it was something to do with sexual abuse of the young siblings by this eldest; Max will never confirm that he was a victim, but he doesn't need to; it's another one of those things that when he tells me, drunk in bed one night at 4am, us having arrived home from a club, falling into bed but rather than jumping on each other, Max jumps on the chance to give me his heart. I can barely believe the offer and accept it without a moment's hesitation. Max's vulnerability only serves to make him more human. He thinks it does the opposite, it makes him inhuman, it makes him the other, and no amount of attempting to convince him otherwise on my part has any affect. So I'll simply stop trying, take him in my arms, and hold him. And that's what I do. For as long as I'm needed to.

Fourteen

A bit of lost summer sunshine finds Leeds this morning; it's 25 degrees, and I'm sweltering as I stand on platform 7 of Leeds Station, waiting for the train doors to open. The station is crowded, as it always is on a Saturday morning, all kinds of people going all kinds of places. There are young families, parents who can't be that much older than me, some chasing to catch up to excited toddlers, children who have just found their legs, and are using them to their full extent, delighted at the chance to poke and probe to find the true strength of another boundary. Other parents push prams, looking calmer than the parents of the running children, but ostensibly being ten times more worked up, laden down with endless bags overflowing with nappies, bottles, toys, a snapshot of the life of a new-ish parent. I always love seeing families like these, who look like they're carting around their every belonging; something inside me just loves to watch them, struggling under massive burdens, but not caring one iota. These parents are so madly, desperately in love with their progeny that they'll do anything; whether it's chase them down the platform, cart all their belongings around, clean up their shit in broad daylight. There's nothing these parents wouldn't do for their children, and for a few moments, as I stand on the long concrete platform, the train stretched out next to me, gleaming in the morning sunshine, I feel some hope. For the future, for our species; for a few moments, things almost seem like they might be worth it. Then there's a high pitched beeping, and snapping out of my reverie I see the button to open the carriage door is flashing. I press the button and lift up my own overnight bag, which seems small and pathetic compared to the luggage of others around me. I hoist it onto my shoulder and step onto the train, shuffling down the aisle to find my assigned seat.

I find it, and I smile when I see I'm in a two-seater and facing backwards. I know half the reason this pleases me; I like being in a two-seater because it means there's less chance I'll end up faced with strangers. And I mean literally faced; the tables and their connected seats occupy such small spaces that when you sit opposite someone, it almost feels like you're wearing each other. Not to mention the lack of legroom; I may not be a giant, but I know for a fact these trains weren't made for people six feet and above. Even in the two-seater, my knees are pressed hard into the grey plastic of the seat in front of me, my discomfort forcing me to sit at an angle, taking up two seats. I hate to do it, but what choice have they left me?

The other reason I smile is unknown to me; the backwards facing seat makes me do it, but why, I don't know. I have no preference, travelling forwards or backwards, so wouldn't be overly disappointed or excited either way. I'll ask my therapist when I next see her; it'll probably be nothing, but I make a mental note to ask anyway. Even if only to kick start the conversation; there are often long, awkward silences at the beginning of my sessions; my therapist sits there patiently, not quite smiling, but almost, patiently waiting for me to begin. I often sit there, wracking my brain for something to say. I almost always do have something, but also almost always forget until I'm prompted. I have the worst memory at the best of times; these days, between the lack of sleep, the inanity of my work and general lack of satisfaction in my life, combined with the general fun that is mental health issues, I might as well have no memory at all, for all the good it does me sometimes.

I'm on the train early, as I always am; I'm the kind of person who would rather be three hours early than a second late, one of those types who thinks being on time is late. I'm the first in the carriage, and the seats slowly fill up around me as time moves ever closer to the moment of our departure. I have the window seat, and from it I can see the big clock on the platform, like an old school alarm clock blown up to massive size, the numbers huge, the seconds folding over, the furthest number from me changing every second, the next one along every ten seconds, the next one every minute, then every ten, etc. I sit there watching the time slip away, watch my life pass by, and I don't even realise how far away from reality I've drifted until I feel a tap on my shoulder, and I come to with a start to see someone gesturing to the empty seat next to me, which my angled body is blocking. Apologising I sit up straight, position my legs in front of me, sitting down all right angles and awkward bones. The person, who turns out to be a woman, thanks me and sits in the no-longer-vacant seat. I smile at her, then turn back to face the window, resume watching the clock, pray the woman won't try and talk to me.

Soon the clock ticks over to precisely 8:32am, and with a shrill whistle from the uniformed officer on the platform, the train begins to slowly pull away. I sigh, watching the clock until I can no longer see it, then just let my eyes drift out into the world. The station is replaced by Leeds itself, which is then replaced by the countryside. I watch it for a while, until boredom overtakes me and reaching down between my legs, I unzip my bag and root around for my book. Finding it I once again sit up straight, redo the zip on my bag, and try and get as comfortable as I can in the tiny space now being occupied by two people.

The trains rattles along, Yorkshire turning into Lincolnshire turning into Nottinghamshire turning into the next county and the next, until we're in London. Before we arrive there, however, I manage to navigate an awkward visit to the dining car and toilet. The woman in the seat next to me has headphones in her ears, and her eyes are closed. I watch her for a minute, trying to get a sense of whether she's awake or asleep. She's so still, her breathing so soft, I have absolutely no idea. She could actually be dead, so little is the life emanating from her body. I take my eyes off her, mindful not to stare at a stranger, particularly a woman, and try and work up the courage to tap her on the shoulder. It's a difficult one; the last thing I want to do is touch her, without her consent; but I'm desperate for a piss, and I can't sit here and hope she opens her eyes, I have to do something.

I'm just reaching out my hand to tap her shoulder when her eyes dart open, and she turns her head and glares at me. I panic, wondering what I must look like; a strange man, reaching out his hand to touch a strange woman, on a train, where there's no escape. My hand flies back into my body, grips my book so I'm grasping it to my chest in two hands like a little child. I want to say something but I'm paralysed, the fear has frozen me. I'm looking at her and can't help it, I need to look away but I'm unable, my muscles and nervous system are no longer responding to the signals my brain is sending. My head is telling my body to look away, stop staring, try and act normal; my body is not responding.

She takes her hands out of her pockets and removes her headphones. I can tell she's going to speak, and I'm terrified at the accusations she's going to level at me, accusations which I'm completely innocent of, but which to a bystander would look very, very bad. I want to say something, speak before her, apologise, explain myself, control the message, but I'm unable. My tongue is as frozen as the rest of me, and all I can do is watch in slow motion as my world falls apart, as my life ends.

"Sorry, did you want to get out?"

She looks at me, gestures to the aisle, starts to get up. In my relief I nearly laugh; of course, she's not going to accuse me of anything, she's just being normal. Not everyone is out to get me; most people are just living their lives, barely aware of my existence, if they even are at all. I think back to what my therapist told me, repeat it like a mantra, even as I remind myself it's meant in a good way, not a bad one. I say it over and over under my breath as I stumble to my feet, awkwardly shamble out of my seat, past hers, and into the aisle. I continue to say it to myself as I thank her, then head to the toilet.

No one thinks about you as much as you, no one thinks about you as much as you, no one thinks about you as much as you, no one thinks about you as much as you.

No one thinks about you as much as you.

Fifteen

I call Max from the train toilet. It's a disabled toilet, which means I have room to pace two or three steps, before turning round and doing so in the opposite direction; each time I reach the door lock button I press it, making sure no one will disturb me. My anxiety levels are through the roof as I listen to the ring from his end, part of me hoping he'll pick up, part of me terrified that he might. I lift the toilet seat and retch once, twice, nothing coming up. I will the train to be as quiet as possible; Max thinks I'm spending the weekend with my mum, in Leeds. I try to think of a cover story for if he asks if I'm on a train, and I realise I can't think of one. The panic is overwhelming me, the toilet shrinking around me, the walls closing in. I'm just about to hang up on Max when he answers, and it's too late, I can't hide from him.

"Hi Noah, is everything ok?" The genuine concern I

can hear in his voice moves me, and I have to choke back a tear before I can answer.

"Hi, you," I'm able to force the words out, before composing myself, clearing my throat and speaking more like myself. I don't want my voice to rat me out. "I'm good thanks, how're you? I'm just bored and wanted to hear your voice."

"That's sweet, but I can barely hear yours. Where are you?"

The dreaded moment. The first thing I do is panic, look about myself as if even *I* don't know where I am. The sight of the toilet around me isn't reassuring, and the calm that I felt upon hearing Max's voice vanishes, and the panic overtakes me, forces me literally to my knees. A small part of my brain is willing me to stand back up, to get my jeans off the dirty, disgusting toilet floor but I can't move. I can't think of any words either, I simply respond to Max with silence. His next words come out with not a small percentage of concern.

"Noah, where are you? Can you hear me? Is everything ok? It's very loud on your end, I don't know if you're talking but if you are I can't hear you. Hold on, let me go outside, it might be the signal in here. Give me two minutes."

Now it's his turn to be silent; well, to be unspoken. Over the din of the train I can just make out his breathing, the sound of doors opening and closing. He's soon back with me.

"There we go, I'm outside. It's absolutely chucking it down, I hope you're happy. Can you hear me?"

I still don't respond. And then it happens, the thing I fear the most.

Ladies and gentlemen, this train will shortly be arriving in Peterborough. Peterborough will be our next stop.

"What's that?"

I hear Max ask this, but from a distance; I feel myself leave my body instantly, that familiar separation from what is happening and what I want to be happening, my anxiety overwhelming me. I manage to stand up, but my legs are so shaky I have to hold onto the door handle to steady myself. I can hear Max talking to me but it's as if he's on another planet, his voice is distant, wavy, like a slightly out of tune radio. I feel the hand holding my phone start to slip, and it's all I can do to hold on to it. I want to say something to Max, say anything, but I can't. So I simply hang up. I quickly send a text to Lucy, it's scrambled but basically says my battery is dying, and I'll see her soon. Once it's sent I turn my phone off, and turning to the sink I splash some water in my face.

The sink is so small that I'm barely able to even get my cheeks a little wet, but I tell myself it's ok, that I'm rinsing my face in cool, calming water, and it helps. I take a minute to compose myself before pressing the button to open the door, and quickly make my way out when I see a few people waiting, throwing me dirty looks. I wonder how long I've been in there for?

I want to go to the dining car, get a drink to steady myself, but I didn't bring my wallet with me. I move back to my seat, and by the time the woman has let me back in, by the time I've sat down and searched through my bag and found my wallet I realise I don't want to move. Instead I simply put my wallet back, close my eyes, and start my grounding exercises.

In through the nose, hold it…out through the mouth. Blow out as much air as possible, really empty your lungs. Even when you think there's no more left, keep pushing, get everything out. Then in through the nose again, and repeat.

I sit there, eyes closed, regulating my breathing, bringing myself back to reality. I may have fucked things up with Max. That's bad, but there's nothing I can do about it now. I can't do anything until I see him, and I won't see him until Tuesday at least; I need to put it out of my mind, to focus on the here and now. I'm on a train. I'm on a train that's just approaching Peterborough. The next stop after this is King's Cross. That's where the train will terminate. I'll get off, and once I'm through the barriers Lucy will greet me. I'm on a train, and soon I'll be with Lucy. On a train, with Lucy.

Train. Lucy.

I think I'm going to be ok. Ha. I've never actually thought that for a second in my life. I *hope* I'm going to be ok.

Sixteen

I haven't been to London since I was 18; fresh faced out of college, uni not starting until September, the entire summer spread out before me like a blank canvas. It was so big, so blank, it was daunting; I dithered and dallied over where to put the first brush stroke, what to do with myself to start the summer off. Then the decision was made for me.

A band I'd loved since I was a young teenager, *Saves the Day*, were playing their first gig in England in years. That it was in London annoyed me; there's a whole country here, you guys; in fact, there's three or four (I'm never quite sure: England vs United Kingdom vs British Isles - what is actually what?). I appreciate you coming over, but that's a long way for one gig. I have to force myself to say *gig* and not *show*, lest I slip fully into American linguistics. It's a show in America, it's a gig in England. Stay true to yourself.

As soon as I found out about the gig I messaged my friend Teddy, who I knew loved *Saves the Day*, and also lived in London; it was a total two birds, one stone situation. I messaged him informing him about the gig, telling him we were going, sending him a screenshot of the email confirmation from the tickets I'd bought. (This was when I still lived at home, and disposable income still existed for me. I didn't have to pay rent or bills, which meant my little part time job allowed me to have some fun. Heady, heady days.) He replied right away, saying he'd also bought tickets, but would be able to sell them. The gig had sold out in mere minutes, and in a surprising turn of events it seemed most tickets had gone to fans, as opposed to touts. Perhaps the band weren't popular enough for the cockroaches to snap up the tickets then immediately sell them at thrice the price. Fucking good. Fuck the touts.

Teddy sold his tickets for face value, actually making a loss after booking fees and all those lovely extra hidden things you're loathe to pay, but can't avoid. Teddy didn't mind; he was 18 then, same age as me. He still is now, in fact. The same age as me, not still 18, obviously. He was from Leeds, like me, but was super smart, and had gone to uni when he was 16. and then had gotten his undergrad and masters in two years. I didn't even think that kind of thing happened in this country; Teddy later told me, after the gig actually, when we were both at least five pints in, and having a good old reminisce, that, actually, that kind of thing *doesn't* happen in this country, they'd gone out of their way to make special arrangements for him. Teddy had been accepted in UCL aged 16, and by 18 held an MA in Politics, Economics, and Sociology. It covers every base, he told me; *I now understand people, money, and politics. What else is there in the world?* Sex, I'd replied, childish in my drunkenness; Teddy laughed so hard he nearly spat beer all over the table and gave me a high five. But you can't learn that at school, he said with a wink and a laugh. I laughed too. Sometimes you have to be crude, you have to let it all out of your system. When Teddy and I get together, we both stop being nice, normal gentlemen, and become lads. Not full lads though; we don't quite start throwing plastic chairs at foreigners, touching up unsuspecting women, try and steal drinks or anything. We just regress, I think, to the age we met; we become 13 again, and act like it. The way we talk about booze, girls, football, fighting, the world, it's very juvenile. I couldn't do it often, but every now and then you just have to. I remember that night with Teddy fondly; most notably because I've only seen him once since, when he was able to take time off work to come see his family, and we had a quick pint before he got the train back to London. Being a genius, prodigy, boy-wonder, whatever you want to call it, Teddy had his pick of the jobs. I was surprised when he took one in the city; I'd always seen him doing something meaningful, something that would improve the world, not just continue to dump on it. I was shocked that Teddy had chosen to use his intellect in the pursuit of wealth, rather than something that actually mattered. I was disappointed, but not overly surprised, when I really thought about it. Teddy had sold his soul, but for a very nice price. I've sold my soul, and for what? For a job that barely feeds me. I'm not jealous. Well, not entirely. Some of it is idealism, some of it is what I know about Teddy; ok, so a lot of it *is* jealousy.

Teddy and I had had a great time at the gig, and then out in London afterwards. The gig had been in Camden, at the Electric Ballroom; one of those places that's fairly low key horrible, but in a charming way. It's dark, a bit dingy, you're wary about where you step, or where you put your phone down, for fear of it sticking and not ever being picked up again; but in spite of all of this, you wouldn't change the place for the world. It's dark, but not too dark. It has dank, but not too much. It's basically the Goldilocks of underground indie venues. Honestly, had a bear walked through it whilst I was there, I don't think I'd have been massively surprised. It was that kind of place where anything could happen.

After the gig we stayed in Camden, went to a bar that's on the side of the canal. The gig was in summer, and even though it was nearly midnight when we left it was still warm enough to sit by the water, to appreciate the last of the day's heat. Teddy got us drinks whilst I found space for us to sit; I dangled my legs over the side of the canal, my feet hanging just above the water line. The river was black, much blacker than the sky reflected in it; looking down upon it, it could have been infinite. I couldn't see what was under the surface, only a reflection of my own face. I had no urge to dive in; Narcissus I am not.

Teddy and I talked some more, and before long the pub was ringing the bell for last orders. I wanted to stay out, take in more of the city, keep the night going, but Teddy was reluctant; it was a Thursday night, and he had work in the morning. I blanched when he told me this; it had been nearly two in the morning, and Teddy was worried about work? I told him that ship had sailed, but he disagreed. He gave me a laundry list of reasons, but half way through I stopped listening; I'd lost the battle, the night was coming to an end. I didn't need Teddy to give me his life story, he'd already won.

He got us a taxi back to his flat; in case you're wondering how much money Teddy made as a member of the city aged only 18, he lived alone in London. That's right, he had a flat to himself. That should tell you all you need to know.

And it wasn't a crap flat either; it had two bedrooms, a good-sized kitchen/living room, and an en suite in addition to the main bathroom. Teddy had made the spare room up for me, but I never made it in there. I'd dumped my bag in the spare room earlier in the day when I first arrived, with every intention of sleeping in there, but once we were back, in the black of night, Teddy said goodnight to me, I watched him walk into his bedroom, and then I watched myself follow him.

Teddy was the first man I ever kissed. Up until that night, I'd suspected I was bisexual, but had never been in a position to find out. That night with Teddy confirmed it for me.

Before Teddy, I'd only been with girls. I'd fantasised about various men, and masturbated to gay porn, but had only physically spent time with women. That all changed with Teddy. He didn't stop me following him, didn't close his bedroom door in my face. In fact, he didn't seem surprised at all; he allowed me to follow him into his bedroom; he went and stood by the floor to ceiling windows which form the boundary of the room opposite the door. To the left was the bed's headboard, against a wall upon which hung some generic, expensive looking artwork, and to the right was another wall upon which hung a huge TV; it was otherwise undecorated save for the door to the en suite, in the far corner. I stood in the doorway, unsure of what to do. I took a step forward and went to close the door behind me, but Teddy softly whispered "don't" and so I stopped my hand, let it fall back down to my side, to hang there limply, expectantly.

I wanted to ask why he wanted the door open, but when he opened the blinds that covered the windows, and turned on a series of lamps and lit a series of candles, I thought I understood. I soon found out that yes, I did understand, I was correct in my deduction; Teddy was a voyeur. Even though his flat was on the 6th floor, and none of the buildings which neighboured the one we stood in stretched this high, Teddy told me he still like to make the flat as bright as possible, make it as visible as possible; a beacon in the night for human attention to flock towards, minds like so many moths, drawn to the brightness, our baser instincts taking over. He had no idea if anyone had ever watched, he told me, but the thrill that they could be, anyone could be watching at any time, is what spurred him on. In my drunkenness I asked if he'd ever thought about being a cam model, setting up a webcam in his bedroom and allowing people to watch that way. Not only could he know for certain that people were watching, via the analytics he'd have insight of when he signed up to whichever cam service, he also might be able to make some money out of it.

"What's that phrase," I slurred to him, still standing in the doorway, Teddy now approaching me having darted to the kitchen to make us each a drink; as if any more alcohol were needed in my system. "*If you're good at something, never do it for free?*"

"I believe that's something people say," Teddy had said to me, and once he put the glass in my hand I took a sip without hesitation, without asking Teddy what the drink was. It turned out to be straight vodka, and it stung, first in my throat, then all the way down my gullet and into my stomach. Once the vodka had been drained the glass contained only ice, and I took a cube into my mouth, sucking on it, drinking what little moisture I could in order to quell my now vodka-upset stomach. It perhaps may have worked, except before I had chance to properly analyse the results Teddy took the glass from my hand, placed it on the hallway table, and kissed me. It all spiralled from there; one moment we're in the doorway, him pushing me up against the frame, kissing me hard, hungrily; me kissing back, fumbling with Teddy's clothes, upon failure fumbling with my own; we're in bed naked, Teddy's hand grasping my penis gently but firmly, moving up and down, me gasping, moaning, savouring the pleasure; me on my hands and knees, Teddy poised behind me, an intake of breath, a sharp pain, then stillness, settling, before Teddy begins to push in and out of me.

I believe Teddy did start doing some online work. I think I remember seeing him in the paper actually; his company found out about his secret second job, and they fired him. Something about maintaining the company's reputation. I think they were more upset that Teddy found a way to make money they weren't involved in; as an employee, they thought they owned Teddy. Independent thought and independent financial gain were not what they had in mind.

I haven't spoken to Teddy for a little while, I should see how he's doing. Not this weekend, not even if I wasn't too scared to turn my phone back on, I'm only in the city for the weekend, and I want to spend the entire weekend with Lucy. All I know about her parents' house is that it's in West London, it's huge, and I can't wait to see it from the inside. I've wandered around Chelsea before; who hasn't? It's one of the joys of London, visiting the natural history museum, learning - for free - all kinds of interesting information, retaining little of it, but having fun nonetheless, then wandering across to Chelsea, admiring the huge houses, wondering who lives in them, remembering they're owned by Russian or Saudi or Emirati millionaires, so no one lives in them; seeing homeless people beg for spare change outside of Lamborghini sales floors, hundreds of thousands of pounds contrasted with a man who just wants to eat, wants somewhere warm to sleep. London is a monument to the greed of the empire; and a monument to the continued hubris and greed of the English nation, a nation full of little Hitlers who can't accept that the empire is gone, that much of the world has independence. People who can't accept that, particularly since Brexit, our little island is an ever-depleting historical relic, a memorial to power now faded, a lament to what we used to call progress.

London still does progress, but only in a very typical way; London no longer produces anything, at least nothing physical anyway. Now it simply produces wealth. But not for the populace, oh no, don't be ridiculous; London is one of the major financial centres of the world, but that has nothing to do with the city's homeless problem. The wealth isn't real and isn't distributed. It's all well and good saying the average income is £10m, but if one person makes £10m and nine make nothing, what good is that? The homeless don't care about the stock market; neither do the working class, and even people like me, the lower middle class. If it goes down, I won't lose any money, but I may lose my job. If it goes up, I won't make any money, but I may still lose my job. I'm human capital, and just like any other capital, I'm a commodity to be bought, sold, traded. All of us outside the upper echelon are. We're pawns for the rich to play with. On the rare occasions they deign to acknowledge our existence, that is.

Seventeen

Lucy has told me her family are quite wealthy, and to prepare myself. No amount of preparation is enough when we arrive there; we're on a street called Tregunter Road and standing outside what Lucy tells me is her parent's house, I'm in shock. I don't even have to ask the obvious question, Lucy knows it's coming so pre-empts me.

"£30m," she says, without even so much as a blanch. "At least, that's when I Googled it a couple of years ago. It might be more now, who knows." She shrugs, looks both ways and crosses the street; she approaches the gate and enters a code into the keypad. After a small delay I hear a buzz, and the gate slowly swings open. Lucy starts to walk through it before realising I'm not with her; she stops and turns around, her hair whipping from one side of her head to the other, momentarily covering her face. I'm still standing across the road, gawping. My mouth isn't hanging open, but it might as well be; Lucy told me to play it cool, to act normal, like I fit in. I don't think she did a good enough job to prepare me.

The house has seven bedrooms, she tells me, and seven bathrooms. It also has a swimming pool, a cinema room, a gym, a library, and perhaps most stunning of all, a garden. Lucy's family are wealthy enough not to just own indoor space in London, but outdoor space too. It's a world I've never seen before, and one that I can't comprehend. It's so far removed from anything in my experience, I just simply can't cope with it. My mind shuts down, refusing to accept what is before my eyes, refusing to entertain new ideas. I withdraw into myself, and Lucy is given the part of me that comes out in a crisis, but one that doesn't present an immediate threat of danger. I don't quite dissociate, but I'm not far off.

Lucy gives me the tour, and by the end of it I'm exhausted, not sure how necessary a gym really is in a house that covers this much space, which requires so much exercise simply to exist in. Lucy barely bats an eye, as if this is all perfectly normal, as if all people come from this sort of background. It makes sense to me now why she had no interest in speaking about work when we met, why she still rarely talks about it now; I work because I have to, I have to pay rent, buy food, have money to have at least some fun each month so I don't go completely mad. Lucy works as a hobby, something she does for fun, to entertain herself, to indulge herself. Lucy doesn't like to talk about money, she says it's 'gauche'. I now see that that's because she has it. It's easy to not be thinking about money constantly when you know it'll always be there, when you never have to worry about the supply running out. The more time I spend in the house, the more time I think about it, a resentment grows in me. How can Lucy and her family have so much, when so many have so little. Literally a ten-minute drive from the building in which I stand sits Grenfell Tower; all I would have to do to get there from Lucy's is walk to Earl's Court and hop on the Piccadilly Line to Hammersmith; change onto the Hammersmith and City Line and get off at Latimer Road. That's it, two trains, six stops, and this vast wealth is replaced by the spectre of death, by a giant monument to inequality. Were Lucy's house taller, you'd probably be able to see the tower from the roof, you could literally look out from your land and see how the other half live. And more importantly, how they die. They certainly don't die from excess, like the people on Tregunter Road may; there's no excess to be found, in the three miles between the tower and this £30m mansion. You leave the excess when you leave Chelsea; it stays there, rotting, corrupting the souls of those to whom it belongs.

I don't say any of this out loud, of course; instead I do what most people do, when faced with a privilege they've never seen before, and know isn't permanent; I bask in it.

How do I even begin to describe what the house is like? It's so unlike anything I've ever seen before that just trying to put it into words is a task I'm not sure I'm capable of. I've stayed in smaller hotels than this; I've lived in entire flats smaller than the swimming pool that lives in the basement of this building. Did you know that if I worked full time in my current job, never paying tax, never spending a single penny, I would have to work for two thousand, three hundred and eight years to be able to afford this house? And that's if I become homeless, somehow manage to survive without food or water, and manage to not only avoid paying tax, but avoid jail for avoiding tax and continue to work full time. Really, it's impossible for someone like me to ever imagine owning a house like this. It just isn't plausible. It isn't just me; there are few people who can afford to live this way. Although there are more and more as time passes, as the wealth gap grows, as more and more money transfers out of the hands of those who really need it, and into the hands of those who simply must have it; there are thousands, if not hundreds of thousands of people in this country, myself included, who struggle to pay rent and bills and still buy food, pay for transport costs, all those little things you must have in order to live. And here I stand, in the hallway of a £30m mansion, far away from the real world.

The hallway is white, stark really, especially in contrast to the grey of the weather fighting its way in through the blind-covered panes of glass either side of the front door behind me. I evidently left the late blooming summer in the north - is this the first time in recorded history that the north of England has something good that the south doesn't?

In front of me is a long hallway, doors opening up to the left, parallel running stairs going up and down to the right. Lucy leads me down the hallway, gently tugging on my hand whenever I stop, see something that demands my attention. It happens very regularly. To the left of us as we walk the hallway are one of the family rooms, the kitchen, the breakfast room, and one of the bedrooms. The hallway ends in large glass doors which open into the garden. The beginning of the hallway has the stairs going up, and once you reach the end, just behind you are the stairs going down. It isn't just the vast number of rooms, the sheer amount of space afforded to one building in central London; it's the size of the rooms themselves. The hallway is wider, much wider than the one in my mum's house, or my flat. The ceilings are high, as in traditional high, towering over us, dwarfing us, making me feel like the proletariat I really am.

Even though I know I'm in a house, in England, the country I was born in, have always lived in, I might as well be on a spaceship. Not just because of how clean the place is; the walls are white, a crisp, bright white that I imagine might hurt your eyes in better weather, when the sun streams in and lights it up. The ceiling is white too, with a grand light fixture hanging from the middle of it. The floor is bare wood, a rich mahogany, dark brown in colour, and with my shoes on it creates a satisfying *tap-tap-tap* as I walk, each step announcing me the way a host might announce a royal at a ball. I pop my head into the kitchen and find my breath taken again; it's long, it must be 40 foot from one end the other. It's brilliant-white like the hallway, the floor not wood but grey tiles, the kind that you can just tell are expensive. They're not off the shelf from B&Q; I'd be willing to bet they're custom made, and potentially from somewhere in Scandinavia. I don't know much about rich people, and what I do is from films and TV, and I'm sure this is how rich people decorate. They throw their money into individuality; yet another thing the rest of us can't afford to have. We must conform to the faceless masses; god forbid we have ideas or hopes or dreams. No, we simply plough on, having the wealth we create from our work stolen so people a hundred miles away from our office can afford to live in this kind of luxury.

The kitchen is all white cabinets and grey, shining, stainless steel units. These gleam, and I again have the thought that if you live in this house in summer, you'd have to permanently wear sunglasses, otherwise your retinas would burn out in a matter of minutes. The kitchen looks like a showroom, like it's never been used; in fact the whole house looks this way, as Lucy gives me the tour. Entire rooms that look like mausoleums, testaments to another time, a period when there might have been some life in this house. Although I know Lucy has just the one sibling, an older sister, so even when Lucy was young and still lived here, there would only have been the four of them? Lucy, her sister, her mother, her father; four people, two of whom share a bed, camped out in a seven-bedroom house. Four spare bedrooms, and five spare bathrooms. Hell, there's a spare *living* room. I'm finally seeing how the other half live - well, it isn't so much half, not so much 50% as it is 1% - and I can't deny I'm jealous. Who wouldn't be? I'd kill to live in a place like this. I'd become another name to add to the number history is littered with, those who socially advance by killing. I don't want to accuse Lucy's parents of murder, but someone in this family must have done something not quite above board at some point; you don't end up living in a house like this fairly. It's impossible to have enough money to buy it without stealing from someone, somewhere, be it taking artefacts from the rest of the world, or exploiting the workforce and stealing the profits for yourself. I don't say this to Lucy; I don't lie to her, I just leave a lot unsaid. I tell her the house is beautiful, stunning really, and I mean it; I'm angry at the size of it, the sheer existence of it, but I'm not hypocrite enough to stand here and pretend it's ugly. It's a lot of things, and one of these is extremely attractive.

It's fascinating seeing Lucy in her natural habitat too. She seems relaxed, but in a different way to normal; she's always relaxed to an extent, generally being a very chill person. I think it's partially her personality, partially being so rich. She'll never have half the worries the rest of us have, and that would make anyone relaxed. Hell, if I never had to worry about having a roof over my head I'd probably be a very chill person. As it is, I worry about it every day, and so I rarely find the time to be chill, and spend most of my time being extremely anxious. It could be a lot worse; at least there's familiarity in the anxiety, a sense of belonging. The relaxed Lucy is in her parent's house is a much bigger, more existential relaxed. It's like when she stepped through the door she stepped onto a spaceship. The rest of the world no longer exists, for here we are in our bubble. I feel it, in a way. All the white walls and ceilings give this house the feel of a spa or something, perhaps a sanitorium, a place where people speak softly, where they place their feet gently on the floor, they walk as opposed to stomping, and even then stroll as opposed to walking. It's a place built for relaxation; even though I know we've just stepped inside off a London street, London already feels miles away. I can see the garden through a vast window in the breakfast room; it's not huge, 90% of it is grass, with some border flowers, and then brick walls. *Vast* brick walls, they must be 15 feet high. These are what really complete the sense of being cut off from the outside world; they provide a sense of isolation, a sense of safety. Looking at these walls, from inside the house, I have a sense of being on the right side of them, of being in the right place. I can imagine these walls being constructed, by the person who paid for the house to be built, I can see him insisting on the walls being much higher than usual garden walls, in order to keep out the lower classes, those walking around London covered in their own - if they're lucky - shit and piss, stinking from a day in a factory, or a slaughterhouse, or something equally vile, with little health and safety, and no hygiene systems in place. I can picture the person who built this house using it to hide from the world; I have no idea how old the house is, but I imagine the original owner is long dead. It's a shame, because I'd like to tell him that he was successful, because that, I now realise, is what I feel in the house. It isn't just relaxation, it's safety. It feels like the world could end, but we'd be protected from it.

Lucy has emerged from god knows where; she's changed, no longer wearing the jeans and t-shirt she was when she met me at Kings Cross. She's now wearing a bathing suit, a one piece; it's a deep blue, warm and enticing, and the suit fits her figure perfectly, highlights just how few flaws her body has. Once again I can make out her pierced nipple through the material covering it, and once again the sight gives me a little electric shock, it causes stirrings inside me.

"I was upstairs getting changed when I realised I haven't been for a swim since I came back. Would you care to join me?"

I'm standing in the breakfast room doorway, my back to the room itself, to the window and the garden; Lucy is in front of me, her back to me, head turned to look over one shoulder. She has one hand on the banister, the other is holding a towel, and her right foot is poised, about to step down; the angle of it shapes her calf and I long to feel the smooth skin, I want to run my hand along it, feel the lack of hair, the tightness of the muscle. The suit also shapes her behind perfectly; it's round and plump, but I also know from experience firm to the touch. I haven't tried, but I bet you could bounced a pound coin off it; the English equivalent to bouncing a quarter.

I'm hypnotised by the sight of her, and the stirring inside me is beginning to be reflected on the outside of me, my jeans are beginning to feel much tighter around my groin. I shift my legs uncomfortably but it's no good, I'll have to try and go to the bathroom or something to rearrange. I could do so now, but I imagine it's easy to get lost in this house; I dread to think, if left to my own devices, how long it'd take me to get out if I woke up in a random room on a random floor. I resolve not to leave Lucy's side for the next two days.

I realise she's looking at me and I drag my eyes from her behind and look her in the face; she's looking at me expectantly, she most likely just said something. I heard absolutely nothing.

"What did you say sorry? I was miles away."

"You were staring at my arse," she says with a smile. My cheeks flush red and I can't deny it.

"I was! Can you blame me, have you seen it in that suit?"

She extends her neck comically, doing her best impression of a chicken or Regan from *The Exorcist*, trying to look at her own behind. I'm embarrassed but can't help but smile at the sight of her; she's equal parts sexy and adorable, and I don't know which side of her I want to deal with first.

"I said," she says, dropping the towel and covering her behind with both her hands in an exaggerated fashion. "Are you joining me in the pool? Feel free to say no; I can show you to my room and you can freshen up or take a nap or whatever, if you'd prefer?"

"I'd love to join you, but I have no shorts or anything," I lament, genuinely sad. I haven't been swimming in forever, not since my first year of uni when I managed to win a year's free entry to the uni pool. I went every day, sometimes two or three times. I was in the final stages of losing my childhood fat, and with the new world uni opens up, i.e. a lot of attractive women looking to have some fun, I worked extra hard to get into shape. I'm still doing ok now; not as good as then, but still ok. I'm still a ways away from dad bod, at least.

"We might have some spare, hold on. Wait there for 2 secs."

She picks up her towel and runs down the stairs, her

bare feet padding on each step, the sound getting quieter the further away she becomes. I can't hear anything from below, but this doesn't surprise me; I imagine when you're rich enough to afford a house such as this, and particularly so when that house is in central London, you invest a lot on noise dampening. I would, anyway; what's the point in having all this money if you can't escape inconvenience?

Just as I'm thinking she might have forgotten about me and gone swimming I hear her voice floating faintly up the stairs. "Noah, I think I have a solution, come on down."

I begin to descend, my socked feet threatening to slip on each step, my right hand clinging on to the banister for dear life, which may be at risk if I'm not careful. Her voice reaches me again.

"So the issue was you don't have a bathing suit, yes?"

"Yes," I call out to the ether, making my way downstairs but not seeing Lucy.

"Ok, no problem." Her voice is louder now, and I turn at the bottom of the stairs and see her standing in front of me, completely naked. She has no embarrassment, she's quite confident in her looks, and this is almost as sexy as her looks themselves.

"Now we both don't have a suit." she puts her hands on her breasts for a moment, covering them briefly, before biting her lip. "So, are you joining me in the pool?"

The second the question finishes she turns on her heel and runs down the hallway, bombing into the pool with a tremendous splash, sprays of water flying in all directions.

"You coming?" I hear shouted down the hallway, and I can't undress fast enough. It takes what feels like several lifetimes but soon I'm finally naked; not quite as

148

confident as Lucy, I cover myself with one hand, and walk to the pool in lieu of her running.

Not being as confident I don't jump in, but lower myself in, moving quicker as I realise the water is heated, then cursing myself for not assuming it would be. Lucy's standing about halfway down the length of the pool, and once I'm in the water she wades up to join me. She wraps her arms around my neck and kisses me deeply, her tongue burrowing into my mouth, mine into hers. We kiss for a long time, before she pulls away and takes a few steps back. I wonder what she's doing until I realise that she's holding one of her breasts, and with her other hand is touching herself. My erection, which was already at fever pitch, threatens to burst, and I walk over to her, pushing my way through the water, and once I'm close enough I reach for the hand touching her breast and place it on my penis. I take her breast in my hand, put my mouth on hers and kiss her again.

We spend a long in the pool, but neither of us do any actual swimming.

Eighteen

I looked up the phrase 'Indian summer'; in a pleasantly surprising turn of events, the phrase's origins aren't racist. I assumed it would be something to do with colonialism, but in actuality the origins of the phrase are unknown, and there's just speculation that it refers to the fact that when it's cold and dark in England, it's still warm and sunny in India. So when the sun comes out unseasonably, it could be said to be an Indian summer. Don't you just love metaphors?

Autumn truly announces its arrival on Sunday; the wind is lashing down so hard, and the wind is so strong, that the weather appears to be moving sideways, as if the whole world has been rotated 90 degrees, and up is no longer up; and yet it isn't down either. We're somewhere in the middle.

Lucy tells me, with regret, that she had some plans

for us but they were outdoors; a picnic, potentially outdoor swimming (she smiles slyly as she says this, her head down, eyes up, mischief all over her face - I'm thinking exactly the same thing), a nice walk. "All of this is out the window then!" She slams her book down on the kitchen island in frustration; she's been up for hours, reading apparently, whereas I've only just rolled out of bed. And I nearly did have to literally roll; I've never been so comfortable, I didn't want to leave the bed. It's vast; even last night, when we were both in it, there was space to spare. It's something called a super king, which I though was a brand of cigarette, but is evidently a size of bed too. We cuddled when we first got in, but we're both separate sleepers, so quite soon she rolled off my chest and over to the edge on her side, and I the edge on mine. I've always had to sleep on my side, right on the edge of the bed; I must remember to ask my therapist about this. I make a note on my phone to do so on Tuesday evening in my next session.

My phone is full of little notes like this, one or two words, or half a garbled sentence. I've also started around six novels on my phone, but I don't have the drive to sit at my laptop and write them. It doesn't help that my laptop is five years old and basically dead. Double clicking on the Word icon causes it to go into near meltdown; it's like in a kids cartoon, a cartoonishly-fat villain trying to get up, and alarms start going off, henchmen start scurrying around, everyone immediately goes into overdrive. That's what I imagine it's like in my laptop, not least because the sound the machine makes when I press the power button gets a little louder each time, and it's basically already deafening. I'm just making excuses, of course; you could give me the best laptop in the history of mankind, and I'd find another reason not to sit and write. And I know exactly why.

When I have an idea in my head, it's more than just that; it's possibility, it's hope, it's a chance for glory. When I have an idea, and I jot down a few key words, a few sentences, I then immediately start to daydream. In these dreams not only do I write the novel but it changes the world, it wins the Booker, I win a Nobel Prize for literature, it sells millions of copies worldwide and becomes the second Bible. I actually do this every time I have what I think is a good idea for a story; I jot it down, and then imagine my perfect fantasy life. The problem I have is that the fantasy is so good, I don't want to destroy it and replace it with the inevitable disappointment of failure. If I actually sat and wrote a book, then most likely, the odds say, it wouldn't win any prizes, wouldn't garner worldwide attention. Hell, if half the articles I've read are true, I'd be lucky if some poor intern sitting in front of a slush pile somewhere even read the first sentence.

I don't think I'd be able to handle the rejections; because in reality that's most likely what I'd be faced with. They say everyone has a book in them, well I fucking wish they didn't. If everyone else would back off, then maybe I could step up. Writing a book is like buying a lottery ticket; after I've bought it, but before I've checked it, hope is alive. I'm Schrodinger's millionaire, both rich and poor at the same time. Of course, checking the numbers reveals I haven't won anything, and destroys the fantasy. But for those few days and hours I get to imagine what life *could* be, and escape from the drudgery that life is.

Being in a luxurious house, I've decided to adopt the luxurious lifestyle, and so I've slept in until nearly midday. "I was going to wake you," Lucy says, "but you looked so peaceful. And plus, with the weather," she gestures with one arm at the rain we can both see falling through the breakfast room window, "there's nothing to get up for. I'm sorry, is that okay? Should I have woken you?"

I smile at her, my best effort at reassurance, and tell her it's fine. Which it is; I was very tired, and I do appreciate the sleep. I move over to where she's standing by the window and take her in my arms; she's small and warm, soft and pleasant, like holding a kitten. She pushes her body against mine and we stand there for who knows how long, in silence, just holding each other. In this moment it's all we need.

That is, until Max forces his way into my head. One second I'm holding Lucy, the smell of her hair drifting into my nostrils, adding to the pleasantness of her embrace; the next my mind conspires to present me with the imagined figure of Max, and my guilt comes back with a vengeance. I'm glad Lucy is smaller than me, so when we hug she can't see my face; she can't see the guilt that must be etched across it, the fear at what I might have done to Max and mine's relationship, at the hurt I may have caused him. I love Max very much, as much as I do Lucy, and I didn't want to lie to him, but I'm also terrified the truth may hurt him more. If you were to ask me in this moment whom I loved more I'd say Lucy without hesitation, but I know that's just because I'm with her. Total recency bias. If you ask me when I'm with Max, I'd say Max without hesitation. I have a lack of object permanence when it comes to people; if they're not there in front of me, by my side, in my peripherals, I forget they exist. My relationship with Max is no stronger than the one I have with Lucy, and no weaker even. It's just that now, this weekend, I'm with Lucy, so Lucy is on my mind. I do my best to put Max out of my mind and try and live in the moment. Practice makes perfect, supposedly. Or is this fake it until you make it? Either way, pretend to be a better person, and one day you may be.

When we eventually separate, Lucy makes us both a coffee, hers white with two sugars, mine just black and sugarless, as it comes, and we move into the main TV room. Lucy puts on the news; it turns out the rain doesn't just look bad, but it really is bad; there's flash flooding in parts of London, images on the screen from a helicopter of water rushing through streets, turning Camden in Venice, you almost wouldn't be surprised to see a gondola float past the reporter, who's on the ground, fighting in vain against the conditions to deliver his report. The things you have to do for your career, I think to myself, and pull my mug into my chest, savouring its warmth. I'm glad we're in here, not out there.

I have a thought; if there's flooding, does that mean no trains? I reach for my phone and pull up the train app; they're all delayed or cancelled, as I suspected. I show my screen to Lucy and she grimaces, she's coming back with me today, is heading to her company's Leeds office for the week. She's supposed to be staying with me, but having been in this house I'm scared to have her in my flat, for her to see the contrasts between us, the different lifestyles we lead, our very opposing backgrounds. I know she's not a snob and doesn't care, but that doesn't stop me from doing so; I can't help it. My brain fucking loves to worry, so will jump on any reason, no matter how small and irrelevant. Anything to add to the anxiety quietly festering away in the depths of my psyche.

"Do you want to stay here another night, and we'll get a train tomorrow? Can you do that?"

I can, and tell her as much. Then I text my boss, telling her I'm in London and unable to leave, and asking if I can take tomorrow off as annual leave. She doesn't reply for hours, which doesn't surprise me; she's a proper woman, with a husband and kids and hobbies and all the stuff adults are supposed to have. She doesn't have time to sit for hours scrolling, closing and reopening the same apps over and over again, replying to messages immediately simply to break the spell of boredom. When she eventually replies later she'll tell me it's fine, and Lucy and I go online and rebook our train, Lucy thankfully (and graciously) covering the admin fees. She has no concept of the struggles I have financially, but she's very generous, and so it hasn't yet become an issue. I'm not dating her for the money, of course I'm not, but I'd be lying if I said it wasn't nice. Even if it does go against everything I believe in.

We half-heartedly make plans for the evening, should the weather improve, but we both know this is in vain; the forecast said rain all day and most of the night, although sunny spells tomorrow morning should see the worst of the groundwater evaporate, and hopefully things will get back to normal. I love that phrase, "back to normal". As if anything about the world, about the systems we've set up, is normal. Do you think fucking turtles have a stock market? Or swans bet on the futures market? Do ants start wars (actually, to be fair they might), do chickens plot genocide? I'm not animal expert, but I think the answer to all of the above, with the possible exception of the ants, is no. It's only humans that seem to have such a fetish for self-destruction. And have had said fetish for so long it's now referred to as 'normal'.

As promised by the BBC Weather app the rain keeps on coming, and so apart from toilet breaks, getting food or drinks, changing the DVD, Lucy and I don't move. It isn't how I imagined spending my weekend in London; I was excited to see the city, explore it for the first time in years, and I'm disappointed that I can't. But spending time with Lucy more than makes up for it; we make love as often as we can - by we, I of course mean I - and in between we eat, nap, silently sit side by side, hand in hand, and watch various films, episodes of *The Simpsons, The Good Place,* myriad other light-hearted American sitcoms. At one point I'm so relaxed that Lucy convinces me to let her have a lie in the following morning, and to take the dog for a walk myself. I look at her concerned; I've been here for about 36 hours by this point and haven't had a single sniff of a dog; I haven't seen her feed one or walk one or do anything even remotely dog-related. I know one lives here, but its absence is such I forgot it even existed. I relay my concerns to Lucy and she tells me not to panic, that he's in a doggy hotel, and is being dropped off in the morning. "My parents were supposed to be back tonight," she explains, "and so Nellie is being dropped off tomorrow, to give them chance to unpack and settle back in and stuff. Their flight has been delayed due to this," (she gestures out of the window again, the rain still falling, it looks infinite, like we could sit here forever and the rain would still be falling, would never stop, it feels like a metaphor for something, though for what I daren't discover), so actually it's good we're here, because her parents won't be back when the dog is dropped off.

Eventually we go to bed, exchanging lying on the couch to lying back in the super king; we cuddle for a little while, Lucy snuggled into me, me in heaven from the comfort I feel on every single part of my bed; pillow, mattress, duvet, Lucy; every inch of me is touching one of these four things, and I'm content as I lay here, I don't ever want to leave, I don't want to burst the bubble we're in and go back to the world.

I wonder how old Lucy's parents are, what her

inheritance looks like. Should I ask her to marry me? We haven't even officially said we're together, I'm still seeing Max, I have no idea if she's seeing anyone, but still; maybe we should get married? I think all of this, don't say it out loud of course. It'd be awkward if I talked about it, and she didn't agree and so we broke up, but then I had nowhere to go, no money for a hotel, no trains running; she'd dump me and then we'd have to live together, at least until tomorrow. Even for someone as awkward as me, that's too much awkwardness.

These are the thoughts running through my head, and soon I slowly drift off to sleep, the sound of the rain lashing at the bedroom windows, the wind howling as it rushes around the outside of the building. The darkness that has been hovering all day takes completely over, and night arrives, spiriting us off for a few hours until the sun comes back to banish her for another day.

On Monday morning the wind wakes me before my alarm. I check my phone (I turned it back on last night in order to use the alarm function, all missed calls and messages not even checked, so I don't know if they exist or not. Which option would make me feel worse: that Max had been desperately trying to contact me, or that he hadn't bothered at all?) and it's 6:33; my alarm was going to go off at 7, so I decide there's no point sleeping for less than half an hour, and I get up. I slowly slide from between the sheets and tip toe my way to the en-suite. The wind is still howling, it must have been doing so all through the night, but a quick glance outside tells me the rain has thankfully, finally stopped. It's difficult to make out because it's still relatively dark outside, but it looks to be dry on the ground. Hopefully the same is true of central London, and I can go home today. Not that I want to leave this palace, but I worry the longer I live like this, the harder it'll be to go back to my regular life. I'm enjoying playing the rich man, I don't want to head back to cold, dark, poverty-stricken real life.

The light switch for the en-suite is on the outside wall, in the bedroom, so I have to quickly turn it on and then close the door as soon as possible in order to not risk disturbing Lucy. I catch a glance of her just before I pull the door to; she's on her back, head turned to one side, hair thrown across her face as if she's been violently thrashing. The sheets have fallen down, and her pyjama top has ridden up, meaning her stomach is on show. Just the sight of it is enough to cause me to catch my breath; even though it's only her stomach, and only for an instant, that flash of porcelain white flesh, slowly rising and falling with the movement of the lungs above it, is everything I could ever need. When I'm hungry it'll nourish me, when I'm thirsty it'll rehydrate me, when I'm horny it'll satisfy me. It sustains my life, and it has the power to kill me, not through withholding itself, but through positive action; I won't die from the lack of it, it'll kill me. Maybe all of this is true, or maybe it's 6.30 in the morning and I'm a little hungover because we shared a bottle of wine before bed and then she fell asleep so we didn't have sex so I'm a little horny too.

The dog is due to be dropped off at 8, but I want to make sure I'm up in plenty of time and ready to receive her. In the en-suite I turn the shower on and climb straight in, the cold water waking me up, before slowly heating up and easing me into the day. My ideal morning is having no alarm set, and upon waking, no matter the hour, however early or late, not getting out of bed but reading, for as long as I want. To wake up with no pressure to go anywhere, to not have to be anywhere; not at a desk making other people even richer, not at the shop calculating the price of all the items in my basket, and cross referencing the amount with the balance of my bank account and how many days it is until I next get paid. My ideal morning has no pressure; after that, my next choice is to wake up early, but not have to go anywhere. I hate my alarm going off at any time, for any reason, but if I at least can hang around after it, I don't have to rush off for a train or to walk to work or whatever, then it's not so bad. This is one of those mornings; I slowly shower, dry, dress, then head downstairs and make myself a coffee, allow myself half a sugar as a reward for doing something nice for Lucy, for being up and having this coffee whilst she sleeps upstairs.

I'm moving the mug to my lips, about to take my first sip when my hand stops; or should I say, my mind stops, and my body goes along with it. It's the sugar; why did I put it in my drink? It's not the calories, it's not the damage it might do to my teeth, which concerns me. It's the moral quandary; I gave myself the sugar as a reward for doing something nice. By rewarding myself, does that mean I haven't done something nice? Does giving myself a prize mean I wasn't offering my service to a friend, but in fact involving myself in a mutually beneficial transaction? Have I helped the woman I'm sleeping with, or have I helped myself? I know it's ridiculous, to think this much about half a spoon of sugar, but I can't help it. I'd like to simply be able to drink my coffee and think no more of it, but that isn't how I work, that isn't how my brain is wired. My brain is wired to need constant justification and approval in order to operate; in a dark kitchen at 7 o'clock in the morning fumbling over a negligible amount of sugar, I find neither of these things. Luckily my phone vibrates in my pocket and snaps me out of my trance, and before I'm even aware what I'm doing I lift the mug back to my lips as I unlock my phone and I take a sip, then another, of the coffee. It's only when I put the mug down that I realise what I've done, but it's fine now; it isn't so much the act I do, it's more of the first steps being where I get caught. Now I've had a sip, I've swallowed some sugar, I've chosen a path of action, all is good. I can quite happily continue down this path. It's the act of choosing that I can't do; in fact, it's even more basic than that. It's doing something without thinking that I'm not capable of.

Making a cup of coffee, adding sugar, and drinking it is far too straightforward, far too easy for me to be able to just do it. I need conflict, I need hurdles to jump, obstacles to surmount. There needs to be an act two, where it seems like things are going to fall apart, before an act three, where I heroically commit to a decision, and then follow it through. Life is so boring so often that I have to change drinking a morning cup of coffee into *Sophie's* fucking *Choice*. It's exhausting being me.

Looking at my phone, the vibration was caused by a missed call from Max. I don't know what scares me more; that now I've checked I have 12 missed calls from him, or the fact he's just tried calling this early on a Monday morning. Upon checking I see I have 23 messages too. It being so early in the morning, I make a fatal mistake: where I mean to just scan the messages in the notification bar, get the gist of them, I accidentally press on one, and it opens the messenger app. And that can only mean one thing: on Max's phone, the conversation will now show as 'seen'. Max will know I've seen his messages. He'll know I'm aware of his missed calls. I already know I'm not going to reply, not yet, not while I'm down here, with Lucy, in heaven. I'll reply to Max once I have to leave heaven, and re-enter hell. The only problem being that means Max knows I know he wants to speak to me, but I'm not speaking to him. Even as I know this will make things much, much worse, I turn off my phone, place it on the island, and try to put it out of my mind whilst I drink my now quickly cooling cup of coffee.

I spend so long dithering - and that's the only word for it - over both my phone and my coffee that I've barely finished drinking it and set the mug down when I hear a buzz coming from down the hallway. I move towards it, and in an alcove between the up and down sets of stairs there's a tiny little monitor with a tiny keyboard. There's an orange light flashing on the keyboard, and above it writing that says, "Gate 1". I look at the monitor and each screen has title; Gate 1, Gate 2, Gate 3, Conservatory N., Conservatory S., Main Entrance 1, Main Entrance 2, Pool, Tennis Courts, etc. I look around at a few of them, seeing little but darkness slowly receding, being replaced by the growing light of day, before turning my focus to Gate 1. In the image being relayed back to me from down the driveway I can see a person, sex indeterminate, standing by the open door of a van. The van has it's hazards on, and though I can't make out what it says on the side I can only assume it's Nellie being returned. I look around on the keyboard until I find a dial labelled "Gate 1"; I flick it from 'Closed' to 'Open' and through the monitor see the gates start to swing inwards, permitting the unknown person to climb back into the van and drive up to the house. I step outside to meet them, wanting to avoid them being in the house, avoid what little chance there is they might wake up Lucy. The same person who rang the bell steps out of the van, and I see it's a man, in his late 30s or early 40s, hunched back, stooping shoulders, wisps of fine hair blowing in the now much calmer wind. He gives me a curt nod I take to be a greeting and makes his way to the rear of the van. I hear him open the doors, the *clatter* and *clacking* of nails on metal, and then before I know it there's a dog in my face. In her excitement at being home she doesn't appear to have noticed she doesn't know who I am; I can only imagine she's taken my proximity to the house to mean I'm a member of it, and so she's more than happy to see me. I hear the van's rear doors slam closed, and the man gives me another curt nod before hopping back into his seat, turning the van around on the gravel in front of the house, and driving away.

I watch him go for a moment, the dog jumping up at me, desperately trying to lick my face, me desperately trying to get her to stop, before I move back inside the house, dog in tow, and approaching the monitor I flick the 'Gate 1' switch back to closed once I watch the van exit on the small, grainy black and white screen.

I grab Nellie's lead from the hallway table and, despite her best efforts, clip it onto her harness. She fights like hell to stop me from putting the lead on; she's only a small dog, I think Lucy said she's a spaniel of some sort, I'm not sure, I don't know dog breeds. She stands about to my shin when she's on all fours, and to just above my waist when her excitement peaks and she has to stand up and hug me, get my attention, do whatever it is she's doing in her excitement. She's brown and black, mostly black, and I have to put extra lighting on in the hallway just to see her.

I've been moving about the house using only the growing natural light to guide me, but Nelly isn't as pale as the inside of the house is, in fact is the opposite, so I need artificial help to keep track of her. Eventually I come out on top, clipping the lead to the harness she's already, thankfully, wearing. Nellie immediately bounds for the front door and heads back out into the morning, pulling me along behind her, a man with a lot less energy than this incredibly excited dog. Am I walking her or is she walking me?

162

Lucy didn't give me any particular instructions about where to walk Nellie, so when I reach what I now know is Gate 1 and step through the smaller, human sized gate built into it, for no reason other than it being the hand I write with I turn left, and walk in whichever direction on the compass it is.

It turns out to be north east, which works very well for me, and even better for Nellie, because it means we soon come to Hyde Park. It's deathly quiet by London standards, and so a regular level of busy by the standards of Leeds or any other city. There are a lot of joggers making their way around the circumference of the park, others bisecting it and running across the diameter, all dressed in various brightly coloured sports items, probably bought with winter safety in mind, and worn in autumn because exercise and fashion aren't closely related. They're related, it'd be foolish to pretend otherwise, but not in the same way as going out and fashion, or sitting around the house but fashionably and fashion are related.

I run myself, when I'm in Leeds, and though I don't put too much effort into what I wear, I put quite a bit of effort in when I buy running clothes. I tend to stick to dark colours, blacks, dark greys, deep blues; I have a few white tops which I try and wear in the winter, but I'm not overly conscious about what my visibility is like in general. I run alongside the Leeds/Liverpool canal, and usually early in the morning; so in the winter it's pitch black, but there's no one else around. Or at least very few people around. I run because it's one of the few forms of free exercise available; I used to swim, as I mentioned, and would like to go to a gym, but it's an expense I can't justify. When I can barely buy enough food most months, a luxury such as the gym is way down on the list. I recently joined my local library as it's the only way I can (legally) access free books; if I'm not willing to pay for books, the gym has no chance.

I love watching runners; there are always a lot like me, casual runners, who do it for health, or perhaps for fun, but don't take it too seriously. I run 8km twice a week, and end each week with a 10km. I'm not particularly bothered about timings; I do have an app on my phone which times me, but it's more out of curiosity than anything else. I'm not Usain Bolt or Mohammed Farah, constantly trying to better myself. I run mostly because I drink a lot of beer, and running helps offset that. I also run because it's the number one thing people preach when it comes to coping with mental health issues. Not running per se, but exercise in general; and again, running is free, at least if you do it out in the world. A woman I work with told me in a recent conversation that road running, which apparently is the official name for what I do, is okay, it's bearable, but nothing compared to running on a treadmill. Apparently I'm missing out, and should run on treadmills as soon as I'm able. When I jokingly asked her if she wanted to sponsor my gym membership so I could, she became noticeably less vocal in her enthusiasm.

I love watching the serious runners too; the ones that wear pieces of gear that are almost like baby carriers; in them they have phones, water, some even have energy bars. They come running with *supplies*, for god's sake, because they *are* inspired by Usain Bolt and Mohammed Farah, they *do* continually try and better themselves.

Each to their own; I'll never do it myself, but I'm glad they do. With something as harmless as running, literally anyone can do anything they like, as far as I'm concerned. Running is the live and let live of sports; maybe that's why I like it, because it's so politically neutral. Football, rugby, tennis, a lot of other major sports are zero sum games. Sure, in football and rugby you get draws, but mostly one team loses and one wins; and you can't win unless someone loses. When it comes to running, particularly for me, it's a battle against my weight. It's not a zero-sum game, because the game never ends. I'll have to keep running, or at least exercising, forever. It isn't over in 90 minutes like football; some mornings this thought almost overwhelms me, but then I put on my trainers, do my stretches, stick on one of the playlists I've curated to run to, and set off.

The best runs are the ones when I'm in my own little world and forget I'm running. The worst runs are the ones where I'm very aware that I'm running, and so neither time nor distance do me any favours. I can run 10km in less than 55 minutes; this sentence is the most competitive I'll ever be.

I have to fight Nellie not to chase each runner as they overtake us. Again, she's only small, but incredibly strong. I switch the hand holding the lead a few times as I fear one or both of my shoulders will be pulled out of its socket by one of her sudden yanks, when the urge to follow someone or something overwhelms her. I manage to keep hold of her each time she makes a bid for freedom, but some of them are close calls, me grasping the lead with the tips of my fingers, centimetres away from disaster. I have no idea what Nellie is like around other people, other animals, and I have absolutely no desire to find out.

Once she calms a bit, her excitement at being back on her own turf changing from being new and incredible to being old hat, we walk slowly around the outside path of the park, entering from the south east and walking anti-clockwise. By the time I'm halfway around the sun has fully risen and is beaming down already. It's going to be a hot one, it looks like; it's 8.30am and already jeans feels like a mistake. It's only going to get hotter as the sun travels across the sky, at least until the evening.

Riding a train in this weather won't be much fun, being crammed in with hundreds of other people in a space made the smallest possible size without being ludicrously uncomfortable. The smallest possible seats without discouraging people from travel. It's the spacial equivalent of the lowest bidder; hell, the carriages probably *were* made by the lowest possible bidder, who made them the smallest possible size. And then the company charges the highest possible amount. And us consumers, those of us that can't afford a car, have the option of riding the train to get where we need to be, or simply not being able to get where we need to be. Don't you just love the free market?

As well as runners there are some cyclists, just as bright in their lycra outfits. There are people heading to work, businessmen and women with their heads down, coffee and phone in one hand, bag or laptop or stack of papers in the other. I even see a couple of barristers in full garb; it's their garb that gives them away, the cloak and wig they have to wear in court. I wonder if they're late for court, which is why they're wearing their get up in the street, they won't have time to change on arrival; perhaps they just like to show off, wear their profession like a badge of honour, want people to know that yes, they're clever, and yes, they earn a lot of money.

I wonder how many of them are from underprivileged backgrounds, came from the north, or the poorer parts of London, and pulled themselves up into a successful career in law. I'd wager not too many. My guess would be the few staff each firm has from lesser backgrounds are in the back office filing papers, making copies, arranging diaries, and generally being allowed nowhere near court, unless to take notes. You put the rich in the front and the poor in the back; everything is a shop window after all.

There are people who must be heading home from work too, young people of all genders in the various uniforms of London hotels, clubs, and other places that open all night. Few, if any, of these people have much optimism. They walk slowly, their heads down; I'm exhausted just watching them, and I try and send waves of sympathy to them. I try and give them my energy; now I'm in the park and walking I'm wide awake, and as my day consists of one dog walk followed by one train ride I'm not sure how much energy I need. I figure I can spare some, even if it isn't a great deal.

As I walk around the far side of the park I pass through trees on either side of the path, and I slow my pace down, much to Nellie's annoyance, in order to bask in the shade. There are a few clouds in the sky but they're sparse, the white objects far apart from each other, as if they're warring factions in a pre-colonial land. You know, before the British turned up and murdered everything they couldn't sell, ruining hundreds of millions of lives under the guise of 'progress'.

Nellie's annoyance at our pace is soon replaced by delight as she sniffs each tree trunk with great vehemence. If anything, my pace here slows virtually to a crawl; I walk three or four paces, Nellie jogging to catch up with me. She then spots the next tree and runs up to it, ears up, tail wagging, nose in top gear. I pause, give her what seems a reasonable amount of smelling time before taking a few more steps onto the next tree, and repeating the process. I'm quite happy to do this; the train we booked is for 1pm, so we don't need to leave Lucy's until midday at the earliest, and that's if we use public transport. I'm half hoping she'll call a car or something, and we'll get to travel in real style. It'll be like a farewell to privilege for me, and I'll love every second of it, but be glad when it's over. Morally at least; in a literal sense, I'm in no rush to get back to poverty life. I can see why people like being rich; if this weekend is anything to go by, it's pretty nice.

As so often happens to me, I'm happily in my own little world, and am only snapped out of it when my phone rings. I don't even remember turning it back on; in fact, didn't I leave it on the island in the kitchen? I must have picked it up, turned it on, and put it in my pocket without even thinking of it. Odd, but not too odd. Just one of those things I suppose. Muscle memory.

I pull the offending object out of my pocket and answer without seeing who it is; I figure it'll be Lucy, out of bed and wondering where I am. I'm correct. Only, she isn't wondering where I am in general, but because it's nearly 10:30 and she's starting to get concerned. I take the phone away from my ear and glance at the time; fucking hell, she isn't kidding. Somehow I've managed to make a walk around Hyde Park last a few hours; I look about myself and see that the runners and workers have gone and have been replaced by tourists; groups of people that are all backpacks, caps, cameras, sunglasses. The locals have gone to live their lives, and the foreign interlopers have snuck in to take over until 5pm and the return of the locals. If you can call people who bring so much money into the city, and the country as a whole, interlopers. And if you labour under the impression that in London, people actually work 9-5, and not like 9 or 10 or whatever, until they're allowed to leave by their benevolent and gracious superiors. Who have been given the permission by their own superiors.

I pull on Nellie's lead and she comes to me, and I set course for home double speed. Nellie is even less impressed with the raising of our pace than she was by the lowering of it, but tough shit. I have to get back, so Lucy and I can think about getting the train.

Funny, I've just realised I've referred to Lucy's parents' house as home. I've been there approximately 48 hours, and apparently it's home now. Being rich must really be nice; it seems to be so nice I've adopted myself into it, rather than face the pressures of real life at my actual home. Turns out I'd rather stay in a 7-bedroom mansion and have literally no worries, than go back to my two-bed flat, both of which are occupied, in which I worry about everything. All the time.

I do have to head back though, even if only to see and feed Sylvia; she was expecting me back yesterday. I text my house mate to let him know the situation, and he's happy to feed her, but still. I miss her little face. I miss her constant judgements; it's nice to be judged on purely good and bad, by something like a cat. It makes a pleasant change from being judged based on my career choice, my wealth, where I live; I suppose what I'm saying is it's nice for my class status to go unnoticed. It's wonderful, when I'm with Sylvia, I can just be myself. It isn't the same with Max or Lucy, or anyone else I know. I have to wear the mask with them, convince them that not only am I a proper person, but I'm one they want to continue spending time with, continue sleeping with. It's exhausting.

Nineteen

I finally call Max from the toilet on the train. When she rebooked our tickets, unbeknownst to me, Lucy upgraded us to first class. Between the glass of champagne I was given when we departed, to the two beers I've surreptitiously drunk in the toilet to steady my nerves, I'm a bit tipsy. I wouldn't normally be feeling this way after such little alcohol, but I haven't had anything to eat, and I can't remember the last time I was so nervous. What the fuck is Max going to say to me? *What am I going to say to him?*

In the toilet cubicle I look at myself in the mirror, really searching my face to see what's there. There's nothing new, it's the same face I've had for the last 20 or so years, and yet it feels unfamiliar. I've never been a huge fan of mirrors; I don't consider myself to be the most attractive man, so don't seek them out. Plus, growing up overweight, I actively avoided them for many years. It's one thing to be constantly reminded of your weight by your peers, you don't need to look in the mirror to confirm if the rumours are true or not. Because of my aversion to mirrors this feels like the first time in a long time that I'm really seeing myself. I don't know what I was expecting, but it's not the face looking back at me. I know it's my face, I recognise it, I've seen it a hundred times before; and yet it feels different, feels alien. I know it's my face looking back at me from the polished metal surface of the mirror, and yet if you told me it was someone else's I'd probably believe you. Of course whether I *actually* believed you, or just chose to believe you because I wanted to, is a different matter.

I put it off for as long as possible, but soon I'm forced to take my phone out of my pocket. It's been mostly turned off for two days now, since I was on the equivalent train to the one upon which I am currently, heading down towards London on Saturday morning, and I now head away from the city on Monday. Since upgrading to a smartphone I've never been without one for this long; even when I've been to multiple day-long festivals, I've always taken a portable charger or a battery pack or something; I don't mind admitting I'm addicted to my smartphone. Although saying that, I've just been basically off it for two days and I haven't felt *too* terrible, so perhaps I'm not actually addicted to it? Or maybe I am, but this is the forced detox I need, and I'm on the road to recovery. It doesn't matter which of these is true, because once the little Apple symbol appears when I've held the power button down for long enough something shifts in me, a piece that I wasn't aware had moved falls back into place. A sense of calm takes over me, and through it I realise that yes, I'm absolutely addicted to my phone. The worry that's been in my stomach for the past two days, which I just assumed was down to how I left

171

things with Max and tried my hardest to ignore, is gone the second the phone is alive in my hand.

As it boots up I brace myself for notifications. I wonder how many more will have come since I last checked; I'm picturing endless missed calls, streams of messages, a tragedy in reverse, receiving the most recent messages first, learning how Max feels today before I learn how he felt on Sunday afternoon, evening, morning. The Apple symbol disappears and is replaced by the picture of a lighthouse which is my background. I'm still braced, and the tension is pulsing up and down my arms, the tightness in my chest threatening to overwhelm me. Should I feel this tense with regards to a piece of technology? I know I shouldn't, but I also know it's disingenuous to think of my phone as just that. Yes it is a piece of technology, sure, but it's so much more than that; in this scenario it isn't just a piece of technology, it's a vehicle for Max's thoughts and feelings. Yes it's made of metal, and under the surface is filled with myriad components, some no larger than the nail on my little finger, but it's so much more than that. It's just the messenger in this scenario, the course Max's words have taken. My fear has nothing to do with the phone itself, but that the phone will allow me to know what Max has said.

A message comes through; I feel the vibration in my hand, and I risk a glance at the screen: a message from Max. I brace myself for the flood, for more to follow, missed calls, voicemails, social notifications, maybe even an email. I stand in the train toilet, swaying with the movement of the carriage as it gently rocks from side to side, bracing myself as we go round corners, reaching for a handle to steady myself when we go over a particularly rough section of track. I stare at my phone all the while, but the dam holds, and the flood never comes. Just the one additional message from Max. I check it and find it's timed and dated just a few hours after the ill-fated notification check, in which I accidentally revealed to Max that I'd read his previous messages. That the message was sent a few hours after I accidentally read his means that he's taken time to compose himself, to put thought into this message.

That it's only one message, and not a slew of them, is somehow worse. I expected Max to be mad, sad, angry, to love me and hate me equally, to be disappointed, and to want to take it out on me. But no, just the one message; this is much, much worse. Rather than feeling a series of emotions, I now have the absolute opposite worry; perhaps Max doesn't care at all? Perhaps I've overblown our entire relationship in my head, and even though he knows I'm lying to him he doesn't care, he doesn't feel in any way about me the way I do about him. This thought threatens to send me into a spiral, and so using my finger print I unlock my phone and open the message. It's not as bad as I expected, whilst simultaneously being much, much worse: *call me when you get home*.

I expected so much from Max, but the flatness of this message devastates me. I had prepared myself for angry messages, him telling me all the things that he probably knows to be true about me but has been hiding behind his feelings for me. I expected diatribes, soliloquies, great declarations and pains at my lying to him, not being able to commit. I wanted him to tell me that whatever I was doing was okay, that I didn't have to keep any secrets from him. I hoped that this might somehow make us stronger, bring us together rather than tearing us apart.

I think I was living in an 80s Rom-com expecting these things. This isn't Hollywood, this is the real world, and in the real world, things don't always go the way you hope. If they ever do. Everything in Hollywood has a beginning, middle, and an end. Real life isn't that simple or straightforward. Real life is messy, non-linear; real life is one event after another, and how we cope with them. Where a film is one overarching story that lasts for perhaps two hours, and is done and dusted once the credits roll, life is a series of small events, one after another. The big events are few and far between, and life is much more like a collection of short stories than it is a novel. If my life were a book, this section would be a story called, "Oh Fuck".

I want to call Max right here, right now, and in fact I almost do, stopping my finger as it hovers above the 'call' button under Max's contact. Instead I close the phone app and open up Instagram, decide to look at his profile first, try and get a feel for what he's been doing, what kind of mood he's likely to be in. Although in this regard I'm kidding myself; firstly, he'll obviously be in a bad mood. And this is the best-case scenario. Much worse scenarios include him being happy, indifferent, include him having dumped me in his head and moved on.

Secondly, social media is absolutely no indication of how a person might be feeling. You never know what's going on behind the frozen smiles, between the pictures of parties and small animals and trips away. Although it's safe to guess that really, everyone is unhappy. Social media has turned even our personal, recreational lives into a competition. Whereas we used to be able to just have fun, to go out and do things and worry about what came next, the world doesn't work like that anymore. At least not my world, the world of a 24-year-old, surrounded by others in their twenties. Now the world works on this simple basis; if you do something, and don't post it to social media, did it actually happen at all? How do you know something was actually fun or enjoyable if you can't measure it in likes, if you can't read it in adoring comments?

Max is what might be commonly known as a social media whore; I hate the phrase myself, well I hate the word 'whore' anyway; it's an outdated word, one that I don't think has any place in modern society. If a woman wants to sleep with a lot of partners, good for her. More power to her. If she wants to sleep with people for money, then that's her prerogative. For far too long women have been judged incredibly harshly when it comes to sexual standards, where men have gotten away with the same behaviours. Let's face it; men get away with much worse. When it comes to the sexual arena, women hold a lot more power than men. Perhaps that's why we men have chosen to demonise them so much? We can't stand the idea of not being dominant, and so we spend our energy trying to tear down those who are. We men are so used to being in control, that where women have control, we must abuse and disavow them. We can't let things happen without our express approval, because that's a slippery slope to god knows where.

So Max is, for want of better terminology, an Instagram whore. But once again, when I check his profile, my expectations are not met. There are no new posts, no new stories. I once again try to figure out if this is better or worse? It certainly makes me feel worse, but then again if he'd posted a thousand pictures, that would also feel worse. I've very much backed myself into a corner here.

Giving up on social media, I read Max's message a few more times, running my eyes over the words until they no longer terrify me. I quickly drink the other two cans I have, then compose myself as best I can before heading back to my seat. Luckily, Lucy has been asleep this whole time, so doesn't ask what took me so long, or why I'm so obviously tipsy. I sneak off to the dining car and buy a single can, just in case Lucy asks me why my eyes are red or my breath smells like beer. "I had a beer," I imagine myself saying, shaking the can to show it as proof, "but only one, so if I look drunk, I'm not!" I imagine myself lying just that easily, the words falling from my mouth without a moment's hesitation on my part.

Lucy wakes just as we pull into Leeds, and she tells me in spite of, or perhaps due to, her lie in this morning, she's super tired. "If it's okay with you I'm going to head to my Airbnb and have a nap. We can catch up later?"

"Absolutely, sounds good to me," I reply, doing my best to smile and act normal. I was going to lie to her anyway, say I was going home then go to Max's. I need to go and see him as soon as possible, get things straightened out.

It's beginning to worry me how easy I'm finding it constantly lying to everyone. Is that what it's like for everyone when you're seeing more than one person? Is your life just lurching from one lie to the next, one bed to the next, no regard for anyone but yourself, no regard for the long-term consequences? I hope not, because if it is I'll have to make a change, I can't go on like this.

Now back in Leeds, Lucy and I make our way through the ticket barriers, and then in front of the station we kiss, before she heads in one direction, and I another. I walk perfectly normally until the first corner; I go around it, and once I'm sure I'm out of sight of Lucy I stop and pull my phone out. I think about ringing Max, but I want the next words we say to each other to be face to face. Instead I text him asking where he is, and he tells me he's still at his parents'. I tell him I'll be right there and summon an Uber. It arrives in a couple of minutes and I get in, sit in the back, and as the car pulls away and starts to eat up the ground between the station and Max's parents' B&B, I try and figure out what the hell I'm going to say to him.

Twenty

Max is waiting outside for me when the Uber pulls up, which I don't take to be a good sign. I thank the driver, giving him a 5* rating as I'm getting out; I have no idea if he was a good driver or not, I was too much in my world little world, wrapped up with my own petty problems, to pay attention.

We made it in what seems like a reasonable amount of time, and the cost is okay, so I'm perfectly happy to give him a 5/5. To be honest, it takes something really bad for me not to give a driver 5*. If they're annoying, or drive a bit fast, or whatever, I don't like it, but I'll still give them a 5; their livelihood depends on it, and I'm not going to put their job in jeopardy just because I'm mildly annoyed. Even in dire circumstances I'll still give them 4/5; I want them to know I wasn't entirely happy, but still I don't want to actually contribute to their ruining. It's incredibly dystopian; a lot of people will point to

Black Mirror, and rightfully so, when talk of ratings comes up. I'm a 4.8/5; I checked on the app earlier. My rating hasn't changed for a while; I know this because I check it regularly, because I'm trying to wrack my brains for something I might have done for a driver to rate me as less than a 5. You can't see individual reviews which is frustrating, but I guess makes sense; far too many people would probably use ratings as a reason to target someone, and it just isn't worth that.

Whilst people point to *Black Mirror*, as I say, when discussing ratings, everyone seems to conveniently forget that China has already adopted a social points system; it isn't fantasy or fiction, it's reality. Those poor bastards, I feel for them. Trapped under an authoritarian government posing as Communist. 'Doctrinal Doublespeak', Chomsky calls it, this adopting and purposefully distorting of words. It isn't new to China, nor is it exclusively a faux-Communist thing; it's been used plenty of times in so called Communist countries such as Russia, and 1970s Cambodia; but these aren't, weren't, never will be Communist countries. They're dictatorships masquerading as communism. A bit like the Nazi calling themselves socialists, or North Korea calling itself democratic. Words seem to have fewer hard meanings these days; look at the rise in fake news, for example. And this is an interesting term in itself, because most people would just use the word lies. But I guess when you're a national TV programme or website or newspaper or whatever, you don't want to run the risk of a lawsuit. And so you use terms like fake news rather than calling people liars. Lying is fine these days but calling someone a liar is not. We seem to have to be kind to these people, our rulers, who want nothing more than to exploit us for their own personal gain. God forbid we offend them as they destroy us.

"Hi," is all I say to Max. It's underwhelming, inappropriate, but also all I can think of. I was doing an okay job of holding myself together until I saw him. Then I lost it. Max doesn't even greet me, just launches straight into it.

"Where have you been? Tell me the truth or I swear to god I'll go back inside and you'll never see me again."

I sigh, trying to say the words. I eventually decided on the truth as the best course of action; I like Max, and I don't want to see him hurt. The problem is I've already hurt him; from here I can be honest, and hope we can carry on, or I can lie to him, to minimise the hurt now, but maximise it in the future. Because if I lie now, it'll all come out eventually. The truth always does, it always catches up with us. For one of the few times in my life, I opt for short-term pain for long-term gain, as opposed to short-term gain and ignore the long-term consequences.

"I've been in London." Max cocks his head like a dog who doesn't understand. "I'm seeing someone else, a woman called Lucy. I've been dog sitting her parents' house with her this weekend."

It feels good to say it, to tell the truth, to get it off my chest even as Max's face begins to fall. I'm not cheating on him, not technically; we never discussed exclusivity, or becoming officially boyfriend and boyfriend or whatever. If I've lied to him - if - it's a lie of omission, rather than an outright lie. I haven't hidden Lucy from him, or vice versa, I just haven't been completely forthcoming with each person when it comes to the other.

"Lucy," he says hesitantly, and I can see him thinking as he does. "Lucy, have I met her?"

"You have, yes, she's the one—"

"—the one with the nieces, was it? When we were shopping for my nephews? And we've seen her a few other times haven't we? She keeps *popping up*, it seems."

He says the words "popping up" with such vehemence I have no idea how to take it. Anger, frustration, and sarcasm all rolled into one is how it sounds.

I nod in answer to his question, my insides threatening to turn to liquid and splash out of me as I see the upset begin to show itself on Max's face. It looks like he's holding back tears, and I immediately start to cry. This sets him off too, and soon we're just two people, standing opposite each other outside a B&B, on a Monday afternoon, crying.

"I, I, I," he stumbles over his words, forcing them out even as he tries to choke back tears. "I've met her?" He finds some incredulity with which to ask this, and it stings. I don't know what to say; there is an answer, even though it's clearly a rhetorical question. Should I answer, or should I leave the air empty for Max to move into, to carry on with? Thankfully he speaks again, so I don't have to decide.

"Oh my god, I can't believe it. I was going to tell my parents about us." He covers his face with his hands, and though I can't see the tears I know they're coming from the way his shoulders rise and fall, sobs wracking his whole body. I am the worst person in the world.

"I've never introduced anyone to them, you were going to be the first, I was so nervous, so terrified, but so excited. It was going to be hard, but I thought with you by my side I could do anything. Well," he spits these last few words out, his lisp more pronounced than ever in his anger, "apparently I was very fucking wrong.

I move towards him but he moves back. I reach out an arm as if to comfort him somehow, but he flinches away from it. I look around, and no one seems to be paying us any special attention. I thank god for this, even if nothing else she's provided is particularly going well for me right now. I envy these people, just going about their days, living their lives. What I wouldn't give for a simple, straightforward existence right now. What I would give to not to be about to be dumped, probably.

"Aren't you going to say anything?"

He's looking at me between his fingers, still hiding from me, but now it seems like his anger has overtaken his sadness; he's glaring at me, and I'm shocked to see genuine hate in his eyes. It's not like I don't deserve it, but still, it feels like a bit much, especially from Max.

"I, I, I," it's now my turn to stutter and stumble over my words.

"You what?" Max barks at me.

"I'm sorry?" In my panic I accidentally phrase it as a question; I pray that Max hasn't heard this, but it's written all over his face that he very obviously has. I want to say something to make it better, but I have no words. And anyway, Max ends the conversation for us. He turns and storms back into the B&B.

"Max…" I call after him, wanting to say something, to fight for him, to not lose him like this. And for a moment, a brief but glorious moment, I think he's actually going to come back to me, that the simple act of saying his name has repaired all the damage I've caused. Of course, I'm mistaken. Just when I think I've lost sight of him, and might never see him again, his face reappears. I have a brief flash of optimism that he might still want me, that his previous love for me is stronger and more durable than his current hatred. I'm mistaken.

"Noah?" I look at him. "Go fuck yourself."

Max doesn't speak to me for six weeks.

Twenty-One

Before long it's Halloween, which I've always taken to signal the end of autumn, and the official coming of winter. Though winter doesn't officially start until December 23rd, with the shortest day of the year - incidentally, I don't feel the same betrayal that the days start getting longer in winter as I do with the shorter ones in summer. So I'm a hypocrite, sue me - it seems to come earlier and earlier every year. I sometimes think Halloween is the only thing stopping people starting to celebrate Christmas in about mid-July.

It makes sense; the year in this country sort of lurches from one holiday to the next; once we're all depressed and back in the office in January, we sit and wait for Easter, and a nice four-day weekend. Then it's a wait for two bank holidays in May, then the end of August. Then it's Halloween, then Christmas, then New Year and the beginning of another revolution. Unfortunately it's only a revolution in a physical, planetary sense; every year follows the same pattern, nothing changes, actually no, things do change but for the worse, and rather than doing anything about it, we humans display our frightening capacity for adapting, and learn to live in an ever so slightly worse world than we used to. I wonder what it would actually take for this country to fight back, to stand up and say "no, things keep getting worse and I'm sick of it. We need to make things better, not just live with them being worse." I don't think it'll ever happen. The root cause of almost every problem this country faces is capitalism, and that system will never be discarded. No matter how terrible it is, as long as it keeps making money for the people at the top, it'll keep being the system by which we live. We can pretend we live in a free democracy all we want, but as long as we're all beholden to the wealth of the shareholders, we're not free at all.

I've never really liked Halloween; when I think about it, it should, in all honesty, be right up my street. You get to wear a costume, which is good because I don't like how I look, so I can hide my true self away. You get to drink, which is always fun; I don't need an excuse, but it's good that there are certain nights, like Halloween, Christmas Eve, New Years, etc. where you can get drunk without any sort of justification. I don't need to tell people it's been a long week, or I haven't had a drink for a while, or one of the other standard excuses. It's funny how going out and getting drunk is fine, but saying you're going out to get drunk is frowned upon. As if we all do it by accident, drink seven beers and pretend we forgot about the alcohol. There's still a stigma about drunk people, which I understand; I've done my fair share of stupid things whilst drunk to justify the general reputation drunk people have. I'm not a major contributor to the reputational problems, I don't think, but I sure don't help matters.

The main thing that should entice me at Halloween is the parade of flesh it has morphed into. Even though it's usually freezing in Leeds at the end of October, and this Halloween is no different, the fact that the temperature might struggle to pass five degrees doesn't stop people putting on their skimpiest outfits and going out into the night. I find myself in a bind sometimes, mentally and morally; I class myself as a feminist, I believe in absolute equality for the sexes. I mean, is there anyone in this day and age who doesn't? Apart from the same sort of backwards people who vote for Trump, even after all he's done in office? Maybe the same people who have watched Brexit ravage this country for the last five years and think "this is good, I like this. My life is exponentially worse, but as long as I'm above brown and black people, socially, in my own mind, then it's worth it."

I consider myself a feminist, which means I am absolutely delighted that a lot of women feel comfortable and empowered enough to wear, or not wear as the case may be, whatever costume they feel. The conflict arises when I can't help but stare; I used to be very confused about the idea of not staring at women. I mean, they're there, looking all pretty, boobs on show, arms and shoulders and legs uncovered, more flesh than clothing on display. And yet, I'm not supposed to stare? Well why would a woman dress like that if she doesn't want to get stared at? Well now I'm a bit older, a bit less naive, I know the answer; women dress like that because they want to dress like that. Growing up, I'd been led to believe by the media, by American TV shows and films, that everything a woman does is to try and impress a man, to try and attract a date. And the same is true for men, everything a man does is to attract a woman, to have sex. I think this is true to an extent for men, but for women? Not a chance. Now I'm an adult, and I've spent time with actual women, rather than fictional characters, had actual conversations with them, I know the truth; women dress up nicely because they want to. Women wear low cut tops, or short skirts, or incredibly form fitting playsuits, because they want to. They want to look good, and they want to feel good. They might want to attract a man, to get laid or whatever, but that will usually be secondary. Women dress sexy because they want to feel sexy. Not for men like me to leer at them. I try not to stare, but I can't help it. I love flesh, all forms of it. I love slutty nurses and slutty cats and slutty Spartans equally. That's one way in which I promote equal rights; I leer at men as much as I do women.

The main problem I have with Halloween is that I wear a mask all the time anyway, at least when I'm around people. I wear the mask of a man who's happy, who's functional, who understands his place and role in the world and is quite content to live and breathe it. I have to wear the mask; there's been a big push in recent years, I've noticed, to allow people to express themselves, to be less strictly business, and be a bit more human. This is great, don't get me wrong, we should be more encouraging when it comes to trying to get the best out of people. Long gone are the days of suits and ties and strict hierarchical offices, that's all very passée now. The business world is slowly and reluctantly coming into the 21st century, and we're all in a better position for it. The problem is, is that it's complete and utter bullshit.

My job constantly tells me they want me to be myself, to be free to express myself, to be happy. They don't want this. If I was truly myself, I'd get fired within the hour. Can you imagine, if your boss tells you to be honest with them, that you actually are? For some reason you have to love your job, and be grateful for it. I don't give a fuck. I work to survive, that's it. If I get rich, if Lucy and I end up marrying and we inherit her parents' vast wealth, am I really expected to sit in an office five days a week and slowly bleed my soul into Microsoft Excel? No fucking thank you. If I won the lottery today I wouldn't even quit my job, I'd just simply stop turning up. They'd figure it out eventually. We live in such a huge, beautiful world, what's this obsession with not only staying in your small part of it, but then giving a large percentage of your waking time to some bullshit company, who really don't care if you live or die? I want to see as much of it as possible; work very much gets in the way of this.

It's nice, on Halloween, to see everyone having fun, to see people in masks and costumes cutting loose, going wild. I'm happy for them. Me personally, no thank you. I go out every year, but I don't celebrate it.

This year I'm out with Lucy, as Max still isn't speaking to me. I've tried calling, and sent him a few texts, but my attempts have dried up at his lack of response. I'm mad at him for ignoring me, but I know this is only a misplaced feeling to override my guilt, because everything that's gone wrong between us is entirely my own fault, and nothing I can do can change that. I want him back, but I'm not going to try and force the issue; I risk pushing him away even further if I do that.

Lucy is dressed as a mermaid; she has on a pair of sparkly purple leggings, high waisted, and a very small turquoise crop top, also sparkly. She's washed and straightened her hair and it looks wonderful hanging down her back, moving with grace each time she turns her head. Despite the fact it's dark and cold Lucy doesn't bother with a jacket; I met her in a bar, we didn't get ready together, and yet I know she isn't wearing a bra, because once again I can see her nipple piercing pushing again the fabric of her top. She looks absolutely stunning, and as much as I don't want to I can't help but stare. It seems like each time I look at her there's something new to take my breath away.

She has glitter on her face, sickle moon shapes either side of her eyes, and it draws attention to them, makes them seem even bigger and brighter than normal. Lucy has beautiful eyes, and I can't help but stare. I stare at her breasts too, in particular her protruding nipple. It's weird, but sometimes I prefer breasts to be covered, rather than just out. There's something in the anticipation, something in them being covered, being hidden, that makes me want them more. Lucy's breasts are small and perfectly formed, and I've spent god knows how long playing with them, but to still see them contained like this drives me wild.

I look at her stomach, at the flat white skin above her leggings and below her top; it's perfectly smooth, and so inviting. I can't see her naval, but I know it's there, just below the waistband of her leggings, and I'm attracted to it in a similar way as I am to her breasts, in that I know it's there but it's hidden from me. And I want to see it, touch it, kiss it. When she turns around I look at her behind, which is perfectly shaped, curved enough to be sexy, not so curved that it's out of shape, or disproportionate to her body. Seeing her in this costume I want her more than I've wanted her in a long time; I whisper this in her ear as we wait to be served in a bar, and she looks up at me and bites her bottom lip, and I nearly ejaculate there and then. I feel her hand move towards my crotch, and there's a brief squeeze which makes my knees wobble. Luckily I'm not wearing skinny jeans for a change, so my erection has room to show itself. I'm dressed in a black suit, white shirt, black tie. In my pocket is a plastic pistol, and a pair of sunglasses, which looked great at home, but now we're out in the world are not helping my vision. The suit is just an everyday one I have, but which I trundle out each Halloween and put on, telling people I'm a Reservoir Dog. It's a quick and easy costume, and people really respond to it. Lucy in particular likes it, and this makes me happy; I put it on for myself, but if it brings cheer to her, then what's not to like?

We've been bar hopping for a few hours, and I'm pretty tired and pretty drunk. Every bar has been absolutely packed, and we've had to fight for service. Luckily, beautiful girls like Lucy don't struggle to get served, so we haven't had to wait for a particularly long time in any place. I've been trying to make it so that the crawls between bars aren't too long; summer is firmly behind us now, and whilst winter hasn't yet arrived, some of its scouts have, bringing a taster of what's to come with them. It's dry, thankfully, but the sun went down around 7pm, and the temperature went down with it. This doesn't discourage people; it isn't just bars, but the streets themselves are teeming with people, groups of men, women, mixed groups, in various stages of dress and undress, various stages of inebriation. It's England at its best and its worst; people out, having fun, coming together to celebrate, boundaries that usually keep people apart forgotten. I think that's why others like Halloween so much; most people don't wear a mask 24/7 like I do, so take pleasure in putting one on. They enjoy stepping out of themselves for an evening, throwing off the shackles of race and class and employment status, and just having fun. On Halloween, for a few hours at least, we're all equal. Equal in our debauchery. Unfortunately, where the equality is what brings out the best in us, the debauchery is what brings out the worst. I don't keep a tally, but if I see fewer than ten people vomiting, crying, or lying in the street, I'll be very surprised. As long as it's neither Lucy or myself I'll be okay; I'm normally a very empathetic person, but once midnight has come and gone, and Halloween winds its way into the early hours, it becomes every man for himself.

I keep thinking I see Max everywhere; whenever we enter a new bar, or turn a corner and walk up a new street, I keep thinking I see flashes of him. I might see the back of his head in front of us, or think I catch his reflection next to us in a shop window. But he's nowhere to be seen, and as much as I try to focus my energies on Lucy, I can't help but be both worried and sad. I miss Max, I miss spending time with him. Don't get me wrong, I love spending time with Lucy, wouldn't change it for the world; but Max, Max is something else. He brings something to the table that Lucy can't. I don't know what it is, some unknown quality that I can't describe, can't place. I probably like both Max and Lucy equally, but for different reasons.

I'm still terrified of all of this blowing up in my face, particularly now that it kind of half has, with me being forced to tell Max about Lucy, and him not speaking to me. I know I need to tell Lucy about Max, but I can't; I'm scared of being so honest with her, and I'm scared of scaring her away. I don't want to go from two wonderful relationships with two wonderful people, to being all by myself again. I've done all by myself, I'm not good at it.

Lucy ends up getting spectacularly drunk, and we're home shortly before 2am. She's staying at my flat, which is good because I feel much more comfortable looking after her in a familiar environment. If we were in her Air BnB it'd be somewhere we were both unsure of, and it might not have all the things we need. As it is, in the flat I have very cold bottled water, paracetamol, various microwavable meals which I offer Lucy in the hope of sobering her up. She isn't interested. When I put her to bed she tries to initiate sex, but thankfully she's so drunk she gives up before I have to reject her. She hasn't brushed her teeth, taken off her make up; she hasn't even taken off her costume. She'll probably be very confused when she wakes up and is still a mermaid. I wonder if I'll be awake to see it; when Lucy's drunk she either wakes up and is wide awake at around 4am, or she sleeps until mid-afternoon. I wonder which tomorrow will bring.

I've just tucked her in, and am heading to the bathroom to brush my teeth before joining her. My back is to her, in the doorway, and when I hear her voice I freeze, panic flooding through me. She didn't say that, did she? She couldn't have. I turn to her and ask her to repeat herself. She does. It turns out she did say it. It turns out I might be completely and utterly fucked. Her last words, which she manages to slur out before she passes out, are:

"How's Max?"

Winter

Twenty-Two

You share your birthday with a man known for being stopped just before he was able to blow up Parliament, many hundreds of years ago. *Remember, remember, the fifth of November*. It's easy for you to remember, because each year it heralds your passage to a new age. This year you turn twenty-five, which is one of those ages where you feel like you're supposed to feel like something, but you don't. Twenty-five feels like a milestone, it feels like you're saying to the world "acknowledge me, oh world, I've been here a quarter of a century, am I not deserving of your acknowledgement, even if I'm unable to claim your respect?" The world, invariably, doesn't notice.

You've always hated having your birthday on this day; no matter how early you make plans each year, most people already have plans. Considering Bonfire Night, or Guy Fawkes Night, isn't really anything, people are always surprisingly busy. Although the surprise is a flaw on your account; the first couple of years of supposed adulthood, the final teen years, things weren't too bad. When you were a student, your friends didn't need much of an excuse to drink, and Bonfire Night was one. When you added your birthday as fuel to the fire, everyone was then delighted because it meant they had two reasons to drink, and thus could drink twice as much. But since you've turned twenty, and people have started to get serious, get real with themselves and their lives, you've struggled to find people to spend the evening with. This year is no exception; you'd planned to spend it either with Max, or with Lucy, or with both; instead, you spend it with neither. Max still hasn't spoken to you following your confession about Lucy; Lucy hasn't spoken to you since your confession about Max. At least the two finally know about each other, you lament; though the information was forced from you, you weren't able to volunteer it, which means you lost control of the message, it got away from you, and so instead of being able to speak reasonably, to present a well thought out argument with reasoning and facts and figures and citations, to each of them you've simply presented a garbled mess of a defence, which does you no favours at all. The jury found you guilty in record time. The deliberations were not long.

A month ago you had a boyfriend and a girlfriend, and tonight, on your birthday, sitting alone in your flat, not even your flatmate for company, you debate how best to go forward. You have no one to go out with, and yet you still want to go out. The rain is hammering on your bedroom window, really lashing down, and yet this makes you want to go out even more; you feel like the rain would be apt punishment, a soaking would be deserved, would be an accurate metaphor on top of the loneliness for how you deserve to feel, based on your actions. Because don't mistake this; you're not the victim here, you're the perpetrator. Whilst what's happening now is awful, you only have yourself to blame. This is the worst of all things; the consequences to your own actions. You were so wrapped up in your own pleasure, for once, you ignored the consequences, you put them to one side as externalities, you forgot. It's good that you chose your own pleasure, for once; the only problem is your pleasure came at the expense of the happiness of others, and that's not ok. You deserve to be happy, but you don't have the right to exploit others to achieve this happiness. Other people have the same right to happiness. Perhaps if we all tried to follow this mantra, the world might be a lot less shitty. Or perhaps it would end up being basically the same. You've never quite agreed with Slipknot, but then again you don't necessarily disagree. What do you think, reader: do people really equal shit?

Not even Sylvia wants to celebrate with you. She's happy that you've been around more recently, spending more face time with her, giving her the attention she's so sure she requires; however tonight the fireworks have her spooked, and she's hiding under your bed, mixed up in the detritus of a now-single man's life. You tried to coax her out earlier, first using just yourself and the promise of your focus, your attention, your love; when this immediately failed you tried biscuits, tuna, you even cooked up a bit of steak that was in the fridge. It's your flatmate's, but he's out tonight, ironically with his girlfriend, and you'll have time to replace it before he's back, before he ever notices it's gone. It was a waste of time anyway; Sylvia normally loves steak, would step over anyone, practically including herself, to get it, but tonight it's no dice; the explosions win out, and she's happier, or at least she's chosen to station herself, lodged deep under the bed.

You're sitting on your bed, wrapped in only a towel, a half-drunk bottle of beer in one hand, your phone in the other. You've been like this for some time; you had a burst of energy earlier and decided that fuck it, you were going out, who cares if you're alone, you can still make a night of it. You're a young, attractive guy, with some birthday cash from your mum and sister; you're ready to paint the town red. That burst of energy carried you to the fridge for a beer, and then into the shower. It lasted just long enough to step out of the shower and wrap a towel around your waist, and then it dissipated. And so here you still are, it's nearly 9pm, the bonfires will be winding down, starting to burn out; people will split into two groups now. One group will go home, content with their evening, wanting to put the kids to bed, get in their warm house and maybe have a hot chocolate to warm themselves up, make them comfortable until it's their own bedtime. The other group will just be getting started; the bonfire will have been the hors d'oeuvres, and now they're ready to move on. Not to the main course, not just yet; there's still the starter, still time for pre-drinking before the clubs open, before it's time to head somewhere dark, where you can seek some flesh.

You sip your beer, and flick back and forth between Max's and Lucy's Instagram feeds. Max is at Roundhay Park, with a few guys, and apparently based on the photos he's posted, and the videos he's been putting in his stories, they're all having a whale of a time. You can't help feeling jealous, and you wonder if this is partly the point; you wonder if Max is truly having this much fun, or if it's exaggerated because he knows you'll be watching. He hasn't blocked you, or unfollowed you, or anything like that, so he must have wanted you to see, to know what he's up to. Either that, or he thinks so little of you he didn't even consider blocking you. You don't know which one would hurt more.

(You're doing a lot of that at the moment: trying to second guess someone's actions, and then wondering which course of action would cause you more pain. You. You. You. Maybe sometimes people act out of their own interests, and the world doesn't revolve around you? As if you ever really thought it did...)

Lucy is at a friend's house somewhere in Leeds; they're having a garden party, their small bonfire has burned itself out, the small amount of fireworks they had have been set off, and they've moved on to the serious drinking portion of the evening. Again, you glean all this information on Instagram, and again, you're not sure where Lucy's mind is, and which state it could be in that would hurt the most. You want to stop, *need* to stop, flicking between their feeds, and yet you can't, the need is impulsive, and even as you get up, the towel falling as you rise, and you open a drawer and put on some underwear, reach for clean socks, find your jeans and slip them on, you leave your room and go to the kitchen for another beer, even as you do all of this your phone is ever present in your hand, palm and four fingers supporting it, thumb free to scroll. Even as you try and coax some life out of yourself, you find you can't stop looking at their feeds. You're much more interested in their life than you are your own. Congratulations Instagram, you win.

You take the fresh beer back to your bedroom and sit back down on your bed. You lean with your back against the headboard, the covers kicked to the bottom of the bed, your knees drawn up so they're under your chin. You're hiding, and though you don't want to admit the fact, as if admitting it might somehow make it more real, you're hiding from your loneliness. The problem is, you can't escape it by sitting here, all alone. And yet you're not sure if you can escape it by going out. Being surrounded by other people might help, but conversely it could end up making you feel significantly lonelier. It's a gamble, and one that you're not sure you're willing to take.

And so you sit, and you sip your beer. And you keep sipping your beer until the bottle is empty, and you go get another one. And you sip that, back on your bed, Instagram still in hand. You drink beer, you occasionally go to the bathroom to piss out beer, and you look at Instagram. You consider going out, getting up off the bed, putting the shower you had to good use. But your fear makes you indecisive, and time slowly slips away, first 10pm, then 11, and before you know it, it's midnight, your birthday is over for another year. But you continue to celebrate, if that's even the word.

You run out of beer and open a bottle of red wine, and as you take your first sip you know it's a mistake, to be mixing drinks like this, sitting home alone, but you don't care. Max has moved into Leeds, is at Belgrave Music Hall. Lucy is still at her friend's house party, and both of them look like they're having the best night of their lives without you. You keep drinking until you realise it's 4am, you're absolutely wasted, and the question of whether to go out or not has been answered for you. Both Max's and Lucy's feeds stopped receiving updates over an hour ago, but this doesn't stop you refreshing them. You switch from one to the other constantly, hoping for an update, praying for one. When Instagram doesn't provide you look through your messages, read your old conversations with the pair of them. You don't realise you're crying until you feel a tear hit your hand, and when you wipe your face your hand comes away wet with the sheen of tears. You finish the bottle of red wine and open another, knowing you

198

shouldn't, knowing it's too late, you should be in bed, you're drinking a month's worth of alcohol in one night, but you're too drunk to care, and you open it and start drinking it. Somewhere in the midst of the third glass you start to fall asleep, all the alcohol and the late hour catching up with you. Your phone still in your hand, the last thing you hear before you pass out is a man's voice, familiar, faintly as if from a great distance, repeating "Hello? Hello? Is anyone there? Hello?"

Twenty-Three

The film *Tremors* (1990) is about a small town in America called Perfection - yes, that's right, Perfection - and how the residents cope when they're attacked by giant, underground, flesh eating worms. It stars Kevin Bacon, and according to Wikipedia was somewhat dismissed upon initial release, but then became a cult classic as more and more people bought and enjoyed watching it on video tape. The film turned thirty last year; it's way older than me, I was born in 1996, I wasn't even a consideration to my parents. My sister probably wasn't either; she was born in 1994, so still years after the release of *Tremors*.

I wonder what my parents' life was like in 1990, when it was just the two of them. I'd love to know, but of course my dad is no longer around to ask, and my mum still doesn't like to be asked about dad, she doesn't like to talk about him, and how things were back when he was alive. She hasn't gotten over it, but I think it's mostly her own fault. I'm not over it, but I'm trying; I'm trying to live my life, to do the best I can do; I hope to be living in a way that would make my dad proud. I haven't set out to live this life, but I just keep trying to do my best, and hope that's good enough. I fall short most of the time, but effort has to count for a lot surely?

My sister and I don't talk about him, don't talk about his death; her being older, she remembers more about him than me. I'm jealous that she got to spend more time with him than I did, those two years feel like aeons when this is the measuring scale. I don't think Emma is over it either, but as with me it isn't for lack of trying. My mum isn't over his loss, purely because she doesn't try to. She lives in a monument to him, a mausoleum; it's been nearly two decades, and yet all his belongings are still in the house. His clothes are all still hung up in the wardrobe; the last book he was reading sits on the bedside table on his side of the bed, bookmark holding his place, giving easy access to the last words he ever read, and the next words he never will. The book is *Dune*, by Frank Herbert. It's a book I'd actually really like to read, but I can't bring myself to. I've gotten so far as taking it off the library shelf, queueing to check it out, and then losing my nerve at the last moment and flinging it onto the counter before running away, running outside, gulping fresh air like a man just saved from drowning. Retching, crying, failing.

I've watched the film *Tremors* three times today. It's a Sunday afternoon, nearly 4pm, in the middle of November; the sun has nearly set already, the darkness drawing in to replace it as it inevitably does. At this time of year, the fact of the sun setting so early feels sinister; I don't know why, but ever since I was young I've always become ill at ease when the sun starts to set; I also struggle with particularly bad weather, how this causes me to think and feel. My therapist thinks that it's somewhere in between being afraid of the dark, being afraid of loss, and the trauma of having lost someone. "If those three were in a Venn diagram, the overlap at the centre would be you," she tells me the first time I tell her about this near constant sense of impending doom. Because that's what it is, at least to me; impending doom. I can't explain it, can't quantify it, can't apply any sort of rationalisation to it; the fact is that I constantly fear some unknown, terrible fate, and there's nothing I can do about it. At least so I believe; my therapist tells me otherwise. I've been seeing her for nearly a year; I've been taking medication for about three or four, it's hard to entirely be sure. Fluoxetine, 40mg per day. I have no idea if it actually works, or if it's just a placebo effect; all I know is the drugs don't cause any noticeable change in me, at least not that I can see; however, if on any given day I don't take the drugs, because I oversleep (unlikely), I've stayed over at Max or Lucy's (very unlikely at the moment), or I've left it so long to re-order my prescription that I've run out (happens far, far too often, much more regularly than I'd like to admit), then it's very noticeable.

I don't know if it is from the outside, but inside the paranoia spikes, the sense of doom becomes almost unbearable. If I had to describe the effect my medication has one me, I'd say it's my spinach. Where Popeye eats it to grow big muscles and save Olive, I take medication to grow my mental muscles, in order to be able to hold back the demons clawing at the gates of my psyche. I use drugs to calm myself, so I can think rationally. "If you think I'm bad now," I want to say to Max, to Lucy, to announce to the entire world, "you should see me without my pills. You'll miss this Noah." I gesture to myself in this imaginary conversation, as if my referring to my body will make the warning I deliver that much more effective.

I didn't mean to watch the film three times; I'm in bed, hungover, and when I see it pop up as I scroll through Netflix I decide to watch it for a laugh. It's a crap film, but in a so-crap-it's-actually-good way, the perfect level for a hungover Sunday afternoon when I don't want to move because I might die, even though right now death doesn't seem the worst option. The film fascinates me, and causes me to keep watching when the credits roll, for one reason; the character of Walter Chang.

According to IMDB, Walter Chang was played by an actor called Victor Wong, born in 1927 and died in 2001 aged 74. You know how when you go in IMDB and search someone, and their profile picture is in black and white, which means they're old, which means you know almost certainly they're dead, before you open their profile and have it confirmed? I knew Victor Wong was going to be dead even before I read it. I mean, even without the black and white profile picture it wouldn't have been hard to deduce; he looked oldish in *Tremors*, perhaps in his 50s maybe (according to IMDB he was actually 63 - he looked good for his age). The film came out 30 years ago, so by my guess he'd be 80 now - and in reality he'd be 93. It's safe to assume that someone who was born 93 years ago may be dead now. It isn't Victor Wong in which I'm interested, however, but Chang, the character he plays in *Tremors*.

The film moves like any other; it's presented in three acts, and once we're introduced to the main characters, then things start to happen. As you can imagine, if you haven't seen it, the residents of Perfection are confused and scared of the worms. By the time their presence is established, the worms have killed multiple people, and even swallowed a car or two. It seems fair enough that people are scared. But Chang? Oh no, he isn't scared. He has something else on the mind: profit. Like a good little capitalist, when the shit hits the fan his first thought is how the collision between fan and faeces can be monetised.

The two characters who discover the worms provide proof of them, in the form of smaller worms, which live within the mouths of the larger worms. Chang offers to buy these worms for $15, and the two discoverers jump at the chance. Later in the film, their delight has turned to regret; Chang has started charging $3 to have your picture taken with the worms, and business is booming. The two main characters are disappointed, but resolved; towards the end of the film - spoiler alert - they kill one of the huge 30 foot worms; their first thought, before even knowing if they're truly alive, or knowing the true extent of the devastation that has been caused, is that they won't be selling this worm to Mr Chang for $15. Not a fucking chance. They high five, and the film plateaus off into the happy ending Hollywood always feels the need to give us, the closure that the media world has that we find so rarely in real life. Hollywood sets us expectations life cannot possibly live up to, but then it's somehow our fault when we find this a bit absolutely fucking not okay.

Mr Chang is a comedy character in the film; good old Mr Chang, who upon being told about flesh eating evil worms decides to buy them and put them to work. Mr Chang, who's only motive is profit, above everything else. Mr Chang, who lives in a town that has a whole 13 other people, where everyone knows each other, and interacts with them daily, is happy to sell them out for his own personal gain.

I found his character to be particularly fascinating

because, as I say, the film presents him and his greed as something comedic, something light hearted to set against the themes of loss and death that are the main drivers of the film. However, Mr Chang isn't a comedic figure; in fact, Mr Chang is everything that's wrong with the world. He's put in a life and death situation, and all he thinks about is profit. He has to pitch in to help his friends and neighbours survive, but instead chooses to focus on money. People are literally dying around him, and his only concern is about making money. Sound familiar?

Mr Chang is late-stage capitalism personified; he's chosen personal gain over human advancement, human success. He's chosen the self over community, chosen to be selfish where he can be helpful. He's a piece of shit, basically, and any normal person can see that. If you asked, most people would agree.

Now ask the average man on the street what they think of stockbrokers and traders. They'll probably have little to no opinion, or maybe even respect them for the huge amounts of wealth they supposedly generate. I say supposedly, because these people do nothing, except get rich off the work of others. Chomsky put it best: *Investors and corporate executives trying to maximise their own wealth regardless of the effect that has on other people.* These are the capitalists, and these are the problem. Stockbrokers, people who work on Wall Street, and in the City in London, and everywhere else, are just as big cunts as Mr Chang. They do what he does, every day, and on a global scale. I say 'supposedly generate', because these people create nothing. What they do is steal. Money, wealth, like other resources, exists in a finite capacity. No one creates wealth; the wealth already exists somewhere, and you just take it from where it is to have it yourself. Stockbrokers, in order to generate such huge tranches of money, must take huge tranches of money from somewhere else. And in steps the working class. Their labour is exploited, the wealth they generate stolen from them, and passed on to others, the already rich. Anyone who tells you social mobility exists is either naive, an idiot, or lying. Or a politician, although I supposed I covered them under 'lying'. Anyone who tells you any stockbroker is anything other than a stupid piece of shit destroying humanity for his own gain is either naive, an idiot, or a liar.

I started watching *Tremors* because I was stoned and thought it'd be funny. As it was, it's gotten a bit too real. Each time I watch it, it hurts me more. Although to be fair, I'm watching it through a haze of smoke so thick I can barely see the TV sometimes, so I may be completely and utterly wrong in everything else I just said. Don't hold it against me.

This isn't the first time I've watched the same film on repeat. When I first saw Cameron Crowe's 1989 coming of age RomCom classic *Say Anything*, I instantly fell in love and watched it 31 times over the following 30 days. I watched it twice on the first day, starting it over immediately once it had finished, and then watched it every day for a month. I'm not kidding, literally once a day for the entire month of June 2019. It wasn't a particularly good month for me, mentally; in terms of films I saw it was flawless, but health-wise, I was in a bad place. I've also recently seen for the first time *Fast Times at Ridgemont High*, and have started a minor obsession with this film. My therapist thinks my dad dying was such a massive trauma that I dissociated, and am only now starting to get back on track. "You're mentally developing," she tells me, "you're just a bit behind your peers. Because you dissociated so early in your life, you missed out on some crucial learnings as a child, and have been playing catch up ever since. That you're routinely obsessed with films aimed at teens, despite being in your twenties, doesn't worry me. I think in many ways you've developed as far as seventeen or eighteen, mentally and emotionally. So watching films for seventeen- and eighteen-year-olds seems about right. Watching them this much probably isn't healthy, but I think that's just your anxiety showing itself in another way. I also think you may suffer from a very mild case of OCD; nothing debilitating, you're lucky in that respect; you just latch onto things once you find they're safe and stay with them until something else safe comes along. I don't think you're in any great danger, to or from yourself, to or from others. You just had a traumatising childhood and are playing catch up."

I take my therapist at her word; she's much smarter than me, not to mention much better trained. I'm a fucking idiot, so I'm willing to listen to her completely, and follow her advice. I think it's working; I'm still fucked up, but I think I'm ever so slightly less fucked up than when I first started seeing her last year. Although saying that, this whole thing with Max and Lucy has me regressing. I haven't spoken to either of them in weeks, and I'm worried.

I'm worried they both hate me for what I've done, to them and to the other person. I'm worried they hate me, and both are going to dump me. I'm worried that, even as they're not talking to me, they're talking to each other, *about* me. I'm worried that I'm falling apart, and that these two have been my scaffolding; now they're gone, I'm going to crack completely. I'm so very worried about so many things. I roll another joint; ironically, I may be the only person in the world that weed makes less paranoid. I think this is because it makes me not care. I know I should care, and I'm learning, but until then I'm happy not to. Especially when finding myself in a circumstance that's not only absolutely horrible, but also completely and utterly my own fault.

Twenty-Four

The morning after the night before; a conversation with Lucy once she's awoken, hungover but not forgetful, in incredible pain, but still hunting for the truth. I do my best to avoid the subject once she's up and about; I've been up for hours of course. I managed a couple of hours of sleep next to her, squeezed onto the side of the bed, clutching on for dear life whilst she, in her drunken sleep/blackout, stretched out like a starfish, monopolising 95% of the bed, leaving me to fight for what feels not just like physical space, but fighting to save the relationship, too. Even as I lay there, before I drifted off, I knew the morning was going to bring some sort of reckoning; I hoped Lucy would forget her question, wouldn't need any information about Max, but I was wrong. I was so, so wrong.

She found me in the living room that morning, just sitting on the couch, Sylvia curled up in my lap, a book in my hand. *Breakfast at Tiffany's*, the novel upon which the film was based, written by Truman Capote. I love this book; it's only about 70 pages long, but it's long enough; one of the major things I learned at uni in a creative writing module I took is that a story is exactly as long as it needs to be. Some might say *Breakfast at Tiffany's* is too short, or that *IT* or *The Stand* by Stephen King, both clocking in at over 1,000 pages, and god knows how many words, are too long. These people are entitled to their opinion; these people are also wrong.

The Stand is exactly as long as it needs to be. Sure, it's an absolute tome, even the paperback probably big and heavy enough to kill a man. But so what? If it's too big for you, you don't have to read it. I personally think *IT* is one of the finest books ever written. I've read it three times now, and it doesn't get any less terrifying, or any less brilliant. My parents were big Stephen King fans, which means I picked up my first of his books when I was probably too young. *Carrie* it was, so not only my first of his, but his first book too. I also walked in on my parents watching the 1990 TV movie adaptation of *IT* starring Tim Curry as the infamous clown when I was far too young to see any of it. I was only in the room for a few seconds before my parents ushered me out, but it was long enough; even now I'm wary when I'm in the shower, lest the drain start to become distended, and an evil shape shifting creature taking the guise of a clown climbs out of it and kills me. One of life's little ironies; I hate being alive, but I don't want to die. It's tough living somewhere in the unknown middle.

So it's Sunday morning and, even though I know what's coming, a sense of peace has washed over me. Perhaps I feel at peace precisely because of what I know is coming. Either way, I'm in a near total state of zen when the door to the hallway opens, and Lucy walks in.

She doesn't creep in like you might in someone else's home, when you don't know who's around, and also you're incredibly hungover and not sure how you acted the night before. No, Lucy walks in with all the confidence in the world. I've heard her in the bathroom, and now I see her I can see that she's splashed some water on her face, tied her hair up so it sits in a bun on top of her head, and has changed from her clothes of the night before into one of my t-shirts. She looks amazing, frankly; if I looked like her, I'd walk in to any room confidently, no matter what circumstances I was about to enter. When you look like Lucy, it must be difficult to be contrite or quiet or withdrawn. People like Lucy, *women* like Lucy, were made to look good. I can't help but stare now, even though I know it's the wrong thing to do, even though I know I should look away, perhaps look at the floor, try and show my shame and fear in my body language. As if she knows what's coming, Sylvia jumps off my lap and darts through the closing door and leaves the living room, leaves Lucy and I alone, at each other's mercy. Or, she leaves me at Lucy's mercy, which, as I sit here awaiting the inevitable, feels closer to the truth.

I close my book and stand up; when I move to touch her on the arm she flinches, and it's then I know for certain that Max is on her mind, and she means to find out what's going on. I sigh internally, bracing myself. I continue to act normal, which I'll do so until she mentions him. I'm not going to bring him up because that feels like it would be an admission of wrongdoing on my part. And whilst I *am* completely in the wrong, whether I admit it or not, I'm in no rush to condemn myself. I'll feign innocence, at least until the evidence stacked against me becomes overwhelming.

"Good morning," I say to her brightly, keeping up my efforts at normalcy even in spite of her flinch. It's not often I can not only make up my mind this easily, but commit to following through as well. I'll maintain my faux joy until it's ripped from my cold, dead hands. Lucy doesn't respond, she simply glares at me.

"Cup of tea?" I say to her even as I'm at the sink filling up the kettle, before putting it back on its stand and turning it on. I reach for the cupboard with crockery in it and take a mug down, just one for her. I then grab a spoon from the cutlery drawer, and a tea bag from the cupboard that does its best impression of a pantry. I do all this with my back to her, fearful of turning round and embracing the silence emanating from her in waves. By this point her rage is so palpable I can almost taste it, and there's a rattle as the hand holding the spoon starts to shake, and I have to put my other hand on top of it to steady it, to dull the noise from the metal of the spoon clashing with the work surface.

What feels like a million years later the kettle boils, and I pass her her tea, using every ounce of will I contain to keep my hand steady; I don't want to spill boiling hot water on her, but even more so I worry that if she sees me shaking she'll take it as an admission of my guilt, and will be able to claim victory before the battle has even started. I fear this because it's true; she hasn't won yet, at least so far as this is a conflict, however she's on the side of truth and justice, whereas I represent lies and deceit. Even though it'll mean my losing, it's imperative that Lucy wins. In a situation like this, the truth needs to prevail. The truth almost always needs to prevail; there are very few circumstances in which a lie is better. Unfortunately, this isn't one of them.

"Is this it?"

I look at the cup of tea she immediately puts down and pretend that's what she's referring to.

"I'm sorry, would you like something to eat?" I move

back to the pantry cupboard and start rifling through it. "We have bread," I call over my shoulder. I open the packet and it's a little stale, but no signs of mould. I relay this back to Lucy. I'm shocked not just by the ferocity of her reply, but the short, sharp, crisp was in which she delivers it.

"Put the fucking bread down." I do. "Turn around." I do, albeit with my eyes on the floor. "Look at me." I do this too, eventually. I don't want to peel my eyes from the floor, but I know I have to; this conversation isn't going anywhere until I do, this whole situation won't move on until I look at her, and the longer I wait, the harder it'll be. I force myself to meet her eye, and I'm shocked when I can see pain in her eyes. I'd expected anger, betrayal, admonishment; for some reason I'd forgotten she's human, she's just a woman, and that this would probably hurt her too. My heart breaks as I see this pain she's carrying. In this moment I hate myself more than I ever have. Which is saying something.

"Who the fuck is Max?"

I hesitate, wondering what to do, how to answer. As I did with Max, I opt for the truth. I owe Lucy that much at least.

"Max is a guy I've been seeing." This feels like a good place to pause, to let what I've said sink in, but I keep going, knowing I need to say it all now or I'll lose my nerve. "We've known each other a little longer than I've known you. In fact, when you and I met, it wasn't long after I'd met Max. I'd given him my number but had just given up on ever hearing from him again, and then I did."

She looks at me, hurt and anger battling for control of her face. That I've caused her to feel this way is killing me; I think of her in the blue dress, *that* blue dress, and for a brief few moments I want to kill myself for what

I've done, I want Lucy to kill me for how I've made her feel. I love her, and I've betrayed her.

"We've been seeing each other since then. I've been seeing him all the time I've been seeing you." I sigh, and hear the next words fall out of my mouth as if of their own accord, as if I'm a bystander in all of this. "I've been cheating on you with Max. And I've been cheating on Max with you."

I stop speaking and wait. I have no idea what Lucy is going to do; whether she's going to be angry and try and hit me, or storm out, or crumple to the floor overwhelmed by sadness. Is she going to call her mum, one of her friends? Is she going to quit her job, the one she doesn't even need, and go away somewhere? This last one is a little bit of wishful thinking on my part; as much as I'd loathe to lose Lucy, it'd be cool to think that I'd literally driven a girl out of the country. It'd make a cool anecdote for the next woman I'm trying to hook up with anyway. Because there will be a next girl.

Even as we stand here, Lucy and I, face to face, my betrayal hanging between us like an axe, I'm thinking about the next woman. I love Lucy, of that I now know, and yet if I were to lose her, I think I could compartmentalise it enough to not let it bother me too much. If my therapist could read my thoughts right now she'd want to kill me. "We've spent so bloody long," she'd say, half amused, half exasperated, "trying to unpack all of your feelings about your dad, about growing up without him, about your mum being repressed, and Emma running away to be a model. We've spent so much time digging this up from your subconscious; we're trying to address things, remember? Repressing them is one of the reasons we see each other in the first place." She'd be exasperated, I'm fairly indifferent. It's amazing how I can dissociate almost at will these days. It's a defence mechanism, for when something gets too much for me to handle. I'm not good at processing emotion, I need more time than most people; dissociating gives me that time. It lets me internalise the emotions, so I can come back to them and understand them later on. That later on never actually comes, that I never take these emotions out and try and cope with them, is neither here nor there.

I snap back into the room and realise Lucy has been talking. I catch the tail end of her diatribe, and it's enough for me to be able to guess what I missed.

"…on me? And with a man? I never expected too much from you, Noah, but this is something else altogether. I know we never officially said we're a couple, we never talked about exclusivity, but did we really need to? We're both adults, I didn't think we needed to sit down and talk and make it official like a couple of teenagers…"

I drift in and out of what she's saying; I can't offer any answers, any justifications. What I hear of what she's saying is 100% the truth, and I have no defence. I will her to stop talking, but each time it seems like she's going to, she's only stopping to take a breath before resuming her monologue. I love this woman. I want this woman to leave.

"…lying to me? How often? When you're tired, or working overtime, or just having a quiet night in, are you actually with him? When I've been sitting at home, having a quiet night in, thinking you're doing the same, have you been fucking someone else? Have you and Max been getting together to laugh at me, stupid and naive Lucy, sitting at home reading a book whilst you're sucking another man's dick." When I don't answer immediately she says, "well?" with such vitriol it nearly breaks me. What little part of me is still whole, that is.

What little part of me I haven't broken off and given to Max, given to Lucy, taken outside of myself.

Lucy continues to look at me, though we both know it's a rhetorical question. But the longer she looks at me, the more I think she actually wants an answer. I start to speak, but she cuts me off; it seems she didn't want an answer per se, just a response she could cut through, to make her exit dramatic. To give her credit, it works. She storms from the living room and I hear her slamming around in the bedroom. Sylvia comes flying in, angry and confused at all the noise. I want to reassure her but I can't; if Lucy walked in now and saw me cuddling the cat like nothing has happened, I dread to think what her reaction might be.

Soon Lucy reappears in the clothes she was wearing last night. Her hair has half come out of its bun and is waving wildly, bouncing from side to side as she moves her head in anger. It's the only part of her that seems to move; she's so angry her body is rigid, her spine straight as a ruler. All her anger is coming out through the jerking movements of her head, and the index finger on her right hand, which she's using to jab at the air between us. I want to say something, say anything, but no words come. She moves to the front door and I trail behind her, her supplicant, needing her presence but no longer able to justify deserving it. She opens the door, and just before she steps through, she turns back to me.

"Noah?" I look at her. "Go fuck yourself."

Twenty-Five

With both Lucy and Max ignoring me, my drinking and smoking go through the roof. At first, it was my overtime that did; I told myself I was stuck in a shitty situation, and I had to make the best of it. I was working 12-, 13-, 14-hour days; I needed the money, yes, but mostly I needed the distraction. Sure, I was bored shitless every day, stuck at my desk moving numbers from one column to another, then perhaps if things got exciting adding them up. I made the rich richer, contrary to everything I stand for, and yet it helped me. I found it comforting, looking at all the numbers. Numbers have order, there are specific laws that govern numbers. Two plus two always equals four. Four plus four always equals eight. Prime numbers can't be even numbers. Pi is 3.1415 recurring infinitely, and it always will be. People, and life, aren't like this. There are rules to life, sure, codes and creeds we both choose to live by, and are ordered to live by the state. But these change, these are flexible, in certain circumstances these rules can be ignored or broken. Murder is illegal, for example, and yet it still happens in every country in the world every day. Theft, fraud, speeding, littering; these things happen every day. No matter how much we legislate against them, people are always going to do them. Thankfully it's a minority of people, but it is people, nonetheless. But that doesn't work with numbers; two plus two will always equal four, every single time. It can be any two, and any other two, and they'll equal four. Two people plus two people will always equal four people, and yet there are nearly eight billion people on this planet; two billion unique combinations of four people, each one being different to any of those before it, or any afterwards. Life is full of variables, and there is none more unpredictable than people.

It was nice at first, taking comfort in the numbers. It was even more comforting when I saw the number my pay would be; much higher than usual, although painfully low still. Barely enough to live on. But since Max and Lucy wanted nothing to do with me, I didn't need to worry about staying solvent. I paid all my bills, my rent, set aside money for food and travel. Once I worked out what was left over, I divided it up across the month, and it became alcohol and drug money. And that's where I am now; I'm still going to work, can't afford not to, but I'm only working my regular hours. I'm coming straight home, and either opening a beer, rolling a joint, or both. My flatmate has expressed concerns, and I can tell from her face that Sylvia isn't happy, but this is what I have to do. I need to escape from the world I've landed myself in. I need to escape from reality, to take illicit substances that allow me to forget, even if only temporarily, the situation I've created for myself. If there's one thing I won't allow myself to do, it's live in denial. The circumstances I'm in are shit, really fucking shit, but I only have myself to blame. That's like a number, that fact will never change.

I lose a bit of weight across November and into early December. I'm not exercising or eating healthily; it's because I'm barely eating at all. At first I'm drinking beer, so initially I gain weight from all the calories it contains; because of this I switch to vodka and cranberry. Perfect drink for if I somehow get a UTI. Although I'm smoking weed, and I get the munchies, the need for food is overridden by my depressive lack of energy, and so no matter how hungry I get, I can't tear myself off the couch, or from my bed, or off the living room floor, where I sometimes lie, feeling like it's the best place for me. My flatmate sometimes finds me on the floor; he's stopped commenting on it, he simply takes what he needs from the kitchen and holes himself up in his room. I don't blame him; I know what it's like to be me, I'd hate to have to deal with me. Although I do tell people, when they get frustrated with me; you think this is bad? I'd estimate roughly 10% of what goes through my head comes out of my mouth, or passes through my body and comes out in my actions. And that's the best, most appropriate 10%. Just try and imagine what the other 90% is like. That usually shuts them up.

I send Max and Lucy daily texts at first; I send the same text to both, making sure not to use their names in case I forget to edit after copying and pasting and make things much worse. Neither of them respond to me. The texts soon fizzle out to every other day, then a couple of times a week, until I give up. I still stalk them digitally, flicking between their respective Insta feeds, watching them both live their best lives, almost as if specifically to fuck with my head. I know it isn't true, that I'm only seeing their highlights, not the times when they're broken up, but it still works. Each time I see a picture of Lucy, her hair down and straight, eyes bright, laughing with some friends, or posing somewhere, perhaps with a cocktail, perhaps with a giant stuffed teddy, it fucking kills me. Every time I see a picture of Max, for some reason regularly shirtless despite the season, hanging with friends, taking cute selfies outside his parents B&B, it fucking kills me. Perhaps I've found a way to commit suicide, it's just happening in real time? Because if I keep looking at these pictures, seeing two people I love happy without me, it will kill me. And again, it will only have been my own fault.

Twenty-Six

It's a Sunday evening and I haven't left the flat since I got home from work on Friday. I've been smoking in my room, much to my flatmate's annoyance. He keeps threatening to tell the landlord and doesn't seem to believe me when I tell him I don't care. I feel bad; I like the guy, we've been friends for a while, he's stuck with me through some of my lowest periods, when I haven't made it easy on him. Same goes to Sylvia; although I haven't had her too long, and this is her first experience of me being really down, she's taking it valiantly. Admittedly, 'taking it valiantly' means avoiding the hell out of me, but that's fair enough. I'd avoid myself too if I could.

It's nearly 9pm; I'm a little drunk, a lot stoned, and stuck somewhere between complete and utter devastation and pure, unadulterated apathy. It's dark outside, and has been for hours. Not that it makes a difference to me, I didn't even open the blinds today. Which is worrying because that's a new addition to my apathy. I stopped showering at the weekend a couple of weeks ago; I stopped socialising even before that. But one thing I've done unfailingly each day of my banishment is get up, open the blinds to let some light in, and open the window to let some fresh air in. I didn't do either today; I'm almost glad it's Sunday, in a way, because as loathe as I am to go to work tomorrow, at least it'll bring me out of my funk. A couple more days in bed not moving and I might never move again, simply lay here until I've run out of either alcohol and drugs, or the money to buy alcohol and drugs. That's the preferable option, but it's the wrong option. Too often, adult life is choosing between what you want to do, and what you should do. Wouldn't it be glorious if just once, these two things were the same? The path of least resistance was also the path of most enjoyment? Those would be the days.

I'm glad I didn't open the window, though wish I had the blinds; it's been bucketing it down all day, without stopping even for two minutes to allow those who absolutely must be outside, to go outside. The rain feels like it's just for me, the way it's constant, and awful. It's lashing against the window, and I feel like I can almost hear each individual drop. The sound is normally comforting, something about the rhythm of the water that calms me; tonight, however, it's having the exact opposite effect. The longer it rains, the more worked up I get. And the more worked up I get, the more it feels like it's raining. I'm stuck in a cycle, me versus the clouds, versus mother nature, versus God. I know I'm not going to win, and yet I keep fighting. Why? Because it's all I can do.

By fighting I, of course, mean staying in bed, drinking vodka, smoking weed, putting on but not watching films, and masturbating through tears to pictures of Max and Lucy. I at first tried to masturbate over my memories with them, but they've become hazy, distant; I can see them through the fugue of alcohol, smoke, mental health problems, but they look like they belong to someone else. When I try and think of a sexy time I had with Max, one that I can get off to, in the few memories I can cobble together I'm outside, looking in. I see the memory in third person; I'm not looking though my own eyes, but watching myself and Max as a third party, as if they're on TV or something. Whether this is because I've been holed up in bed for two days with the TV on, Netflix blaring away one thing after another, or whether it's purely because my mental health is much worse than even I realise, I don't know. All I know is these memories are mine but they don't belong to me. They belong to a stranger, the person I used to be, before all of this.

My phone rings but I barely flinch. I used to leap up, thinking it may be Max or Lucy wanting to talk, maybe even to reconcile. I haven't heard from either of them. So when my phone goes now, I acknowledge it with a look, but that's about it. I'll check it eventually, but there's no reason to now. Whatever message is there will be there later.

I turn back to the joint burning between my fingertips, and as I take a drag on it my phone pings again. When I ignore it, it pings a third time, and a fourth. I soon realise that it isn't messages coming through, but it's ringing. I reluctantly lean over and, digging through the pile of sheets that once resembled a well-made bed, I find it and pick it up. 'Mum' shows on the home screen, it's her that's calling me. I'm a bit alarmed at the day and time of the call; she's normally settled in by now, ready to go to bed any minute. She normally takes this time for herself, so I'm concerned that she's ringing me.

I just about make up my mind to answer when the ringing stops. I wait to see if it'll start again, which would tell me that something really is wrong, but nothing happens. I stare at the phone for a minute; it sits in my palm, a black rectangle, smaller and more expensive than anything else I own. This phone is my life; it has my friends, my email, my banking, my social calendar. Not that there's much in that at the moment, mind you. I couldn't live without it. And yet I'd like to. Just as I'm about to put it down I feel the phone vibrate in my hand, and I move to answer it. When I look at it though it isn't ringing, it's a notification telling me I have a voicemail. I stop; this really doesn't bode well. I slowly, reluctantly unlock it with my fingerprint and then tap on the notification. My phone turns into an actual phone, one of the rare occasions it does, and calls the voicemail. I listen with horror and heartbreak at what my mother has to say. I was right, it's an emergency.

"Hi Noah, it's your mum. I need you to come home right now. I don't know if trains or buses are still running, but if not get a taxi and I'll pay when you get here. If there's any problem give me a ring. I love you."

The message ends and is replaced by a robotic voice telling me to press one to hear it again, two to save it, or three to delete it. I do none of these things, and evidently the voicemail service gets mad at me, and hangs up. I'm too stunned to move; or should that read stoned? I'm panicking, which is actually a tremendous effort considering how drunk and stoned I am. It's a miracle I can feel anything, let alone anything bad, with this many happy substances inside me. I know I should get up, pack a bag, check the train times, but I don't move. Once again, my brain and my body are disconnected, The mind is willing but the flesh is weak. I don't know how long I sit there for, but it's long enough for my mum to call again. This time I answer, although I wish I hadn't.

Where she'd been reserved on the voicemail, a bit clipped sounding but basically okay, on a live phone call she's a wreck. I can barely get two words from her; that is, until she manages to string together five, and it changes my life forever.

All thoughts of Max and Lucy vanish from my head, and I'm next door to sober immediately. My mum was right, I need to get up and get over there asap. My mum needs me, but it isn't just me, it's Emma too. She needs me more than ever. I tell my mum I'll see her soon and hang up, then run to the toilet and vomit. It's all liquid, and once all the alcohol is out of my stomach I'm throwing up bile, feeling it burn my throat, hating the feeling but appreciating how it too sobers me up. Once nothing more is coming and I'm retching, I burst into tears. My flatmate comes and knocks on the door to see if I'm alright, but I couldn't answer even if I wanted to. My mum's words are still ringing in my ears, the sound of her tears is haunting me. I eventually get up, start packing, and summon an Uber, my mum's words haunting my every movement.

"Your sister has been raped."

The American band Fenix TX have a song titled 'Phoebe Cates'; it's from the soundtrack to the film American Pie 2. *It's named after the actress, and the lyrics refer to, amongst other things, the band's singer's teenage exploits masturbating to the famous pool scene in* Fast Times at Ridgemont High.

Noah decides to walk to his mother's house. It'll take about an hour and a half, and though he'd rather be there much sooner, right now if it were possible, he doesn't want his mother or his sister to see him like this. He's still stoned off his face, incredibly drunk, and hasn't washed for going on 66 hours. He has a lightning quick shower, making a terrible mess as he does so but not caring, figuring that's a problem to be addressed at a future time, gets dressed, packs a bag, and is out the door fifteen minutes after hanging up on his mother. He didn't *hang up* on her, merely put the phone down after they'd both agreed the conversation had reached its end.

Now Noah is walking with a purpose. He takes frequent, large strides, not running but not far off it. He's not going to win the gold for the 100m, but he'll give professional speed walkers a run for their money. The streets are quiet, a few cars pass and the occasional bus, but that's about it. Noah barely notices. His head is down and he's watching his feet fall in front of him, watching the ground swallowed up underneath him. There's a light drizzle in the air, the strange kind of rain that feels incredibly light, and yet leaves you somehow soaking wet. Noah welcomes it; he's already had a shower, but this is the best thing nature can offer him in terms of cleanliness and refreshment, and he accepts it gratefully onto his face, his arms, hands, all the skin he hasn't covered in clothing. He also likes it because it masks the tears falling from his eyes. He isn't crying, there are no sobs, his shoulders don't heave up and down, his breath isn't ragged, and yet the tears keep coming. They've been flowing in a steady stream since his mother said those five words to him, and he doesn't think they're ever going to stop.

The American band Hidden in Plain View opened their debut album, their first full length release following their self-titled ep, with the song 'Bleed For You'. In it, the singer laments that he couldn't take his friend's place when she was raped, that he couldn't bleed for her.

He reaches his mother's house and before he's even closed the garden gate she's thrown the front door open and stands, the light coming from behind her casting her as a silhouette. She stands, still as a statue, in a dressing gown and slippers, hair dishevelled, and waits. When he approaches the doorway in which she stands she grabs him and pulls him into a hug, one with such ferocity as he hasn't felt from his mother in years, perhaps decades; perhaps since his father died. He hugs her back, grabbing the back of her dressing down and holding on like a drowning man finally rescued, afraid to let go in case he sinks again. They hold each other in the doorway, light coming from within the house, darkness from without, and soon her tears seep into him and he's crying too.

How long they stand like this neither of them know. He wants to go inside and see his sister, but he isn't ready to face her, doesn't know what he'll do, and so this hug provides an excellent means of procrastinating, of delaying the inevitable. But it can't last forever, and despite his grip on her, he soon feels his mother pulling away. He lets her go and she blows her nose on a tissue he hadn't noticed she was holding; the sound is loud in the quiet of the night, obtrusive almost. He imagines that any nearby people or animals that are disturbed by the sound have long fled, because she'll have been making it for hours. He doesn't know any of the circumstances yet; what happened to his sister, how she ended up back here, how she told their mum. He'll learn all this in the very near future, he imagines. There are a million things he wants to know, but he won't be going into this as a speaker. He'll be going as a listener, as an ear. He and his mother exchange one more look before she stands to the side and ushers him out of the night and into the house.

Other than the hallway light, the only light in the house is coming from the kitchen at the end of the hall.

He can't see his sister but can sense her presence, and after taking off his shoes, bending down to untie the laces and slipping them off his feet, feeling wonderfully normal in this incredibly not normal situation, he pads down the wooden floorboards in just his socks. He stands in the doorway for a moment and looks at her; she hasn't seen him, her back is to him, she's standing at the sink, looking out the windows into the garden. She's clutching a mug of something hot, steam rising from it and engulfing her, and as she takes a sip he's surprised to see her hand isn't shaking. In fact, although he's only seeing her from behind and at a distance, she seems remarkably calm, at least in her body language. He hadn't expected this; he'd tried to prepare himself for her being a wreck, for her throwing herself at him and weeping, him also weeping, his mother joining in, until all three died of dehydration. But no, she seems calm even when he moves into the room. She jumps slightly when he puts his hand on her shoulder, but she soon puts hers on top, and they stand like that for a time, it could be five minutes, it could be two hours. Neither of them know, nor do they care. Just to be together is enough in this moment.

Funeral for a Friend's second album, Hours, *released in 2005, has a track on it titled 'Roses for the Dead'. The song seems to be about suicide; the video certainly is, it shows a young man jumping from the top of a building, a woman we assume to be his mother later mourning him. It's a terribly moving portrait of grief.*

Emma is much calmer than I anticipated; I'm not sure exactly what I expected, but it wasn't this. I make her another cup of tea, as well as one for myself. My mum says no, saying she needs something stronger, and when I join the two of them in the living room, passing Emma her tea before sitting down, I see she has a glass of what looks to be whiskey. I didn't know she liked the stuff; perhaps she doesn't, but desperate times and all that. I'd quite like a whiskey myself, but despite appearing relatively sober I still probably have a tonne of alcohol in my system, and one drink may wake it all up again. I need to be sober now; I'm the man of the family, and even though it's 2021 and we're a pretty open, progressive trio, at times like these, times of crisis, sometimes you just need to fall back into the comfort of a stereotypical role. My mother will no doubt be much happier now that I'm here, to at least share the burden, if not accept it in totality. My sister, once she's told the story, can obviously do whatever she wants. She's the victim here, so we need to make sure her immediate needs are met. That leaves me, the man of the house, the youngest and least self-assured, least responsible. But I don't have a choice, and despite how much of a wreck I am, I'll do my best to step up, to look after these two women who mean so much to me.

Once we're all sitting down, silence descends. Emma is on the couch; I'm in an arm chair at one end of the room, my mother is in another at the opposite end. I keep putting my tea down on the coffee table before picking it up again; I want to drink it but it's too hot, but I keep forgetting. I put the mug down as it heats my fingers, forget right away why I put it down and pick it back up, only to put it down again a moment later. I do this over and over until Emma, her voice remarkably steady, asks me to stop. I'm halfway to putting the mug down and I freeze, hunched over, mug hovering a few feet above the table. I don't know what the correct move is; do I put it down, or keep it in my hands and sit back with it? I know that once I've made a decision I won't be able to change it. The pressure is too much, the weight of the evening for some reason coming down on me in this one decision. I want to cry. I eventually decide to commit to what I was doing and put the mug down; the second I sit back I regret it, but it's too late, the mug is down, and I don't want to bother Emma by picking it up again.

I want to break the silence, and judging by the look on my mum's face she does too, but neither of us do. This isn't our time to talk; we're here as support functions, to provide comfort to someone we love who's suffering. So instead we sit, and we wait, and before long Emma starts to speak. Her tale is as unsurprising as it is harrowing; as she tells it I cycle through so many emotions I don't know what to do with myself. Anger, frustration, sadness, devastation, fear, lust for revenge, a complete lack of surprise. It's another story from a beautiful woman to be added to the pile of similar stories from beautiful women. Not every man, but definitely every woman. The lack of originality in what I'm hearing is astounding. The more things change, the more they stay the same I suppose. Men have been attacking women for 10,000 years, and sadly they'll most likely attack them for 10,000 more. It isn't any worse, that it's my sister, it just hits much closer to home. I should have been there to protect her. I've let her down.

There's a song that's been in my head a lot lately: 'Lady in a Blue Dress', by the band Senses Fail. I highly doubt I have to explain that one to you.

As Emma tells her story, my mother and I alternate between tears, moans, and unutterable silence. The story is harrowing, absolutely devastating. And doubly so for not being surprising. I am Jack's complete lack of surprise.

"I'm 27 now," Emma begins, eventually. My mother

and I have waited for this without pushing; it's the kind of story you can't ask for, you can only accept if offered it. Besides, what am I going to do, sit there and be like, "hey sis, how's it going? How's New York? Heard you got raped? Tell me all about it. Nice to see you"? But Emma is incredibly brave, and tells it all from start to finish without hesitation. Afterwards, we three fall back into that uncomfortable, dazed silence that can only follow hearing something like this from someone you're close to.

"I'm 27 now, and in the modelling business I might as well be 107. I'm still working, and working a lot, don't get me wrong, however I'm losing more and more jobs to girls who can surely be no more than 14, yet agencies and photographers happily believe them when they say they're 18. Some have parental consent, like I did, and so can be honest. Most just lie. The agencies don't care; your age is only a problem when you're old. When you're young, there's no such thing as too young. As long as you look the part, and people will see you on a poster and buy what you're selling, it doesn't matter if you're 14 or 18. It doesn't matter how young you are, it only matters how old you are."

She's repeating herself a lot, but that's okay. No matter how calm she looks on the outside, she's just undergone an incredibly traumatic attack. I'm surprised she's as coherent as she is, in all honesty.

"In the past few months, especially since my birthday, I've had to start thinking seriously about what's next. 27 years old in the modelling industry? I might as well be dead. I've had offers in the past, you know, TV and films and stuff, but I've always turned them down, it never interested me. I don't even really like modelling that much, but it pays well and I'm good at it, so why not?

"I asked around at first, putting feelers out, you

know, making my intentions semi-known and wondering if anyone would bite. And they did, one of the big studios said they had a project coming up that had a role for which I'd be perfect. It wasn't massive or anything, only a little screen time, not too many lines, but I'd get to keep all my clothes on, and it'd be a start. I jumped at the chance; the pay was shit too, but it was supposed to be a foot in the door, nothing else.

"My agent sorted it all; I was to fly to LA for three nights, three days, and I'd have a screen test, which would double as an audition. I wasn't really auditioning per se, more like they just wanted to make sure all would be okay, that I wouldn't go to pieces in front of the camera, or immediately forget my handful of lines and be a blubbering, stuttering mess. I wasn't concerned; I've been in plenty of ads, so wasn't nervous about that part. Besides, I've spent basically every day since I was 15, the last 12 years of my life, in front of one camera or another. If I'm not ready for them now, I never will be."

She pauses here, takes a tissue out of the box she's holding, blows her nose. She scrunches the used tissue up and puts it in her pocket. She grabs another, but instead of blowing her nose with this one she holds it in her hands, the box put aside so there's room for her hands in her lap. As she resumes speaking, her fingers begin to knead and knot the tissue, alternately scrunching it into a small ball in her palm, then stretching it back out, the material taut and straining from the external force being applied to it. Soon she begins to shred the tissue, the only sound other than her voice the very quiet sound of the paper ripping. Pieces of the shredded tissue fall into her lap like snow or confetti, something much more exciting, much more hopeful, much more positive than the situation calls for. My mother and I just watch, enraptured, unsure of what to do. I'm unsure at least, though I can't speak for my mother, can only guess. I want to reach out for Emma, to take her hand, put my arm around her, to do something. It's difficult though; as much as I think she needs comfort, I'm not sure that she'll want me to touch her. Only now do I notice that there hasn't been any contact between us, other than my briefly touching her shoulder and her briefly touching my hand; normally upon seeing each other we run towards each other, she leaps at me and I catch her in my arms, like lovers reunited. But that didn't happen today. This realisation brings the sting of tears back into my eyes; now the sobs really begin.

"When I arrived at the studio, everything seemed fine. My agent had sent a car to my hotel to pick me up, and we breezed past security and onto the lot. The driver was obviously a veteran of the studios, because he drove us to the correct sound stage with zero hesitation.

"He drove slowly once upon the lot, signs everywhere calling out the 5mph speed limit. I pressed my face up against the window like a small child; I wanted to take in as much as possible, but I couldn't be seen to have my head hanging out of the window like a dog, I have a reputation to keep up. I stared, well, no, let's be honest, I *gawped* at everything we drove past; some buildings had the names of famous TV shows or upcoming movies chalked next to their entrances. One had the name of an incredibly famous sitcom on it, and the driver, as if reading my mind, told me that when that sitcom eventually ended, they named that particular stage after it, to honour it. As a fan of the show, I was thrilled to learn this information, it felt like a secret of which I was now part, and the giddy glee in my stomach grew and grew. By the time the car pulled up outside a stage and the driver turned and smiled at me, I wasn't entirely sure if my legs would be able to support me. I opened the door, thankfully distracted enough by the LA heat that I forgot about the jelly in my legs, and was able to exit the car and walk up to the studio door no problem.

"As I reached the door I raised my hand to knock, but before I got chance the door swung open, and a young lady holding clipboard and wearing a headset smiled at me. I smiled back, and I saw a flash across her face, only momentarily, and then it was gone as quickly as it arrived. But it was there, it had definitely been there. I know what was coming even before she opened her mouth. 'Oh my god,' she'd said, trying her best to keep herself calm, keep her emotions in check. 'Emma, I mean Miss Paris, it's such an honour to have you here.' She reached out one of her hands to shake mine, but in doing so she dropped her pen. In bending to pick it up, she then dropped her clipboard. She bent down to retrieve her items, but was struggling. I think she was so nervous to meet me that she couldn't help it. I didn't mind, it happens to me plenty."

Emma smiled at this, though the smile looked more like a lament for what once was, rather than happiness for what still is. The longer it stayed on her face, the more grimace-like it became, until I had to tear my eyes from her and look out the window, almost as if to remind myself that there is some good in the world, there are still some people who just do the right thing, rather than the easy or the fun thing.

"I bent over to help her gather her things; once she had them all we both stood up and I touched her wrist, told her it was fine, shit happens, if the worst thing she did that day was drop her pen, then it was probably going to be a good day.

"She thanked me, then bade me follow her into the studio. I did so, initially blinded by the darkness of the building, compared with the brightness of the outside.

One thing about LA; everyone knows it's always sunny, but did you also know the majority of the buildings in the city are white, or anyway very lightly coloured. It's bright enough with the sun, but when every surface reflects its light back at you? I reckon going without sunglasses in LA, you'd go blind within a day or two. So I stood in the entrance to the studio for a minute whilst my eyes adjusted to the much lower light level. The assistant or intern or whatever she was, I never found out, soon realised that she was walking across the studio floor by herself and stopped to wait for me. Once my eyes were adjusted enough, i.e. I could see anything at all, I caught up with her.

"It wasn't much past ten in the morning but the place was already abuzz with action. Men and women floated around, moving across the space, doing whatever it was they had to do to make sure things ran smoothly that day. I saw a caterer unpacking various containers and laying them out on a big fold-out picnic table. I saw two famous actors sitting in chairs opposite each other, I assume running lines. I meet a lot of very famous people in my line of work, as you can probably imagine, but seeing these two was amazing, even for me. I wanted to go over and introduce myself, say hello, take a selfie and stick it on Insta, but the intern woman was moving so quickly I didn't have chance.

"The building was vast, like an airplane hangar or something. The ceiling stretched way above us, to the point where I almost couldn't see it. I couldn't see walls to either side of me, only bits of set, either built and ready to go, or in pieces, having either been taken apart, or waiting to be assembled. After what felt like an age of walking, although when I checked my phone I realised it had been no more than two minutes, we reached a door at the back of the studio. The intern stopped, and when I stood alongside her she reached up the hand not holding the clipboard and knocked three times. We waited, and then the door opened, and a man stepped out. I vaguely recognised his face and was just trying to place it when the intern said his name, and I made the connection in my head.

" 'Good morning Mr Ward,' she said to him. 'Miss Paris is here for her screen test.' 'Thank you Rebecca,' he smiled at her before turning to me. I heard her quietly say 'it's Rachael' under her breath before I was ushered into the room, and the producer closed the door behind me.

"It was just the two of us in the room, and as soon as I stepped inside I got a bad feeling. I'd been wondering about this room, tucked away at the back of the studio, seeming very out of place. I had assumed it was the producer's office, one he must use when filming was taking place, so he had a quiet place to work, but one that wasn't far away from the action. However, when I looked around it, I knew I was wrong. The room was practically empty; there was a chair at a desk, which had nothing on it, an arm chair pressed against the left-hand side wall, and a small couch. The producer gestured to the couch, and in spite of the bad feeling in me, which was growing all the time, I took a seat."

Emma hesitated here; she'd long since shredded the first tissue, and there was now a small pile of discarded paper in her lap. It was a small mountain of frustration, anger, sadness, regret; that much I knew without Emma saying a word. I looked at my mother, but there was no definable expression on her face. She was a blank; only the shredded tissue in *her* lap gave any sign that anything was amiss.

"He sat on the edge of his desk, perched as if to pounce; that's the thought that went through my head, that he was ready to *pounce* on me. If I'd have known then

236

what was going to happen, I might have used different terminology in my head. Not that it would have any effect on the events that followed.

"Things started off just fine. He welcomed me, offered me a drink, and when I declined he proceeded straight into things; he talked about how honoured he was that I was there, how delighted he was that I'd finally accepted his offer of a screen test. 'I don't know if your agent told you,' he said to me, 'but I've been trying to get you in this office for years and years. I'm so glad you finally said yes.' This made me uncomfortable, but I smiled through it. As I remember it now, it's like everything he said and did was a red flag; sitting on the edge of the desk, telling me he wanted me in his office, not in a *film*, but in his office, the way he'd hugged me instead of shaking my hand when I entered, and above all else the way he was looking at me. I mostly ignored it; I've gotten used to the looks of men over the years, and have gotten pretty good at ignoring them. Perhaps that's what got me in trouble with him? Perhaps because I ignored his look, I didn't see that it was over and above what I usually see in the eyes of men, and was something much more menacing, much more sinister. It's funny," she sobs as she says this, still managing to smile, "I'm left-handed, I thought I was supposed to be the sinister one."

She's emptied the box of tissues, and her hand comes back empty when she grabs for another one. There's a pile of shredded paper on the floor next to her, and looking at it breaks my heart. *He did this*, I think to myself. This pile of paper is his fault; it contains all of his misdeeds, all of his wrongdoing. Emma pauses her story for a moment whilst our mother goes into the kitchen and returns with a fresh box of tissues. Emma grabs for it the second she sees it, and immediately begins to shred a fresh tissue. Which seems to give her the confidence or reassurance or whatever to keep telling the story. Looking back now, I almost wish she hadn't. I couldn't live without knowing what had happened, and yet living *with* knowing probably isn't any better. I'm cursed with knowing what happened to Emma, and that's something I'll have to live with for the rest of my life.

"We were just talking about films, my career, mutual acquaintances, when all of a sudden he stood up. He did it so quickly that it caught me off guard, and before I could regain my composure he'd thrust a script into my hands. I looked down at it; it was for the movie version of *Lolita*, yet another red flag now I look back. A fucking massive, absolutely stupidly unsubtle one. But at the time, I just thought it was the script closest to hand, and that the actual film it was, was unimportant. He told me to turn to a certain page, I don't remember which, and we'd do a scene together. I was to play Lolita herself; whilst I found the page and read my lines, he started to set up a video camera. Again, nothing odd here, I assumed he was filming it so that if I was any good he could show it to other people, people like the director, and casting agents, that kind of thing. Things felt odd, but they were also normal enough that I just rolled with it. I was in unfamiliar territory; modelling was my forte, I could have guided anyone through that with my eyes closed. When it comes to film, I'm completely inexperienced, so had no idea that what this producer was doing was anything out of the ordinary. I just assumed, made a stupid, stupid assumption, that he was doing all of this for me, and that he genuinely wanted to help me in my career. I'm such an idiot."

I reach out for her when she says this and she grasps my hand, but only for a second before letting it drop. It's enough; my tears come harder and faster than ever, and hers really start to fall in earnest. I can hear our mother weeping too; what a trio we must look like from the outside. Which is anything and everything; we three are a family, we belong to each other and each other alone. I've never really felt at home in my mother's house, we've never felt like much of a family unit, not since dad died. But this has brought us together. It's taken a tragedy, but here we are.

"Once he had the camera set up, he pulled up a chair and put it next to mine. The scene he'd picked out was one of the many ones in which Humbert Humbert and Lolita are driving in his car, moving from city to city, motel to motel, carrying out their illicit affair. And by that I of course mean one of the scenes after Humbert has abducted Lolita and is taking her from town to town raping her all the while. This should have set off all kinds of warning signals in my head, but all it actually did was explain to me why he was sitting next to me.

"I had the first line, and so once he said action I read it. Then he read his line, and I mine, and so on. Things were going okay, I was pleased with how I was performing, so much so that when the script called for him to put his hand on my leg, and he did, I didn't think anything of it. We continued exchanging lines, until the script called for his hand, which had been on my leg for a little while now, to start crawling up my leg. In the story Lolita is wearing a skirt, but I was wearing jeans, so the scene couldn't quite play out between us as it had in the script. Not that it should have gotten anything like that far; but he did indeed proceed to move his hand up my leg, from my knee up my thigh and uncomfortably close to my crotch. I shifted in my seat, trying to dislodge his grip, but he held firm. I began to worry a great deal, but persevered; he was just being thorough, I told myself, and anyway he was only acting, as was I. We were both just doing what the script said, like good little actors. I tried hard to rationalise it, when it was so irrational it was beyond even thinking about really.

"The scene soon devolved into one of Humbert raping Dolly; I kept reading my lines as the event approached; I kept expecting him to say 'that's enough' or 'that'll do' or 'cut' or something, but he just kept reading. And as I was being auditioned, I didn't want to be the one to stop, to put my chances of success at risk. I don't know if I was being too slow for him, or if this is how he always did it, or what, but he soon threw his script down in frustration, and turned and addressed me directly.

" 'Take off your clothes please, Miss Paris.' He said it just like that, just like it was the most normal thing in the world to say. As if he'd asked me to pass him a pen or something. 'Take off your clothes', as if we were in a dressing room before a show or something. I laughed uncomfortably, but when I looked at him I could see he was serious. My laugh didn't last long.

" 'Take off your clothes woman, and don't make me tell you again.' He said this with such authority that before I even knew what I was doing I started unbuttoning my blouse. I'd undone two or three buttons before I came to my senses and realised where I was and what I was doing, but it was too late. I stopped, and he obviously noticed me doing so and so grabbed my blouse and ripped it open. Buttons flew off in every direction, and I remember briefly being sad, because I really liked that blouse and now he'd ruined it.

"I wasn't wearing a bra, a fact which I'd completely forgotten until I saw the salacious look on his face. And he licked his lips; I was I wish kidding, *he literally licked his lips when he saw my boobs*. I tried to pull my blouse closed, to cover myself, but he was too quick; he pulled it off my

240

arms and left me there topless, using my hands to cover myself. He reached out for me, it was almost cartoonish, like he was zombie or something, all hands and mouth. I tried to push him away but he was too strong, I barely even moved him.

"I stood up, wanting to grab my jacket and run away, but the second I was on my feet he had me. He grabbed me by the shoulders and spun me around so I had my back to him; he reached around and started fumbling with the button to my jeans. I tried to stop him, tried to hold the button closed, but he was too strong, and he soon had my jeans undone, and then he yanked them down so they were at my knees. He pushed me by the shoulders so I was bent over the empty desk. I tried my hardest not to let him, I tried to stand up, to move to either side, I even tried to kick out at him, but the jeans had rendered me immobile, and so all I could do was stand there as he held me down. He didn't even take my pants off, just pulled them to the side as he clumsily shoved himself inside me.

"I don't know how long it went on for; the second I felt him inside me, I left my body. I felt myself float out of myself, and I was suddenly on the ceiling, looking down at him raping me. I wanted to stop him, I wanted to scream, to kick and punch and fight, I wanted to do anything, but I was powerless. All I could do was watch and pray it would be quick. Whether it was or not I have no idea, but it felt like it lasted a thousand years.

"Eventually I felt him come. I don't know what's worse, that I could feel it inside me, or that I could feel him reaching climax, his hands on my hips gripping me so hard it hurt, his thrusts become so fast it began to burn. I tried to stay as still as possible, almost as if I could disappear, and eventually he pulled out of me, and pulled up and buckled his trousers with a satisfied smile. I couldn't move; I was still bent over his desk, my breasts on his discarded copy of the script. I could see the world *Lolita* screaming at me from the title page and it felt like a taunt, like it was saying to me 'I was your first clue, I tried to warn you to get out, but you didn't listen, so this is your fault.'

"Because that's how I initially felt: guilty. I can't explain it, but as I stood there, hands covering my nipples, his come dripping down my leg, I felt like *I'd* done something wrong. Particularly when he sat at his desk and looked at me with an odd look and said 'what are you doing? Cover yourself up woman.' He actually called me woman, as if that's all I was to him, just some woman. Not a woman he'd invited for a screen test, not a world-famous model. Not even just a human, another person deserving of the bare minimum of his respect. No, the way he said 'woman' I could tell he didn't consider me to be human, at least not to his level.

"And then, somehow, things got worse. I pulled my jeans up, found my blouse under his desk and put it back on. It still had just enough buttons that I could cover myself, and I did. Once I was dressed I didn't know what to do. I wanted to leave, but my legs wouldn't work. I wanted to sit down, not in the office but anywhere else in the world. I wanted to die. And then it got worse. He looked at me and said, 'that was great, thanks for coming, we'll be in touch'. *And that was it.* He pulled some papers from a bag I hadn't previously noticed and began to read. He was done with me, literally. He'd raped me, and now he was dismissing me. I think what makes it so much worse is how casually he did it; he'd just violated me, in a way that I already knew had changed me, and to him it was nothing. That was the worst thing that has ever happened to me, and the worst day of my life, and to him it was just another day at the office."

Twenty-Seven

When Emma finished speaking, the three of us sat in silence. Emma looked exhausted; she'd clearly said all she had in her to say, and looked relieved to have done so. I'm so proud of her for sharing her story, and I want to tell her, but I can't find my voice. I fear it's buried under an ocean of tears, and if I open my mouth to try and speak all that'll happen is my voice will crack, and then I'll burst into fresh tears. Because I am crying now; it isn't just the tears falling from my eyes, but all the rest too. I am devastated.

Mum is quiet too. From the look on her face I think she wants to say something, to say anything, but she doesn't seem to be able to either. She's been sharing the box of tissues with Emma; she hasn't been destroying them, but using them for their actual function. Both women have a pile of tissues at their feet, and I feel left out not having one myself. I've been letting my tears fall where they may, and I look down at my jeans and see they're wet through. Now that I've noticed they're wet I can feel it, and it suddenly is making me very uncomfortable. I jump to my feet, like a sleeping soldier called to attention, afraid of being reprimanded. Emma and mum both look at me, surprised by my sudden movement. They both look expectant, as if I'm going to do something, as if I have a plan. They have no idea I was just uncomfortable. Or perhaps they do; these women have known me all my life, and probably know me better than anyone. Not that they know everything about me, not by any means; neither of them know the extent to which I struggle, with drink, alcohol, and just life in general, but that's because I've kept it to myself. As far as they know, I'm still the same person I was when I was a child, aren't I? I'm just the grown-up version of him? So my family knows me, and so perhaps knows I'm just moving for the sake of moving, because it's something I've been doing most of my life.

Their expectant faces are looking to me with some hope now, that I might control the situation. I don't know what to do, so I do what any self-respecting British person does when they're with company and there's a lull, or a moment of awkwardness:

"Does anyone want a cup of tea?"

Noah moves into the kitchen and fills the kettle up before turning it on. He reaches into the cupboard and produces three mugs, popping a teabag in each. Once the water has come to the boil he fills each mug, and then waits whilst the teabags do their thing. Once he's happy he removes the bags, adds a splash of milk to all three mugs, a spoonful of sugar to his and Emma's, and picking up all three moves back into the living room.

He moves robotically, looking like a human but

barely acting like one. He doesn't know how to act, how he should be; there's nothing in any of his programming, either the information hard coded into him at birth, or the information he's picked up as he's grown and lived and experienced the world. There's no advised way to respond in this situation. So Noah just does his best.

As he enters the living room he sees his mother has moved from her chair to sit beside Emma on the couch, and he's very glad for it. His mum has her arms around Emma, who looks deflated; or does she look like a woman who has surrendered, who even though she's an adult has found comfort in the arms of her mother? Noah watches them for a moment, enjoying their closeness, hating what it's taken to bring it out. Emma sees him first, then his mum, and their looking at him breaks the spell, and he enters the room proper and puts the three mugs on the coffee table. He slides the mug without sugar to his mother, one of the ones with to Emma, and keeps one for himself. He sits in the chair his mum had been in, the one closest to the couch. Technically the couch is a three-seater, but Noah knows that whoever decided this has never seen three people all together. It fits two comfortably, and that's the way it's used. Noah doesn't mind; as much as he's empathising with Emma, and is devastated and angry and horrified at what that piece of shit producer did to her, he knows that rape is a different thing to men than it is to women. To men it's something abhorrent, but something abstract. Men do get raped, of course, but the number who do is small. It's terrible, but it's in no way comparable to what rape is like for women. Every woman fears being raped, Noah knows this. Women live their lives in ways that discourage rape; where men exist and hope it won't happen, and have the odds in their favour, women must live every second as if they're about to be raped. Imagine coming to a park late at night and not being able to walk through it. Absolutely absurd. The world is an absurd place to be if you're a woman, and not for the first time Noah is glad that he isn't.

Emma and Noah's mum both pick their mugs up, so all three are now holding their cups of tea, cradling them. Silence descends again, but it's the silence of a room of tea drinkers now, rather than the silence of people hearing a story about rape. It's much less uncomfortable, though the silence is still fairly palpable, and the air in the room hangs like a weight above their heads.

Noah is the first to finish, and as he places his mug back on the coffee table he looks at Emma, meeting her eyes with his, and begins the next steps of what will now be a shared experience with a question.

"Emma, I know this is hard, but can you tell me who he was? Who did this to you?" He pauses, before continuing. "Can you give me a name?"

"I can," Emma replies, "but it wouldn't do any good. He's too big, he's too powerful."

"That's fine," Noah says, "one thing at a time. All we need now is a name. We don't have to do anything else, we don't have to worry about what comes next. And besides," he continues, "look at what happened to Harvey Weinstein. Things are different now, Emma, things are changing. We're still thousands of years behind where we want to be, yes, but at least there's some accountability. Tell me his name, please, and we can go from there."

Emma says a name that even their mother, who would herself admit to not knowing the first thing about films, especially American ones, gasps in shock. Neither Noah nor his mother can believe what they've heard. Not him? Surely not him?

"Okay, okay, not who I expected but okay." Noah is

floundering, the name has clearly knocked him off kilter and he's trying to regain his composure. "How old is he, late 40s, early 50s?"

Emma shrugs.

"It doesn't matter; what I'm getting at is whether he's done this before. I mean, logic tells me he has; men who do this to one woman usually do it to many. And if they're going to, at his age they've been doing it for a while. With his power too, they're not going to let that go to waste. Do you know if he's done this before?"

Emma shakes her head as fresh tears pour from her eyes. Her mother reaches for her hands and they hold each other, both now looking at Noah like he's their saviour. Or perhaps they both want him to shut up, stop talking, to stop trying to be their saviour. Perhaps he can save Emma. Perhaps she doesn't even need saving.

"Okay, no problem. It'd be easier if we knew he had, but it's probably safe to assume. It'd be better if we could contact other survivors, and all go public at the same time. That'd give us more credibility. But still, hopefully us coming forward will encourage others, if there have been."

Emma looks shocked. Come forward? Tell the press what happened?

"Noah," she whispers, her voice fading. "I don't want to tell anyone. I didn't even want to tell you two," she looks at Noah and her mum "but I couldn't think of a story to explain why I'd flown 5,000 miles seemingly at random, and so just told the truth."

"Emma please-" Noah begins, but Emma cuts him off.

"No, Noah, no. I'm sorry, I know you're just trying to help, but I can't do it. I'm too famous, it'll be everywhere. I won't be able to move without being reminded of the worst thing that's ever happened to me.

I don't think I can live with that."

Noah looks exasperated. He understands what his sister is saying and supports her. Unfortunately, as much as he wants to support her 100%, he's unable to right now.

"But Emma-" he begins. Emma tries to interrupt him but he ploughs on regardless. He has something to say, and he's going to say it. If Emma still doesn't want to come forward, then that's fine, ultimately it's her decision. Noah just wants to make sure she considers every factor before making her decision.

"Please, Emma, just listen to me. Let me say what I want to say, and then I'll shut up." Emma gestures for him to continue talking. "I am so sorry for what's happened to you, truly I am. If I had the money, I'd book a flight right now and go and kill the piece of shit." This makes Emma smile, and Noah is heartened to see her doing so.

"I love you big sister, I love you more than life itself. I'm sorry to have to say this though, but this isn't all about you. This is about more than just you, this is about all women, but particular future women who may come across his path.

"Imagine you're 18, just moved to Hollywood, looking to make it big. Imagine you walk into his office, wide eyed and bushy tailed, and before you know it he has you bending over the desk and is raping you."

Emma is flinching, and as much as Noah hates to cause her to do so, he continues speaking. He has to say his piece.

"Now if you're that girl, wouldn't you be incredibly upset if you found out that people knew what he was capable of, hell knew what he had done, and yet let you walk in there anyway?"

Emma sobs again, unable to answer. Noah hates how

direct he's had to be, the language he's had to use, but he needed to make his point without any room for interpretation. Satisfied that he's done so, he sits back and leaves the ball in Emma's court. It's a long time before she's able to speak, but when she does, the three of them end up talking long into the night. It's nearly 2am before Noah drags his tired body to bed, but he doesn't mind; he knows that if he'd gone to bed at a normal time he wouldn't have slept anyway, so tiring himself out this much may be a good thing.

His phone has been in the kitchen this entire time, and he grabbed it before heading upstairs. Sitting down on the bed that used to be his but now functions as a spare, he presses the button on the side and the screen lights up. He's surprised to see he has seven missed calls and four messages, all from Lucy. He thought she still hated him, so why would she try to contact him? As he reads the messages it becomes clear why: she's drunk. Just as he's about to put the phone down, it lights up with a call coming in from Lucy. He hesitates, unsure if he has the energy to answer it, before deciding he does. In spite of all that's happened to Emma, Lucy and Max are still on his mind. He doesn't want to choose between them, doesn't want to lose either of them. If he has to, so be it, but he'll be devastated. That he's speaking to Lucy first is purely because she's tried to contact him; if this were Max ringing, it'd be Max he was speaking to first.

"Hey," he says when he answers, saying it tentatively, no idea what to expect from Lucy. He gets an answer he wasn't prepared for.

"Hi Noah," she slurs, clearly well beyond tipsy and completely at home in drunk. "I fucking hate you."

Eet, by Russian-American singer songwriter Regina Spektor, is from the album Far, *released in 2009. The lyrics tell a particularly poignant tale of loss; Spektor's voice haunts with its beauty, and she tells a tale of woe so real it nearly surpasses any actual feelings a person may have. "It's like forgetting the words to your favourite song…"*

Noah ends up talking to Lucy long into the night; it turns out she's outside his building and wants to thrash the whole thing out. He tells her he's at his mum's, his sister is there too, but he doesn't say why. It's not his information to share. Lucy, in her drunken state, doesn't believe him; she accuses him of cowardice, of hiding from her, of hiding from the consequences of his actions. He protests over and over that he's telling the truth, even going so far as to take a picture of the dark street out of his bedroom window. He sends it to her whilst they're still on the phone, and Lucy becomes silent as she studies it. Reluctantly, she decides he's telling the truth, and that she'd better go back to her Airbnb before she starts upsetting Noah's neighbours.

Noah wants her to get a taxi, but as she's drunk Lucy is feeling pig headed, so despite his protestations to the contrary, she insists on walking. It's only an hours walk, Lucy says, and nothing Noah can say can talk her out of it. But it turns out to not be so bad; unlike Emma, Lucy is lucky and manages to avoid the perverts of this world, fly under their radar, and makes it safely back to her temporary home unmolested.

The pair have been talking all the time; well, it's mostly been Lucy talking and Noah listening, but he doesn't mind. He's just happy she's talking to him, even if it is a stream of consciousness mixed up with frequent insults and admonishments. She cries a lot too, which surprises Noah, because he never had her pegged as a particularly lachrymose person, but he supposes when you hurt a person as much as he has, whatever tendencies that person used to have when you knew them might switch, they might over time morph into something they didn't used to be. And you have to carry the guilt for that change, be it for better or for worse.

As tired as Noah is, he's happy to stay awake and stay talking to Lucy. He doubts she'll remember much of the conversation when she wakes up, but that's okay; they're not exactly thrashing out the Paris Peace Accord or trying to get her to memorise an Oscar acceptance speech or something; this is a conversation between two former lovers, one incredibly drunk, in the early hours of the morning. Perhaps it's better left forgotten.

Noah has apologised myriad times, but he knows these aren't enough. He knows he needs to apologise in person, when Lucy is sober. That's the beginning of trying to make things right. If he wants to be with Lucy, he also needs to end things with Max. If Max hasn't already done that. He knows he can't be faithful to Lucy if he has a boyfriend on the side; he can never truly be honest with her, or with him, and most likely they'll all end up getting hurt again. But that's another part of the conversation that's for another day. Right now, Noah is just happy to have Lucy's attention.

When the conversation finally ends, Noah is surprised to hear movement in the house; he's shocked when he glances at the clock to see it's 6am. Between Emma and Lucy, the whole night has been talked away. He's tired, deathly tired, but he leaves the safety of his bedroom regardless to investigate the movement in the house. He isn't surprised when he finds Emma sitting on the back step, wearing only a dressing gown and slippers, half smoked cigarette in one hand and steaming mug of tea in the other. This is one of those rare problems that can't be solved by nicotine and tea; however, they also can't make the situation worse. Noah plucks the cigarette from between his sister's fingers and takes a drag, before passing it back to her and sitting beside her. Emma doesn't say anything, so neither does Noah. He's quite happy to let her take the lead. Plus he doesn't know what to say anyway, so he's quite happy to be spared trying to find words. What do you say to a person, your sister, when the last conversation you had was her describing her rape? Noah is in unprecedented territory; territory he hoped he'd never be in, but territory he's in nonetheless, and needs to find a way to navigate.

The silence isn't uncomfortable, and Noah smiles when Emma stubs out her cigarette, and lays her head on his shoulder. They sit like this, brother and sister, for as long as they need to. Neither of them have anywhere to be, so they choose to be with each other. For a little while, until normality returns, it's enough.

Holly Humberstone, like Regina Spektor, is a singer-songwriter who is probably best described as haunting and beautiful. To be moved by someone so young, who feels such emotions, is something else altogether. Her song titled The Walls Are Way Too Thin *is a beautiful piece of music about trying to wrestle the one you love out of the arms of someone else. She's new on the scene, but is going to make a huge splash. Remember the name.*

The house becomes a tomb; Noah almost begins to miss the mausoleum it used to be. Noah, Emma, and their mother float around like ghosts, three souls occupying the same space, but not knowing what to do either with it, or each other. Noah tries to look after his sister without babying her. He rings his work and tells them he needs to take some time off, family emergency, and though his boss doesn't believe him, and insists he comes in, Noah stands his ground, and his boss eventually backs down. He says he needs at least a week, maybe more. She gives him two, and says to let her know towards the end of the fortnight whether he'll be returning, or if he'll need more time off. He thanks her, and that's that.

Emma spends her days sleeping, lying in the bath, or sitting on the couch staring listlessly at the TV, her phone, her iPad, whichever device she decides to give her attention to. She eats very little, and the weight loss is obvious on her. She was already model-thin to begin with, so didn't have much room to work with. Her hips, always pushing at the surface of her skin, become like awkward corners in the middle of her body. Her arms and legs become dangerously thin, and whenever she moves it looks like it's costing her much, much more than just physical effort. Noah masturbates every night. That his sister is even skinnier turns him on for reasons he doesn't think 100 trained professionals would be able to explain. Noah tries to tell himself it isn't Emma he's thinking of when he masturbates; she's his sister, for god's sake, that would be disgusting. He isn't even masturbating over her femininity, all of her female attributes, with the fact she's his sister disconnected. No, he thinks he's masturbating over her helplessness. And he hates himself for it. And he can't stop.

Christmas in the Paris house is a quiet affair. It's just the three of them, and though they decorate the house, put up the tree together one Sunday afternoon, a fire roaring in the fireplace, *Home Alone* playing in the background, it's just not the same. It's like they're a facsimile of a real family, like they're playing pretend. In fact, it's like they're a group of children in a play, who have been assigned the roles of a family. They're not sure why they're there, what's going on, or what they're supposed to be feeling; they're acting in the ways they think they should be, in the ways they imagine the others expect them to. There's no celebration; the lights are on, but there are no souls home. There are three people, but three people who all have come to the conclusion, separately, that what little good there is in the world, what little hope and optimism they had for the future, has been snuffed out. None of them want to feel this way; particularly Emma, who worries that the more she lets this ruin her life, the more he wins. She knows it isn't a case of win or lose, not really, but that's how it feels to her. Life feels less like a life since she was raped, and more like a game.

Noah has spoken to his boss again and they've agreed he can take Christmas and the New Year, but he must be back in the office on January second, or they'll have to have a conversation about his future at the company. *Great*, Noah thinks, *just what I need. My sister has been raped, but we can't let that get in the way of profits.* It's terrible, we're so sorry, blah blah blah generic platitudes, please open Excel and put enough numbers into enough cells until we profit from it somehow. Noah is furious but doesn't have the heart to argue. What little emotional stamina he has, he's trying to save for his sister.

Noah and Lucy speak every couple of days; after their initial phone call, he called her the next afternoon, and they hashed things out. They're still not on the best of terms, but they're far from the worst; plus, Noah has explained where he is, what's happened, and Lucy has been very understanding. She wants to see him, she tells him, and she misses him, but she understands he has other things going on. She isn't going anywhere; her company have recently got a new account, which means Lucy will be in Leeds for at least the next six months, with the possibility of it being extended. He tells her he's supposed to be back just after new year, and she says that sounds nice, and she's looking forward to seeing him.

He doesn't hear from Max, with the exception of one

message. Noah's just going to bed one evening, not expecting to sleep, but figuring if he gets ready, turns off the lights, and lies down, when he's inevitably tired in the morning, at least it won't be his actions that are to blame. His phone *pings*, and he almost doesn't check it. He's spoken to Lucy recently, so guesses it won't be her messaging. And other than her, and his sister and mother, there isn't anyone he's really interested in speaking to. He's long since given up on Max; Noah messaged him not long after arriving home, saying he was staying with his mum for a bit, and could they catch up when he was back around. He got no response. He sent another message a few days later, asking Max if he'd received the previous message. Again, no answer. So Noah gave up. As much as he still likes Max, and misses him, you can't have a relationship with someone who doesn't want one. And besides, after all that's happened with Emma, he doesn't have the time, effort, or even the inclination for any drama. The recent drama has been too fucking real, he's happy for that to be not just the beginning but the end too.

He decides on a whim to check his phone and is pleased and surprised when he does. Max has finally replied. Although if you can call it a reply Noah doesn't know; Max hasn't addressed the two messages Noah sent, makes no reference to them; nor does he make any reference to the relationship they had, what Noah did to end it, any of that. The message is political, but Noah is grateful for it, nonetheless. It's just a short message saying, *I heard what happened and I'm so sorry. If there's anything I can do let me know x.*

The kiss at the end fills Noah with joy; he wonders how Max found out, but then assumes Lucy told him; she told Noah, on their afternoon reconciliation phone call, that she'd drunkenly tracked Max down and sent him a bunch of abusive messages. She said Max took it remarkably well, didn't throw anything back in her face, and strangely, Lucy and Max have become friends of a sort. The idea both delights and terrifies Noah in equal measure. Noah doesn't focus on how Max knows about Emma; instead he focuses on the 'x', the simple little kiss that probably took very little for Max to type, but means so much to Noah. In that kiss is possibility, is hope. In that kiss is the notion that perhaps not all is lost, and Noah shouldn't give up hope just yet.

Noah presses reply and types out *thank you*. He's about to hit send when he hesitates; he doesn't want to waste this opportunity. This horrible scenario has brought about some hope in the form of a partial reconciliation with Lucy, perhaps it can do the same with Max. And if not, Noah had already written him off, so he has nothing to lose. He adds to the end of the message *I miss you* and presses send. Noah immediately puts his phone down and tries to sleep, patently ignoring his phone. He needn't; Max doesn't reply.

Twenty-Eight

It's that strange week between Christmas and New Year's, when time loses all meaning, the days bleed into one, and life becomes a blur of food, drink, and television, some of it festive, most of it not. Noah and Emma are watching TV one evening, their mother long since gone to bed, and Noah is about to get up and go to bed as well when Emma moves down the couch and leans against him. She lifts his arm and drapes it across her chest, and Noah can't help but feel her breasts under his forearm. He starts to get an erection and crosses his legs, trying to temper it, to hide it. He worries that if she notices it, he'll ruin their entire relationship. Not to mention the idea of an unwanted erection around a woman who has recently been raped; he dreads to think how it would affect her on that level.

They sit for a while, the celebratory TV programme ending and being replaced by some crappy film neither of them care enough about to watch, but don't hate enough to turn off. They sit in silence, but for the first time in a long time it's comfortable. When Emma reaches for his hand Noah lets her take it, and when she squeezes it he squeezes back. He kisses the top of her head, and she makes a noise of delight and snuggles into him. Noah is just starting to nod off, such is his sense of calm, but Emma's words shock him back awake. Did he hear her right? He must have done. But she can't be serious, she can't have meant it? He says nothing, not sure how to respond, and when she asks him again he knows it was real, and he didn't imagine the question. He still doesn't know how to answer, but it's okay, because they'll talk in the morning, and figure it out. He'll find a way to say no, that he can't possibly afford to do so, let alone any of the other complications, finances aside.

The question Emma has asked him is "Noah, will you come back to New York with me?"

Whitney Houston was a powerhouse of popular music in the 1980s and 90s. Her untimely death was a tragedy that robbed the world of someone who possessed extreme and incredibly enviable talent. One thing that has always raised a question, however, is this: in one song Whitney states that loving yourself is the greatest love of all, and yet in another she states there must be a higher love, something from above. Which is it, Whitney? Which?

Noah can't go to New York, and it breaks his heart. He wants to go, because he never wants to leave his sister's side again, but there are too many practical considerations. Firstly, he can't afford it. It isn't just the flight, but accommodation too, living expenses, all of that stuff. No matter how much Emma says he can of course stay with her for free, and she'll take care of him, he can't bring himself to do it. Something he doesn't too often feel - pride - wells up inside him and, as tempting as the offer is, he can't accept.

He also has Sylvia to think about; he's already neglecting her just being here at his mother's house, leaving her in the flat with his flatmate; he can hardly just flit off to New York, abandoning her in totality. Besides, it isn't just that he has a responsibility to her, it's also that he loves her, and doesn't want to leave her. He loves his sister more so, but a greater love doesn't necessarily always triumph.

He has his job too, and his flat. He's contracted until the summer, so at least another six months; as much as he hates landlords and wouldn't mind fucking his over, he also believes in honouring a deal you've made; like it or not he signed a contract, and so he believes he owes the money. Come the summer when the contract expires, who knows, but until then he's on the hook for the flat. Plus he doesn't want to leave his flatmate in the lurch, that wouldn't be fair. Yes, you have to do what's best for you, but you can't sacrifice others in the process. You can affect people negatively with your actions to a point; abandoning his flatmate to pay the rent alone is beyond that point. And therefore, unfortunately, unattainable.

There are also little things like his phone; he's tied into a contract on that too, and if he moves to New York he'll have to pay it, though his phone won't even work. He recently did a big-ish food shop and doesn't want to see that go to waste. The fresh stuff will already need to be chucked out as a result of his impromptu stay at his mother's, but the rest of the food, the non-perishable stuff, will need dealing with. He doesn't often have money to splash out on food like this, but his mother gave him some of his Christmas money early; he'd spent it on food in the hopes of following through his original plan, which was to have Lucy and Max over, if they'd come. He wanted all three to spend some time together, in the hopes of forcing a reconciliation. He was even going to cook; he'd never had a Christmas away from his mum and was going to make it a big deal. Because it was going to be a big deal. As such, he didn't even get to send the invites; life happened, and he spent another Christmas with his mother, and a long overdue one with Emma.

It's funny, Noah thinks to himself; when it comes to the big decisions, like moving to New York, he doesn't question it. However, when he has to make a series of small decisions, like what to do with his cat, his flat, his job, suddenly the water becomes murky, and he's no longer so sure. He wonders if he's unique in this sense, that the big questions are answered easily without a second thought, but it's the small ones that hold you back. He thinks he probably isn't; there are enough people on this planet that surely no trait is unique? Even the incredibly rare ones must, by the law of averages, affect at least two people? He doesn't know what his basis for this thought is, but he finds it reassuring, so sticks to it. It's good to not be alone sometimes.

Emma is distraught when he says no, and she doesn't speak to him until New Year's Eve. It makes the atmosphere in the house incredibly toxic, and Noah hates this; he hates it for his mother, he hates it for his sister who, despite being the cause of the toxicity, is still a victim of it. He hates it for himself; he feels like shit all the time, even more so than usual, and a negative atmosphere in the home isn't going to help anything. Thankfully, Emma's mood soon passes. Noah can't be sure, but he thinks his mother might have something to do with this; a couple of times he's caught the two most important women in his life in hushed conversations which stop immediately as they notice his presence. Noah is paranoid at the best of times, but in these moments his anxiety threatens to overwhelm him. Eventually Emma thaws; she finds Noah trying to read in the study and tells him it's okay, she forgives him, she'll be okay. He starts to speak, he wants to explain himself, to justify himself, but Emma stops him. She comes and climbs into the armchair in which Noah sits; she doesn't really fit, has to wedge herself half next to him and half on top of him, but she seems to be comfortable, and though Noah isn't, he doesn't say anything to let on to this fact. He puts his bookmark in his book, places the book down on the small coffee table to the side of the chair, and extricating his arms from underneath Emma he wraps them around her, pulling her into the biggest, warmest, safest hug he can manage. He feels Emma relax into him and enjoys her warmth, her smell, and her surrender. It makes him feel useful and needed, two things he doesn't feel often.

How long they sit like this Noah doesn't know; it's only when he feels Emma shift slightly that he realises he's been going to sleep. *This must be a good thing*, he thinks to himself, *I must be nice and relaxed for this to happen*. He doesn't *feel* relaxed, but the evidence states that he is, so he tries to be. A few more minutes pass, but Emma is growing restless, and soon she lifts her head from off his shoulder and shifts her position until she's sitting on his lap, facing him. He's uncomfortable, because the pose is much more of that of lovers than siblings, particularly adult siblings, but his confused feelings for his sister quickly arise again, and his penis starts to once it realises what's going on. He needs to move, now, needs to extricate himself from the situation, but for the first time in a long time Emma looks happy, at least contented, and he doesn't want to end this. So he relinquishes control; he looks at Emma and smiles, and she smiles back at him. Before he knows what's happening she leans forward and plants a soft kiss on his lips. It's clearly only an affectionate kiss between siblings, but Noah forgets where he is and kisses her a second time, with more force, less like a sibling and more like a hopeful lover. He does it before he even realises, and even as their lips are still touching he braces himself for her to pull away, for her to freak out, rightly so, and jump up and leave. But she doesn't; at first she doesn't react at all, but then Noah feels her kiss back. They both have their lips pushed tightly together, tongues firmly still in their respective mouths, and yet the siblings do kiss, a little, awkwardly, like a pair of teenagers sharing their first ever kiss.

Without realising what he's doing, Noah moves his right hand and places it on his sister's left breast. She emits a soft moan when he does, and this is enough to break the spell. It's as if they both break from a trance; Noah pulls his hand from his sister's breast with such speed that he nearly shatters his elbow in a collision with the wall behind him. Emma jumps up and climbs off him, moving faster than he's ever seen her move. Once she's off him she stands up and so does he, and now they're facing each other on their feet. They make eye contact briefly, but both flick their eyes to the floor, embarrassed, confused, a little excited. Neither of them knows what to say, so they stand there, not speaking, not moving, just looking at each other. They may perhaps stay this way forever if their mother hadn't knocked and then let herself in; her knock startles both of her children, and when she enters the room they both look awkward and uncomfortable, but even as she tries to work out why the atmosphere passes, and soon it's just the remaining three members of the family in the study, and everything is okay. Well, it's as okay as it can be, given the circumstances.

No one says anything until Emma opens her mouth,

and says words even she wasn't expecting:
"I have to go back to New York tomorrow."

The soundtrack to the film Drive *is dripping in excellency. Be it Kavinsky, Desire, Electric Youth, or just the instrumentals and atmospheric music by Cliff Martinez, each song is perfect for the scenes it's set to. In what is already an incredibly atmospheric, not to mention brilliant film, the soundtrack adds yet more weight to proceedings. As Desire sing,* you keep me under your spell…

Emma doesn't go home the next day. In the confusion about what the fuck just happened to them, and between them, both Emma and Noah have forgotten that the next day is New Year's Day, and travelling will not only be expensive, but a logistical nightmare.

New Year's Eve is an even quieter affair than Christmas. None one says anything, but it's understood the three of them will stay at home, and ring in the new year together. It ends up just being Noah and Emma; their mother tries, but hearing what happened to her only daughter has aged her 20 years in a matter of weeks, and so she drags her exhausted body up to bed at 10.30pm.

Noah and Emma sit at opposite ends of the couch, Emma drinking wine, Noah beer, both staring at the TV, both staring through it. They talk half-heartedly, but neither one is fully present. They're staying up to midnight out of duty to the holiday; unless Emma does something to show she wants him to stay up with her, Noah plans to go to bed at 12:01am. If Emma wasn't here, he'd be in bed already.

Midnight comes and goes, and the two siblings sit silently as the TV presenter counts down from 10, at 0 the entire country exploding with joy. Fireworks are set off, both on TV and in real life; Noah can hear them from all directions. He normally loves fireworks, but right now they seem pointless, a waste of time and effort and money. A lot of things seem like that at the moment.

Noah wishes his sister a happy new year's. He wants to kiss her, not just because it's new year's tradition to kiss someone, but also just because. He can't get their first kiss out of his mind, and he's dying for a second. Even though thinking about it disgusts him as much as it arouses him. But he doesn't do anything; they haven't talked about the kiss, it hasn't even been hinted at; Noah wonders if Emma is purposefully ignoring it, pretending it never happened, because she wishes it hadn't. He's glad it did, but won't do it again unless Emma starts it. The ball is in her court as far as he's concerned. He'll love Emma forever no matter what she chooses; because, how could he not?

Twenty-Nine

Emma clarifies to her mother and brother that she's going to fly back to New York on 2nd January, rather than the 1st. Noah and his mother are reluctant, and wish she'd stay longer, but Emma is adamant; she has to get back on the horse, she tells her family. As terrified as she is of going back, of getting back into *that* world, she has to. It's been lovely being back home and spending the holiday period with the two people she loves most in the world; however, she explains, being here is like being in a bubble. She feels safe, but only because she's in a safe place. She needs to put herself in situations that she can't guarantee are safe, though knows they most likely will be, in order to see if she's actually ready to face the world, or is just on the outside looking in.

Noah is sitting on the couch in the living room with a book in his hands, not reading it. He's watching his sister out of the corner of his eye as she books her flight; 2nd

January, 4.30pm, London Heathrow to New York JFK. Noah is distraught at the fact he's losing her, but he also knows he needs to let her go. The kiss they shared was too real, it was too close to Noah's real feelings, which he'd never thought Emma reciprocated even in the slightest. He still isn't sure she does, in fact thinks it's probably the opposite; she thinks of him as a brother, nothing more. Being here, it being Christmas, and with what happened to her just before, she's confused, unmoored, doesn't have too firm a grip on reality. Noah supposes she forgot herself, forgot where she is, forgot who he is. That they haven't discussed it, or come close to doing it again, tells Noah he's probably right in his suspicions.

Emma soon puts her laptop to one side, and when she sees her brother watching her she smiles at him and tells him it's all sorted. Noah can't help but notice it isn't a full smile, that there's something missing; he's trying to figure out what it could be when it hits him. The kiss has changed their relationship forever; where they were previously brother and sister, and no more, now something more has passed between them, and nothing can ever change that. Emma's smile doesn't reach all the way to her eyes like it used to, it's only 90% genuine affection and warmth, where it used to be 100%. He doesn't like this change, but knows he can live with it, because he has no choice but to do so. Plus, if it's the kiss that ends up getting Emma back on her feet, even if it's much sooner than either of them anticipated, then surely it's a good thing. Good things done for bad reasons are still good things right? Noah wishes it was that black and white.

Emma stands up, stretching as she does so. She leans forward on her toes and lifts her arms up to the ceiling; she's dressed in pyjamas, and as she raises her arms her top lifts, and Noah can see she isn't wearing a bra. He's seen her breasts before on adverts, in magazines and on billboards and online, but he's never seen them in the flesh. As her shirt rides up, he can't help but stare; her stomach is so flat, so soft looking, he's dying to run his hands over it. His eyes travel upwards, and he can just see them bottom of her breasts, the gentle curve they have, the gathering of flesh and muscle that somehow, to Noah, is perhaps the greatest thing to ever have existed on this planet. Just as quickly as they're exposed, Emma lowers her arms and they're gone again. She smiles at Noah one more time before picking up her laptop and leaving the room, going where, Noah has no idea. He gives it a minute before getting up himself; he's gotten yet another erection at the sight of his sister. At what point does it become a serious problem?

He makes his way upstairs, knowing he's going to masturbate to the memory of what he's just seen and hating himself for it. He locks the door behind him as he enters the spare room that was once his childhood bedroom, and is just unbuttoning his jeans to free his penis when his phone vibrates. He ignores it, wanting to climax before the mental images fade too much, but when it vibrates again he picks it up. The two vibrations were two messages; he's surprised to see Lucy has messaged him, and downright shocked that Max has too. All thoughts of his sister drop from his mind as he reads the messages, which, whether by coincidence or design, are identical. It's probably just coincidence as they're both short messages, and they come in the form of a question:

"When will you be back home?"

When will you be back home?
I'm not sure. Emma flies back tomorrow, so depending on how

my mum is it'll probably be quite soon. Why do you ask?

Because I want to see you, obviously.

I want to see you too. Are you doing anything this weekend, Saturday afternoon?

I don't think I have any plans.

Can we meet then?

Yes, absolutely. Although not at your flat, somewhere else.

How come?

Somewhere neutral. We need to have a proper talk before anything else happens.

That's fair. Shall we say Cross Keys, 4pm?

Perfect, see you then x

xxx

When will you be back home?

I'm not sure. Emma flies back tomorrow, so depending on how my mum is it'll probably be quite soon. Why do you ask?

I'm so bored. I've been at the B&B for a couple of weeks now, helping out over the Christmas and that, but now it's January again everyone has gone home, and so I'm going to go home too. It'd be nice to see you. We have a lot to talk about.

We do. Are you available this Saturday?

I am. I wasn't sure when I'd be coming home so the next few weeks are clear in my diary.

Sounds good to me. Let's definitely meet on Saturday then.

I can't wait. I'm still mad at you btw. Lol

And I'm still sorry.

You can make it up to me…

I'd like that. Tell me how?

Come over now.

I can't do that, I'm sorry.

Please?

I'd love to, believe me I would, but Emma is still here, and I can't leave before her. She still needs me, at least until she's back on a train down to London.

Maybe…

Maybe what?

Maybe I could come to you?

I'm sorry. I'd love for you to be here, but it isn't a good time. Once Emma's gone we'll meet up. But we need to meet somewhere else first, we need to have a big old chat on neutral ground.

Sounds good. Where and when?

The Cross Keys, 4pm?

Perfect, I'll see you then x

xxx

Thirty

Noah returns to Leeds on the 3rd of January, and spends the next few days before Saturday wondering why he's choosing to meet them both in the same place at the same time. Especially when *that* is what has caused all of this. They're both mad at him because they didn't know about each other, but now both want to reconcile; Noah has decided to reconcile with them both at the same time. He doesn't know why with complete certainty, but he thinks he does know; Noah has a self-destructive streak, he's afraid of happiness and much more at home in misery. But he can't make himself miserable because that would be self-defeating. However, he can put himself in situations that will most likely end up as miserable, and he's good to go.

Things go even worse than he'd anticipated; Max arrives first, a little before 3.50pm. Noah has been there since

3.30pm and is nursing a pint, hoping it'll make things easier. If anything, it makes things much, much worse. Things are awkward at first with Max; they're both tentative, cautious, wanting to be with each other but aware of what's between them, they both know it's an obstacle that, ignored now, will have to be addressed at some point.

Eventually things thaw, and just as it looks like they might be able to get on, Lucy arrives. She sees Noah and Max before they see her; her mood changes from hopeful to furious in a second; she of course knows who Max is, is even kind of sort of friends with him, internet friends anyway. But she didn't expect to see him here. She thought this was her own private time with Noah, she had no idea Max would be there, has no idea why.

Noah sees her and smiles, but his smile quickly vanishes when he sees how angry she is. As she stalks over to the table Noah stands up, hands out in front of him in a gesture of innocence, of calm. He starts to speak, to say Lucy's name, to explain what's going on, but before he can do so Lucy has reached the table and she grabs his pint and pours it on his head.

The speed at which Lucy does this takes Noah by surprise; he's barely time to acknowledge that he's wet, before Max turns his own pint up and over Noah's head. Max had no idea Lucy would be coming, he also thought it would be just himself and Noah, and his mood quickly becomes one of incandescent rage too. He follows Lucy's lead in dumping his drink over Noah's head. He can't believe what Noah has done, that he'd bring them both here at the same time. The rapport that has been built between them in these last ten or so minutes vanishes in an instant. So too does the rapport that he and Lucy have built up over text the last few days. Noah knows he's well and truly fucked it.

Max and Lucy exit the pub, one stomping after the other, and Noah chases after them. When he gets outside he just has time to shout their names as he sees them getting into a taxi, *the same taxi*. A bolt of fear joins the bolt of pain in his heart, and he runs across the road, but before he reaches it the taxi pulls away from the curb and is gone. He can see the backs of his two former lovers' heads, but neither turns to look at him. Instead they're gone, leaving Noah standing in the middle of the road, cars honking at him as they swerve around him, some drivers being kind enough to roll down their windows and swear at him.

Well, Noah thinks to himself, *that's that then. I officially have no one*. Nothing certain has been said, nothing official, but Noah thinks he's probably finally single, once and for all.

The rest of the weekend just gets stranger and stranger. Noah goes home, stopping to buy a large bottle of vodka on the way, and proceeds to get incredibly drunk.

He's watching TV in the early evening when his front door buzzer sounds. He ignores it, but it goes a second, a third time, the loud ringing harsh in Noah's ears, giving him a headache the longer he has to endure it. He eventually drags himself off the couch, and not bothering to put his bottle of vodka down moves to the intercom, and says gruffly "hullo?"

He's shocked when his greeting is answered by his sister, the one he believed to be in New York. He can't think of anything to say and so he presses the button to open the building's front door, and then opens his flat's door, standing in the doorway, waiting for his sister. He realises he's still clutching the bottle of vodka, but rather than put it down, or try and hide it, he takes a swig from it. Soon Emma appears, a vision in front of him, and he

272

moves towards her to hug her but she dodges him, and deftly taking the bottle from him takes a swig as she enters his flat.

He wants to ask her what's going on but Emma simply says, "don't ask" and Noah, wanting to respect her wishes, doesn't. Instead they just sit side by side on the couch, and drink, Noah switching from vodka to a bottle of beer, Emma with a gin and lemonade in her glass, both bottles produced from her suitcase. Noah drains what's left of his beer and gets up to get another, asking Emma if she wants one. She says she does, but she'll come with him, she isn't sure what she wants to drink so she needs to investigate what her options are.

Noah trudges into the kitchen, the alcohol and tiredness catching up on him, causing his already low mood to sink even lower. Not even Emma's presence can bring him out of this funk. He opens the fridge and grabs another beer regardless, popping the cap off and taking a swig. As he lowers the bottle from his mouth Emma, giggling, takes it from his hand and has a drink herself. Standing up seems to have made her even drunker than she realised, and she finds the whole scenario ridiculous. She begins to giggle, but when Noah moves to ask her what she's giggling at she shushes him and takes another sip of beer. Noah, thirsty himself, takes the beer from her, fighting her playfully, and has a drink. When Emma reaches for it again he holds it away from her; she's older, but he's taller and stronger, and he holds her off easily with one hand.

Emma knows she won't win a fight against her brother directly, so she tries a different plan. She stops fighting, waits for Noah to lower his guard, and when he does she slaps him in the crotch. He doubles over immediately, the bottle falling from his hand. Emma is able to catch it before it drops to the floor, where it would either bounce or simply shatter, either way making a racket loud enough to wake the neighbours up. Even though they're both in their mid-20s, they regress to teenagers when they're together, especially when they're both drunk. They sneak around the flat as if they're back at their mother's house, trying not to wake their one remaining parent. Emma drinks the beer, victorious, whilst Noah crumples into a heap in the middle of the kitchen floor, holding his groin. He's moaning, and Emma knows she should feel bad, but instead she continues to giggle between sips of the beer. Eventually Noah sits up, and he gingerly asks for a sip of beer, not wanting to engage his sister in a fight again now he knows her tactics.

Smiling somewhat sinisterly, Emma hands Noah the bottle. The reason for her smile soon becomes apparent to Noah: the bottle is empty. Emma watches his face, and as he realises the bottle is empty she creases up with laughter; this time it's her holding herself and dropping to the floor, although she falls with great delight, rather than great pain. Noah is drunk, tired, thirsty, and his balls hurt. He's in no mood for Emma's antics. He waits for her to come to a rest on the floor, and then he makes his move. He takes her by surprise, pushing her from the sitting position she's in so she's lying on her back. Noah straddles her and they end up face to face, their noses only a few inches apart. Noah wants to kiss her, suddenly wants to stop fighting and do the exact opposite; he's drunk, but not so drunk he's going to make a move. Emma lays there, her intentions unclear. They stay like this for several seconds until Noah seems to come to his senses and climbs off his sister, stands up, moves away from Emma, stands leaning on the counter at the opposite side of the room. It takes Emma a little longer to get up; she stays laying down for a couple more minutes, before reluctantly pulling herself to her feet using one of the dining chairs. She stands leaning on a counter too, and the pair face each other, as if they're cowboys duelling at dawn. Neither wants to make the first move. Neither knows how to.

They might have stood here all night, but luckily the tension is broken by the sound of a toilet flushing in a neighbouring flat. They both glance up at the noise, and when they look back down they make eye contact, and both break into fresh fits of giggles. They laugh as quietly as they can until the spell passes; Noah snaps out of it first, and still smiling he moves across the kitchen and envelops his sister in a huge bear hug.

"I love you Emma, I love you so much."

"I love you too Noah," Emma replies, returning the hug. "I'm sorry."

"For what?" He releases her from the hug but grips her shoulders, holding her at arm's length so he can look into her face.

"For…for everything. For being here, now, for telling you my story, for the kiss the other day, for the fact I'm sure you've had to see me topless at some point. I'm sorry for it all, I'm sorry for being the worst sister ever."

Noah is shocked, he can't believe what he's hearing. The world is so patriarchal that he's standing with a rape victim, and she's apologising for having been raped. He feels a momentary murderous rage that someone would make his sister feel this way, but it's quickly replaced by an overwhelming and bottomless sadness. He wraps Emma in his arms again, and between kisses he plants on the top of her head he tells her it's okay, she has nothing to apologise for, she's done nothing wrong.

Emma is crying, and he hands her a tissue; she blows her nose and dabs at her eyes, doing the best she can whilst still in her brother's embrace. When Noah thinks she has herself under control, he releases her again, and asks if she is okay, if she wants to go to bed.

"I think that might be a good idea," Emma says with no sarcasm, smiling through her tears. "But would you stay with me tonight?"

Noah hadn't been expecting this and doesn't know what to say.

"It's just," Emma continues, "I don't want to be alone. I want to be with the man I love most in the world."

Noah is unsure, but he agrees. He loves Emma more than anyone, and if she needs him he's going to be there. They sleep in his room; Noah had planned to give it to her and to take the couch for himself, but he's much happier to be in a bed, especially his own.

Before climbing into bed they brush their teeth side by side in the bathroom, just like when they were kids. Noah stays in the bathroom and puts on his pyjamas, whilst Emma goes into the bedroom to change. After a couple of minutes she messages him it's okay to come in, and he leaves the bathroom, turning off the light behind him, and padding across the hall slowly opens his bedroom door.

Emma is already in bed, laying on her side looking at her phone. Noah slips into the other side and instinctively checks his own phone. Nothing to look at, no notifications, not being bothered with social media in this moment, Noah soon puts his phone down and lays on his side facing his sister. Her back is to him, and soon she puts her own phone down, turns off her lamp, and lays still without facing him.

"Good night, Emma. I love you."

"Noah?"

"Yes?"

"Would you…"

"Would I what?"

"Would you mind spooning me?"

Noah is hesitant, but it's just spooning right? Surely siblings do it all the time.

He scoots across the bed until his body is pressed against hers. He puts one arm under her neck, and he drapes the other across his sister's body. She makes a contented noise and snuggles into him; her behind is pressing against his crotch, and he wills himself more than he's ever willed himself before to not get an erection. He's actually doing a decent job until Emma takes his hand and guides it to her breast. Noah freezes, unsure what to do. The touch of his sister's nipple leaves him firmly erect, and there's surely no way Emma can't feel it. In fact, she presses into it, and moans softly. Noah doesn't move; he's terrified, he might finally be about to get everything he wants, everything he isn't allowed. His level of fear and excitement is so high he wants to cry, he doesn't know what to do with himself.

Emma clearly gets frustrated at his lack of involvement and takes matters into her own hands. She lifts his hand from her breast and puts it down the shorts she's wearing. Noah's heart is beating at approximately 10,000bpm as he feels his hand slide down his sister's body. He feels her pubic region, completely smooth, and then before he knows it his hand is on her vagina. It's already wet, and so warm, and she moans and continues to shift against him as he touches her. Noah, drunk, confused, recently dumped by two people of different sexes, gives in, and starts to gently massage his sister. Her moans increase, and as they do so, so does his participation. Soon she pushes away from him and lies on her back so she can spread her legs. Noah moves his hand from her clitoris and inserts one, then two fingers inside his sister's vagina. She moans properly now, her

277

body moving with his rhythm. His erection is throbbing so hard it hurts, and he takes his hand out of his sister and before he knows what he's doing he takes her clothes off.

He sees her breasts in the flesh for the first time, and he can't stop himself from touching them, from taking first one, then the other nipple in his mouth. He knows what he's doing is so wrong, he knows that his therapist, hell any psychologist in the world, would have a field day trying to decode a grown man imitating breast feeding with his older sister, and yet he doesn't care. He might end up having sex with his sister, and he's okay with that. She seems to be too.

In fact, things are quickly moving in that direction when Noah ruins everything. Emma pushes him onto his back and moves down his body until her head is level with his penis. She moves it out of his shorts and looks at it briefly, before taking it in her mouth. Noah nearly orgasms right then from pure ecstasy, but manages to hold it in. It feels amazing, that his sister is giving him a blow job. He thinks this is what his life has been heading towards, every decision he's ever made, every word he's said and movement he's made has led them here. This is why he was born, he's fulfilling his life's goal. He's moving closer and closer to orgasm when it happens; he's moaning, and he makes to say Emma's name, but what comes out of his mouth is, "oh my god, Lucy."

Emma looks up at him, his penis still in her mouth. She looks furious, and after a second she takes his dick out of her mouth, moves back into her previous position and lies still, clearly trying to sleep. Noah tries to spoon her again but she pushes him away this time. In the silent darkness of the room Noah can hear his sister snivelling, can imagine her tears. But what can he do? She doesn't want him to touch her, and there's nothing to say, surely? What can you say to a woman who you've just called the wrong name? What do you do when that woman, who has just given you three quarters of a blow job, is your sister?

What is any of this?

Noah's head is spinning, and he realises he's going to be sick. He runs for the bathroom and makes it just in time; luckily he left the toilet seat up, and so even though he starts vomiting from halfway across the bathroom it all ends up in the toilet. He wipes his mouth and sits on the floor cradling the toilet, his head hanging in the bowl. How long he sits there he doesn't know; he eventually decides he isn't going to vomit again, and as he stands up he realises he's maintained an erection this entire time. He takes off his shorts and masturbates, knowing that his erection won't go away, that he won't be able to sleep, until he does. Tears fall from his eyes as he strokes his cock, and when he ejaculates he doesn't bother with any tissue, he doesn't care enough.

When he's done he gets up, washes his hands, and leaves the bathroom. He once again pads across the hallway, but his bedroom door is now shut, and when he tries to open it, it doesn't move. Whilst he's been vomiting and masturbating, Emma has gotten up and locked him out. He tries the handle a couple more times and when he's sure it isn't going to open he sighs, gives up, goes into the living room and lays on the couch. Thinking he'll be awake for hours, Noah falls asleep almost immediately.

When he wakes up in the morning, Emma has gone; there's no note that he can see, she hasn't messaged or called him. He tries to call her and it goes straight to voicemail; her phone must be turned off. She can't be on a plane already, surely?

As he's reeling from this discovery, he gets a message from his mum, who drops an even bigger bombshell on him; she's decided it's time to sell the house, and to move into some place smaller. She doesn't say it, but she doesn't need to; Noah knows that his mother has finally accepted her husband's death and has realised she can no longer live with his ghost but needs to move on. Seemingly the trauma of Emma being raped has superseded the trauma of her husband dying. Noah's mother has potentially put the one to the side to deal with the other. Or maybe she just finally got the kick up the arse she needed to continue living her life.

Noah tells her he's delighted for her, ignoring the fact he actually doesn't know how he feels. He sends her virtual hugs, and he goes in the shower, because pretty soon he has to acknowledge the inevitable: he has to get back to real life. Then he needs to think about going back to work. He doesn't want to, but with Emma gone, and his mother selling the house, he needs to join in their behaviour, and carry on. He isn't ready, but then he never was the first time around, when he turned into an adult. It didn't stop time then, and it won't now.

When he gets out of the shower Sylvia is waiting for him, and Noah spends the rest of the day fawning over her. Because he's realised something, today, in the short space of time between waking up now; he's realised he's rootless. With his mum selling the house he grew up in, he no longer has a base. Even though he hasn't felt at home there for a single second since his dad died, it's at least been a source of consistency in his otherwise hectic life. That this little consistency is being taken from him almost makes him feel seasick. He used to think that home might be Emma; no matter where they were, home is where they're together. But she isn't answering his calls or replying to his texts; by the time he goes to bed 14 hours have passed since his first attempt at contact; she may not have replied to that, or the next few, because she was on her flight, but by now the flight will be long over, she'll definitely have her phone turned on. If she's not replying, it's because she's choosing not to.

Noah hates winter; in this winter alone he's lost Max, Lucy, Emma, and the home he grew up in. He's become relationship-less, friendless, even more alone than he's ever been. He has nothing, he has no one, he has nowhere to go. If not for Sylvia, Noah wouldn't even be sure he was alive. Her miaowing keeps him present, although he wishes he wasn't. Can't something good just happen, just once? Without him fucking it up?

Spring

Thirty-One

If winter is the death of the old year, spring is the birth of
the new. Green shoots start to appear, falling into the
company of perennials, those hardy plants and trees
whose leaves survive the worst winter has to throw at
them, and come out smiling on the other side. The plants
that aren't so lucky use the springtime to replenish
themselves, turning towards a sun that feels like it's
barely risen at all over the last three or four or five
months. It now comes out with a vengeance, and flora
and fauna both are grateful for it.

Copses of trees that have been barren since autumn
made its exit come back to life. They haven't been
hibernating per se, but the next best thing, which is to
shut themselves down and ride it out. Because often,
that's what winter is all about in England; survival. Plants,
animals, buildings, people; mostly, when winter comes,
and darkness outweighs light, everyone and everything

just tries to get through it. Sure, there are those who prefer the winter months, who thrive in them, but they're in the quiet minority, and everyone else just leaves those strange people to it. Perennial people, like perennial plants, seem to defy nature. And as much as everyone likes something new, something different, secretly everyone likes things to stay the same, consistency is king, change is new and scary and, more than anything, unknown.

Spring isn't just about what comes naturally though, but what comes metaphorically. Spring is the season of hope, the season of better things to come. Spring is a blank slate for us all, a canvas on which we project our hopes, our fears, things we're excited for in the New Year, things we're dreading. There's a sense of possibility, of anything being able to happen. Murphy's Law never feels more relevant than in the springtime; when the sun stays up past 4pm, when you can shed your winter coat, although you better keep it close just in case. England doesn't complete the full transition away from winter until the summer; spring is just the country warming up, preparing itself for what's to come. But this is okay; spring is the warm up act, you didn't pay to see her, but you enjoy her nonetheless, and she awakens the excitement within you that has lain dormant for a long time.

Spring exists in and of itself, but this isn't its function. Spring's essential function is to get you ready, to prepare you. It's the season of leaving behind the winter blues and finding a little bit of optimism you didn't know you had left. Spring is about watering this optimism, working on it in the hope that it'll find a way to flourish in the new year, that it'll find a way to grow and bloom, and whatever happened the previous year, those ghosts are left in the past where they belong. Spring is hope. Spring is promise. Spring is very fine, once she comes to us.

I try to have hope, to have optimism, to convince myself everything is going to be fine. I fail. I feel like a refugee in my own life; I used to have a girlfriend, but no more. I used to have a boyfriend, but no more. I used to have a sister, but, seemingly, no more. I used to have a mother, but for the time being she's too busy sorting her affairs out, finally moving on with her life, that she doesn't have time to get into the minutiae of my everyday life. Which I secretly find frustrating, but outwardly, and even mostly inwardly, I'm delighted by. As much as I miss my mum in these months, I'm glad she's finally moving on. It's taken longer than anyone could have anticipated, and probably much longer than is healthy, but it's better late than never. I go over a few Saturdays to help her, but there isn't much to do. I mean, there's a whole house to clean out, to decide what's staying, what's going, what's worth selling, what's worth no more than a landfill; there's a lot to be done, and it'd go much quicker if I were able to properly help, but my mum wants to do most of it herself, and I'm happy to let her. I think this is less about selling the house, and more about a spiritual goodbye. If I'm right, then it's something incredibly personal, and I'm happy to leave her to it. I said my goodbyes years ago.

I haven't heard from Emma since she gave me half a blow job and I called her by the wrong name. I've text nearly every day, sometimes multiple times. I've tried ringing, getting her on Insta; hell, I even got desperate enough to email her management company, hoping they might give her a prod, to at least let me know she's alive and okay. But I haven't heard a peep from anyone. I'm obviously keen to repair our relationship, to have a big old talk about everything, or to forget everything, I'm happy either way. However, mostly I'm keen to make sure she's okay; only a few weeks before we did what we did, she was raped. I think that fact got lost between us, in all the noise of what we were doing; I'm scared Emma has gone back to America too soon, and that this will end up doing more harm than good. She isn't exactly, as far as I'm aware, going to be in many situations that are healthy and stable. I don't know it in great detail, but I'm struggling to picture the New York modelling scene as a place of great healing and catharsis, of both body- and sexual-positivity. My biggest fear? She gets raped again. I'll keep trying to contact her, in the hope she gives up and lets me in. I miss her, terribly. I've known her all my life, and even if we've never been overly close, at least not geographically, I love her to pieces, and I hate not having her in my life.

With regards to Max and Lucy, I wanted to address them separately, but the fact that they've started appearing on each other's Insta feeds, and with alarming regularity, means I need to take them as a pair. As a couple. Because that's what I think they are. I mean, there's little evidence to point to this; all the pictures they're in are innocent, there's no kissing, no holding hands, nothing to prove they're in a relationship. But in my heart I know they are, I can feel it. My heart is sending waves out, and the waves coming back are not positive. I want to be happy for them. I'm trying to be happy for them. If they've found each other because of how badly I treated them, then I'm glad something good has come from the shit storm that is my actions. I'm glad the time they spent with me wasn't a complete waste. I wish either, or both, of them was with me, but it's my fault, and mine alone, that they're not.

The four most important people in my life are drifting away from me, and there's nothing I can do about it. Or at least, nothing I think I can. Something may change; the future is a dark unknown with infinite possibilities. Perhaps in one of them I'll be able to overcome my own personality, my own craving for destruction and unhappiness, and be able to make some positive changes, make some positive decisions. Perhaps, as much as it feels like this is all killing me, it'll actually be the making of me. I'll come out the other side completely and utterly alone, but also capable of dealing with this loneliness. I won't emerge from the dark winter months with everything I want, but I will emerge a better person, one more able to handle things, more able to live life on life's terms, rather than constantly trying to have things on my own terms and having a tantrum when things don't work out exactly the way I wanted.

Because that's my problem a lot of the time, I'm unwilling to compromise. My therapist tells me I'm still stuck in some ways, psychologically a large part of me is still a child, and a stubborn one at that. She tells me one of my major problems is I expect the world to work for me and haven't yet accepted that life is actually the other way around. Life is never going to work for me, not as long as I'm rigid in my expectations. She tells me I need to focus on compromise, on sacrifice. I can't have everything I want all the time, but that doesn't mean I get nothing. It just means I'll be able to have some, but not all, of the things I want. And that I have to work for them, they won't simply be handed to me. And the things I want but don't get, I have to let go. It's no good mourning them, becoming fixated on them, because then I spend so much time lamenting what I don't have, that I waste what I do.

And as always, she tells me the clocks only run in one direction, and so what has happened has happened, will always have happened, and there's nothing me, her, or anyone else on the planet can do about it. I may have driven Max and Lucy into each other's arms, and I'm allowed to be upset about it, but the fact is they have each other, and no amount of my moaning and no number of temper tantrums will change this fact. All my unhappiness is doing is making me unhappy; the way I act is only affecting me, is only bringing me down, is having absolutely no positive impact on anything. I'm ruining my own life fighting a battle against opponents who don't even know I'm there. I need to make a choice; I need to choose whether to be unhappy, or to be happy. The problem is, I've spent my entire life choosing to be unhappy to the extent it's second nature to me now, and my first instinct. Which is okay, my therapist tells me. It's all a learning curve. I can't expect to wake up one day loving myself. But I can gradually stop hating myself. And work from there.

I can't imagine a time where I don't hate myself, but I'll keep working. I'll keep doing what my therapist tells me, and keep trying to make better decisions, and who knows. Maybe one day I'll wake up, and I won't find the mere fact of my existence abhorrent.

Thirty-Two

One major thing does happen in spring; I quit my job. I hadn't been planning to, but one Friday afternoon, at the end of what I thought had been just another week, my boss called me into a meeting. I followed her, no particular worries in my mind, no thoughts really at all in my head except how I would spend the weekend. Would I spend it pining over Max, over Lucy, missing Emma? Or would I do something constructive, spend the time wisely, make some aspect of my life better. I knew which was the better option. I also knew which option I was much more likely to take up. Hint: the one that required no effort on my part.

I'd followed my boss into one of the many identical meeting rooms, and as she held the door for me and I passed her, I was surprised to see someone already in the room. I was just turning to ask my boss if she was sure we were in the right room when she closed the door, smiled at me in a way that was at least 80% grimace, and told me to take a seat. I did so, not wanting to continue floundering, which is what I had been doing. I recognised the man who was sitting at the table, but couldn't place him right away. Then it hit me; he worked in HR. My heart began to pound, for you see as much as I hated that job, I couldn't afford to lose it. Which, it turns out, was exactly what was going to happen, they told me. That is, if I didn't quit. They had everything they needed to fire me, they said, but they didn't want to unless I left them no option. I didn't want to quit, but I immediately knew I had to; I wasn't looking at any sort of severance package either way, so in quitting I wasn't forfeiting anything. What I was doing, was avoiding a bad reference. They told me if I quit now, the reasons for my firing, in fact that very idea that I had been fired, would never leave this room. When future employers contacted them, they'd pass along all the necessary facts, omitting this piece of information. The alternative, they said, was them telling any company who asked for a reference that they'd had to bin me off, and they didn't need to tell me how much that would affect my chances of future employment. And so I did the smart thing and quit. I jumped before I was pushed. I left the only source of income I had. I hated the job yes and thought my mental health would improve by being rid of it. But then again, the prospect of not being able to pay my rent or any of my bills would probably have a similar sized, if not much bigger, detriment on my mental health. I don't think there was much positive spin I could put on the whole situation. But it showed personal growth I was at least trying. That's another thing my therapist and I have been working on: praising myself. I thought it was ridiculous at first, but then she asked me one question which made it all so obvious, and made me feel very stupid: *when you do something bad, do you chastise yourself?* Of course the answer is yes, who doesn't? And then it became painstakingly obvious. If I chastise myself, why don't I praise myself? You have to take the bad and the good equally; all I've been doing is taking the bad as my own responsibility, making myself feel like shit by blaming myself, and then when something good happens, praising and thanking external sources, not recognising my own hard work. I've spent so long hating myself it's difficult to say nice things to me, about me, but I'm doing my best. Because that's all I can do.

And so I'd spent the weekend pining. I pined for the loss of my sister, and how much I missed her. I pined for the loss of my family home; despite it not once feeling like a home after dad died, it still turned out I was attached to it, and loathed to let it go. I pined for Max, and for Lucy, who were now absolutely in a relationship with each other, I'd confirmed that through a mutual friend on Insta. It didn't hurt me as much as I'd expected. I suppose I dissociated again, I think most likely when Emma was recounting the story of her rape.

I should have been devastated about Max and Lucy hooking up. Or, had I been a better man, I would have been happy for them, I would have been glad two people I care about have found each other, and found happiness, particularly after the unhappiness I'd put them through. As it was, the revelation of their getting together caused me to feel a whole lot of nothing. I knew it wasn't healthy to feel this way, but it was, still is, easy. And I'll take the easy option any day of the week. Finally, I pined not the loss of my job, but the loss of my source of income. I wouldn't miss the job even one iota; those poor rich fucks would soon have someone else putting their numbers into Excel, making sure the wealth they had and did nothing with grew even larger. I mean fuck the people starving on the streets right, as long as the 1% are happy? That seems to be how the world works, it becomes more apparent to me every day. And I am a hostage to it.

I wasn't going to mention this, but the reason I was asked to leave my job was because of my attitude. My boss, whose name I forget, and the dude from HR, whose name I also have since forgotten, both told me that my work was to an excellent standard, and there were no problems there as far as they were concerned. The issue was, I was told, that I had a toxic personality; when I was in the office I walked around under a giant cloud, and when people were near me, or spent time with me, they fell under the influence of the cloud. No matter how good I was at my job, I was informed, I could never justify the attitude I carried. I wasn't surprised to hear this news; if anything, I was surprised that it took them so long to pull me up on it. I knew I had a shitty attitude; I hated that job and made no attempt to hide it. I had no plans to work there for 40 years, have my boss at my wedding, give my retirement speech from the same shitty office chair. I had absolutely no love for the job and didn't care who knew it. Which ended up being my downfall. Vonnegut said it best: *so it goes.*

The more I think about it though, in the time since it's happened, the more pissed off I am. Imagine being fired from a job that the company admits you're amazing at, because you don't love them enough. Imagine how insecure that company must be, to give up an excellent worker, because he isn't sycophantic enough. How fucking pathetic. But that's the essence of capitalism; the only ones who succeed are the ones with Stockholm Syndrome. Because no matter how good you are at your job, no matter how much value you provide, it's all about saying the right things and acting in the right way. The people at the top want to exploit the value of your labour, *and they want you to thank them while they fucking do it*. Oh thank you Mr CEO, for enhancing your personal wealth using my blood and sweat. By the way, are those new boots? I'd sure love to kiss them. I can't help but notice you're treading on me, thank you so much. I love you Mr CEO of Shitty Fucking Shit Incorporated, and I love Shitty Fucking Shit Incorporated even more. Long live the masters!

One good thing did come of my leaving my job; it forced a reconciliation between Emma and myself. Well, perhaps reconciliation is the wrong word, seeing as we never fell out in the first place. My leaving my job meant that Emma spoke to me again, which almost made the whole shitty situation worth it. How it came to pass was this: I rang my mum on my way home from my now former work, telling her what had happened. I wasn't that bothered in her knowing, per se, but I had to lay the groundwork for when I inevitably needed to borrow some money. I called up under the pretence of asking how the house selling was going, and eventually got around to my own circumstances. I told her I was okay (lie), that I didn't need money (lie), and that I was sure something would be on the horizon (lie). I told these lies to appease her, and to try and convince her I was an adult. I don't think she really believed me, but I think selling the house, plus the ever-present worries of Emma being taken advantage of and abused again, meant she convinced herself to believe I was fine, so she'd have one less thing to worry about. For my part, it meant when I rang her a week later and asked if I could perhaps borrow some money, she wasn't at all surprised.

She asked how much and baulked when I asked for £1,000. I didn't need that much, not that soon, but it

couldn't hurt to ask. I was shocked when she said yes.
Also a little confused, as I hadn't known she had that
kind of money lying around. It turns out she didn't,
which is how Emma and I ended up back on speaking
terms. After my mum put the phone down, saying the
money would be with me soon, I went to open a beer to
celebrate. I had four in my fridge which I'd been saving;
as much as I wanted to drink them, I hadn't wanted to
leave myself in a situation where I had no alcohol, nor
any access to it. I'm not an alcoholic, not at all, I just like
the option. After the phone call, knowing I'd shortly be
able to afford many, many beers, I finally cracked into
them. I was just sitting down on the couch, trying not to
smile too much at how lucky I was to have this kind of
familial support, when my phone started ringing again. I
assumed it would be my mother, saying she needed my
bank details, or something other admin related, and so I
answered without looking. I was shocked to hear not my
mother's voice, but Emma's.

"Hello, you," she said to me quietly, timidly. It was
early evening for me, which meant mid-afternoon in New
York. I wondered what she was doing, how she was
spending her days, that one in particular, but her days in
general too. I wanted to tell her I loved her, I missed her,
I was so sorry for what I'd done, that I'd driven a wedge
between us. I wanted to say a thousand different things,
but in the end all that came out of my mouth was a tiny,
high-pitched squeak of a hello. My nerves won out.

"How are you?" Emma asked but continued speaking
before I could answer. "I'm sorry I haven't been in
touch, it's just things got a little, you know." I did know.
Saying things 'got a little you know' was perhaps the
understatement of the century.

"I'm sorry-" I started, but she talked over me.

"I really am sorry, Noah, about what happened. I'm

sorry for locking you out, sorry for taking off while you slept. I'm sorry for running away."

"It's-"

"Please, Noah, please let me finish. I need to say this now, or I don't think I'll ever be able to." I didn't reply, obeying her wish to have the floor.

"What we did was so wrong, so stupid, so fucking weird, and yet I haven't been able to stop thinking about it. It was so gross, really, when you think about it, and yet I've never been happier than when we were together. I've always loved you, Noah, since the day you were born, and I always will. You're my brother, my only brother, the only consistent man I've had in my life since dad…" Emma trails off; even after all this time she's unable to say it.

"I don't know what not having a dad did to me, psychologically. I could sit here and say I saw a father figure in you, and I wanted comfort and support, and it came out in a weird way, but I'd be lying. I miss dad, of course I do, but not once have I felt like I was missing something from my life. You, mum, my work, it was enough for me. It always has been, I don't know why it wasn't that night. Maybe it was the time of year, or because of what happened to me, I don't know. But I do know one thing; I don't regret it. We shouldn't have done it, but I'm glad we did. I'm just sorry for how it all ended."

After she finishes speaking there's silence between us. I'm waiting to see if she has any more to add before I jump in, and I imagine she's waiting for me to jump in. When it becomes clear she isn't going to say anything else, I speak.

"I love you too Emma. You don't have to apologise to me, you never do. I've been wanting to apologise to you; I was so worried that I took advantage of you that night. I've been so scared that between what happened to you, and the alcohol, you weren't thinking straight, and I attacked you. I'm so glad you don't think this way, I'm so relieved. Not just for me, but for you. I couldn't live with myself if I ever made you feel anything other than safe. I also don't like how that night ended, but I understand. It's a situation for which there are no rules, and so, even though neither of us liked it, you did nothing wrong. I love you as much now as I ever have, and ever will. I'll never not care about you."

It was Emma's turn to wait to see if I had finished. Whether she couldn't make her mind up, or had nothing to say, I don't know, but I spoke next. Something had been niggling at me, and I wanted Emma's answer.

"Why now?"

"Why what now?"

"Why have you like called me now? I've been trying to get into contact with you for months. Then I speak to mum and tell her I need help, and then you ring. It surely can't be a coincidence?"

"It isn't, of course it isn't. Mum rang me as soon as you were off the phone and explained what was happening. I rang you as soon as she and I were off the phone. Mum doesn't have much money, at least not while she's in the process of selling the house, it's all tied up with solicitors and the bank and stuff. She rang me to ask if I could lend you some money. And I'd be happy to Noah, you're my brother and I'll always help you. I'm always here for you."

I hadn't known what to say; I wanted to tell her she clearly wouldn't always be there for me, as she hadn't been for weeks, but there was no point mentioning that. Emma isn't stupid, she'll have known the inconsistencies in her words. She didn't need me to point out her flaws, she was adept enough at doing that for herself. I spoke eventually; I was embarrassed at borrowing money from my older sister, embarrassed that in my mid-20s I was in that situation. But at the same time, relief swept over me like a wave. Things were going to be okay. Perhaps only for a month, yes, but for the next month I'd be fine. I'd worry about the following month when it was more real, when it was closer.

It was wonderful to speak to Emma. I wanted to carry on the conversation but she explained she was actually in a shoot, and the director was calling her back to the set. I told her I loved her and I missed her, and as I was about to hung up she said something to me which made my heart skip a beat.

"I'll lend you the money, Noah, any time. But on one condition."

"Anything, Emma, just say the word." I said it, and I meant it.

"I'll give you the money on condition that you come to New York and see me and accompany me on a trip to LA I have coming up. Obviously I'll pay for everything, you don't need to worry about that. I want to pay, if that's what it takes to get your butt out here."

I didn't know what to say. My first instinct was to say no, for no other reason than I had forgotten I had no reason not to say yes. When I thought about it, what was holding me back? Max and Lucy had each other and didn't need me. I had no job, few friends, and I'd been so absent recently that Sylvia much preferred my flatmate to me. She was a great lover of consistency, and as much as I love her, I can't provide that for her. I can barely look after myself, let alone anyone else.

I was silent on the phone for a minute, as if in thought, though the answer was obvious, and Emma squealed with delight when I gave it to her.

"I'd love to come out." I meant it. We hung up, and a

minute later I got a text from my bank: £2,000 deposited 03/03/2022. Ref: *here you go :) come see me any time, the sooner the better. Just let me know when to meet you at JFK. Love you xxx.*

I love my sister very much. I can't wait to see her.

Thirty-Three

Whilst spring brings hope and optimism, it isn't without
its challenges. As the sun returns for the year, fresh from
her stint in the southern hemisphere, she warms the city
up. It's wonderful, of course, to have some light and
warmth, after what feels like three plus months of cold
and dark; people respond to the warmth, to the
appearances of the sun. I walk into town the day after
Emma sends me the money, and it kills me.

I don't need much, just some travel toiletries; even
though Emma gave me twice the amount I requested, the
majority of it will still go on bills. I hold back £500 for a
plane ticket, but otherwise the rest is accounted for. The
pain of spring comes as I walk through town; everywhere
I look, in every direction, I see flesh. Shoulders, arms,
midriffs; things that have been missing from my life for a
long time now come flooding back, and as much as it
excites me, the promise this flesh suggests, the

anticipation, it hurts too.

Whenever I see a woman's flat stomach, or the curve of her breasts just popping out the top of her blouse or halter neck or whatever, it reminds me of Lucy. Whenever I see a woman with long blonde hair, or a beautiful, natural smile, it reminds me of Lucy. In fact, in this short trip to pick up some supplies, which lasts only just over an hour, I think I see Lucy 14 times. Fourteen. Not one of them is her.

Flashes of blonde hair, a piercing stare, a woman of complete and utter beauty walking with confidence; amongst these things my mind torments me with jagged memories of Lucy. The way she used to smile at me when I was being foolish. The way her hair would fall after a shower, long and sleek with wetness, shining in the artificial light from the bedroom bulb, as she sat on the floor in front of the mirror, applying her face. The sight of her nipples poking at the fabric of whatever top she was wearing, as we got more and more comfortable in each other's presence; she started wearing bras less and less because, she told me, bras are mainly for support yes? Well when you have little to support, and it's able to support itself, why wear something incredibly uncomfortable for no reason. Her logic was fine and dandy as far as I was concerned; the more I saw of her flesh, and the more I was tempted by what I couldn't see, the happier I was. Lucy and I spent a lot of our short period of time together jumping onto each other, ripping our clothes off, fucking hard and fast. Sure we made love regularly, but mostly we fucked. I couldn't help it, she's just so fucking sexy. I could never control myself around her.

Just as I'm heading home, laden with my supplies, thinking about getting home, booking a flight, heading down to London to catch it, I see Max. I've been so focused on Lucy, so worried and excited about the prospect of bumping into her, that Max hasn't once popped into my head. I start at seeing him; he's waiting on the street outside my flat, which fills me either with excitement or dread, I can't quite decide. I soon realise that probably it's both. Is there an equivalent word for *schadenfreude* when it's your own pain and misfortune your take pleasure from? Because if there is, that's my life. That's how to describe me in one word. Seeing Max terrified me, but this terror excited me. All thoughts of Lucy were pushed from my head as I got closer to Max, as he spotted me and walked over to me, putting himself between me and my building, blocking my entrance as it were.

When we finally stand within a few feet of each other, neither of us says anything. This is the first time I've seen him since the pub and his marvellous and yet completely understandable decision to pour a drink over my head, since Lucy turned up at the pub as well and each stormed away from me.

When we're close enough that I can read the expression on his face I can see that he's nervous, he's worried; when we come to a halt face to face he doesn't stay still. He fidgets, twitches his fingers, taps the floor with his foot, pulls at his impeccable clothing, actually making himself look worse as opposed to better. I have so many things that I want to say, that I need to say to him, but no words come out. I'm still reeling from the surprise of seeing him, particularly here, right outside where I live. Luckily he breaks the silence which has defeated me.

"Hi Noah," he says tentatively, unable to look me in the eye, instead looking at the ground, his shoes, at anything and anywhere other than directly at me. "How're you?"

I assume this is a rhetorical question, in the same vein as "how was your weekend?" and "how's the family?" but the fact he pauses, giving me an opening to answer, changes my mind. Because I assumed the question was rhetorical I don't have an answer ready. I could answer honestly, I suppose, but Max has probably had to summon up a lot of courage to be here, to speak to me, and the last thing I want to do is scare him away. I must be silent for too long, because before I know it Max has moved the conversation on, is talking again.

"I'm sorry to just appear like this, but you weren't replying to any of my messages, and I need to speak to you."

Messages? What messages? I pull my phone out of my pocket and when I open Insta, something I haven't done a great deal since the pictures of Max and Lucy started appearing, that's when I see a little red '5' in the top right corner, transposed on top of the arrow indicating direct messages. I click the notification and see that indeed, yes, Max has messaged me several times, and I haven't seen them. My heart plummets; what if he wanted a reconciliation, but I've missed my opportunity? What if one of the messages was him asking to meet to thrash things out, but then the next was Max, frustrated, telling me fine, ignore him, let's not bother talking about 'us'.

I want to read the messages now, but I have the real Max here, now, in front of me; he probably should be the focus of my attention. What little focus I can muster, that is. Ever since I fucked things up with Max, with Lucy, generally fucked up my whole life, I've been finding it harder and harder to concentrate on one thing. I can't sit still for too long or focus on any one thing for a protracted period of time. I know it's because my anxiety is through the roof. I also know I'm not going to do anything about it; I'm going to meet my sister in New York and then accompany her to LA, and if that doesn't relax me, nothing will. Except industrial strength medicine, which I'll investigate upon my return to this country, should I still need it.

"I'm so sorry, Max," I say to him, meeting his eye for a second before he looks away, meaning every word. "I haven't been checking my Insta much since, you know…"

I trail off, hoping he'll finish the thought for me, or even that it doesn't need to be finished, but he just looks at me, confused, like a small puppy who doesn't understand a command. I'm forced to elaborate.

"Since you and Lucy started spending a lot of time together."

Max's face twists into fury for a second, and I hear him mutter something to himself about having told her, knew this would happen.

"I'm sorry you had to find out through Insta, Noah. I wanted to avoid putting pictures up until we spoke to you, but Lucy insisted. You know how she is when she wants something."

I did, I do know, and remembering makes me want to cry. I used to be the one trying to calm her when things weren't going her way. I used to be the one hiding behind her when she'd be giving someone a dressing down in a shop or restaurant or something. I used to be her poor boytoy, following her heels like a lost little urchin, loving every second of our life together. That I no longer am devastates me.

"I'm sorry you found out through social media before we were able to tell you. That's the main bulk of the messages, is me trying to arrange to meet, so I could tell you to your face."

"Well," I smile, gesturing at nothing with my hands,

"here we are. You've told me, you're released from your obligation. You and Lucy can spend all the time in the world now together, knowing you've done the right thing."

The last couple of words come out in a stutter, and before I realise what's happening I do started to cry now, and once the tears come it's like the floodgates have been opened. I cry for Max and Lucy, for my loss of them, for my having driven them together. As we stand in the street, in the middle of the afternoon, people passing us on both sides as we stand in the middle of the pavement, I weep. Most people who pass slow down, try to steal furtive glances, listen intently to what we may be saying, as if they can find out what's happening simply by taking in Max's and mines respective demeanours. Some stare outright, not trying to hide their interest, clearly feeling absolutely no shame whatsoever. I almost respect them for their brazenness, but I can't focus on them, or anyone else who passes by for that matter, enough to care.

I cry for Emma's rape; I cry for losing my job, and at 25 years old being unable to support myself, for all intents and purposes being a failure. I cry for Sylvia, who has officially adopted my flatmate, who has adopted her in return. I told him I was going to see Emma and he dove in before I got a chance to and told me he'd like to keep Sylvia. He was moving, he said, once the contract was up, and thought she'd be better with him. I didn't want to let her go, but if I was being honest with myself, which I'm trying to more and more, she's better with him. He can provide Sylvia the consistency I'm unable. I'll miss her terribly, but knowing she's well looked after will help. Not that it can distract me from the fact that I've driven away yet another creature I love, for no reason other than I'm incapable of living a proper adult life.

"I know you know, obviously, but here it is: Lucy and I are together."

Even though I know, this isn't new information to me, hearing Max say it brings the reality of it crashing home to me. I've lost Max and Lucy, both of them, forever. They'll always exist to me but be out of reach. And I only have myself to blame. And I know I'll do a lot of that.

"Thank you for telling me," I manage to choke out to Max, before I stop, unsure if I'm even able to say any more. Even if I have the words, which I don't, I just want this conversation to be over, I want to run away. But I'm frozen to the spot, I can't leave. I can only stay where I am, and live my worst nightmare.

"There's something else, too." I dread what he's about to say. "Lucy's parents bought the B&B from mine. They stayed in it, when Lucy and I wanted our parents to meet, and they absolutely fell in love. My parents were reluctant to sell, but the offer was high enough that they can retire comfortably. I'm happy for them, they deserve this."

I'm not sure where Max is going with this, so I don't say anything, just let him speak. I can tell from his face that saying this to me isn't easy, and my heart goes out to him. What little of it is still left alive, anyway.

"My parents are moving to Cornwall, they've bought a cottage there. I'm taking over running the B&B, well Lucy and I are."

Ah, so that's what he wanted to tell me. That's why he's so nervous. Max talks faster and faster as the information falls out of him; it's like now he's started talking, the truth, the whole truth, and nothing but the truth is the order of the day. I'm happy for him, happy for Lucy, and devastated for myself. I wish I was dead.

"We're getting married, too. She's pregnant."

Before I know what's happening, I feel a swelling in my chest, then my throat, and turning away from Max I vomit. Right here in the middle of the street, through my tears, I'm now being sick. Max has made all my worst nightmares come true; Lucy is pregnant, and they're getting married? The Lucy I know never wanted to marry, said it was too much of a burden, too tiresome, it impinged on her freedom. She didn't want kids either, instead wanting to not have her body ravished by pregnancy and then birth, perhaps adopting when she was a little older. This is the Lucy I thought I knew; I guess I never really knew her at all.

Max hasn't said anything whilst I've been vomiting; when I finally stop, wiping my mouth with the back of my hand look at him, I can see he's been waiting for this sickness spell to pass, in the hope I'll say something to him. I think he wants, of all things, my approval, and my absolution, as if I'm a person capable of giving either. I'm not even sure why he'd want them from me, why my blessing would be something he and Lucy are seeking. Why can't they move on? I'm trying, shouldn't they be? Max wants me to say that everything's fine, that I'm happy for them, and so much more, but once the vomit has subsided, nothing comes out of my mouth. I stand there a moment longer, and Max must finally see I'm not going to say anything, because he moves to speak. I cut him off before he has chance to.

There's nothing he could do, nothing he could say, I tell him, that would make things any better. At worst, things will stay as they are right now. Right now, things are terrible, and if they don't change I might drop dead here in the street. The thought gains traction in my head, and I can feel my airways starting to close up, the path of air in and out of my lungs becoming restricted. I'm hot and dizzy, and I know that if I don't sit down soon I'm going to faint. Max is still waiting for me to say something, and whilst there are a million things floating around in my head, a million things I'd like to say to him, I need to leave. I need to extricate myself from the situation and focus on my own immediate wellbeing. I push past Max, knocking him back more with surprise than strength, and let myself into the building. As I make my way down the ground floor corridor to my flat I can hear a knocking on the front door, and know it's Max trying to get my attention. Even though I have nothing to say to him and have clearly left the conversation, he seems to think we're not done.

I stumble to my flat, pulling out my keys and seemingly aeons later finding the right one, letting myself in. I make it to the bathroom just in time to vomit again, and once this spell passes I curl up on the bathroom floor in the foetal position. The tiles are nice and cold, and the contrast of the cold on my cheeks versus the heat of my flash fever is wonderful; I close my eyes, and I must drop off, because before I know it my flatmate is prodding me with his toe, asking if I'm okay.

I don't know how to answer him.

Thirty-Four

My life in the UK has seemingly come to an end. Emma messages whilst I'm sitting in Heathrow departures, waiting for my flight to board. She tells me she's got me an internship at a very famous literary magazine. She tells me not to worry about where I'll stay, about my visa, about the fact the job pays nothing. She has it all in hand, she tells me. As I read and re-read her message, I look at my meagre hand luggage, and think of my not-much-less-meagre suitcase that I checked into the plane's hold. I've under packed; I assumed I was only flying out for a week or so, to make sure Emma is okay, to make sure everything in LA is okay. It seems I won't be coming back.

Mum eventually found a buyer for the house, and decided that rather than stay in Leeds, or indeed England, she was moving to Spain. I have no idea how it works being an expat post-Brexit, but she seemed confident.

Good luck to her. She didn't tell us much about the people buying her house, only that they were a young couple, just had their first baby. She said she hopes they can make lots of happy memories in the house, and their lives will paper over the cracks that are our ghosts. I hope she's right. I wish them luck.

In a strange turn of events, Max and Lucy asked me to be their unborn child's godfather. I was as shocked as I was honoured to be asked, but I unfortunately had to say no. I would have loved to have been there for that child, but I don't know that I'm going to be able to be. I don't know what the future holds, but I know this; I'm making no plans, and I'm going where my life takes me. I've spent too long trying to live by my own ideals, trying to manage my own affairs. I've fucked up at every turn. I'll see Max and Lucy whenever I'm back in England I'm sure; they said they wanted to keep in touch, and I think they actually meant it. I think they've put the past long behind them, and rather than me being an ex to both of them, as well as having cheated on both of them, I've taken the position of matchmaker in their narrative. No matter how absurd and grotesque the circumstances, they met because of me. Their child exists because of me. Because of my fuck up. Maybe not everything I do turns to shit? Maybe there is a reason I exist?

If that's true, and the reason I exist is for the enjoyment of others, so be it. I gave up on my own happiness long ago, but I'll happily (pun intended) seek that of others. And who knows, maybe New York will bring better luck for me. Maybe things will be different on the other side of the pond. Maybe if I'm there, Emma won't get raped in LA. I'm excited to live with her. Her apartment has two bedrooms, but I think we might double up every now and then. Strictly platonic though. That ship has sailed.

Maybe I'll build a home in New York. I have to try. I can't let the fact I've failed everywhere else put me off. I'm 25 years old, I have a lot of life ahead of me. I should probably try and live it.

ACKNOWLEDGEMENTS

My aforementioned wife, for everything.

My parents, for existing. My mother does not live in a mausoleum, and my father is very much alive. Two things I'm unassailably grateful for.

My pets, for their comfort and softness. Nellie and Sylvia are both real animals, both wonderful little terrors.

Elliot Harper, for not letting me not write.

Izzy Grace, for beta reading this novel in its infancy and making sure the same Christmas doesn't happen twice, amongst many other things.

Dr. Wilby, for listening.

Stephen King, Bret Easton Ellis, AM Homes, Irvine Welsh, Shirley Jackson, Hermione Hoby, Kurt Vonnegut, Heather O'Neill, Nick Hornby, John Steinbeck, and too many other writers to list; thank you for inspiring me.

For those I've missed, I apologise. Writing acknowledgements for a book is like when someone asks you your favourite song; suddenly, you couldn't name a single song that's ever been written in the history of the world if your life depended on it.